in my rhythm

CM CAMPBELL

For permissions, inquiries, or business inquiries, please contact:
authorcmcampbell@gmail.com

First Edition: 2025

ISBN: 979-8-218-69948-2

Cover Design: CM Campbell

Formatting: CM Campbell

Cover Art: CM Campbell

Printed in the United States of America

acknowledgments

Writing this story cracked me open in ways I didn't expect, and I'm endlessly grateful to the village that held me while I put these words down.

To my readers: Y'all are the heartbeat. Every message, every review, every time you put this book in someone's hands—you keep me grounded and bold. Thank you for trusting me with your time and hearts.

To my beta and sensitivity readers: You caught what I couldn't see and gave me language for what mattered. Your care made this book safer, deeper, richer.

To my circle—my chosen family and day ones: Your belief never wavered, even when mine did. Thank you for the check-ins, the "you got this" texts, and the space to fall apart when I needed. Every word here carries a piece of your love.

To Austin: Thank you for being the man I didn't think I'd find. Your steady love and support—both emotional and practical—let me chase these dreams full-out. You make me feel seen, valued, and held. I love you.

To my readers on the spectrum: This is personal. I wrote Darius with y'all in my heart because I see you. I know what it means to move through a world that demands your performance, that shrinks your brilliance. This story is my love letter to your resilience and softness— your right to be held exactly as you are. Thank you for existing in your fullness.

To every Black woman who's ever been told she's too much: This is for you. For your softness and strength, your fire and

tenderness. For the way you keep choosing yourself. I see you.
I honor you.
And to myself: You kept going. Even when it was hard.
Especially then. Proof that survival blooms.
Thank you for being here.

trigger warnings

Before you read:
This story grows wild—rooted in love, tangled in grief, and not afraid to get messy. It moves through dark places and tender ones, holding space for both pain and healing. Check the trigger warnings to
care for your heart how you need. Your peace matters here.
Foster care trauma and abandonment
Emotional neglect and childhood emotional abuse
Grief and loss
Murder and physical violence
Kidnapping and captivity
Threats and intimidation
Workplace sabotage/theft
PTSD responses and anxiety spirals
Explicit, consensual sex scenes rooted in trust and communication
Strong language and raw discussions around trauma and healing

playlist

This playlist is a heartbeat.
Every song in was chosen with care—to echo the ache, *In My Rhythm* was chosen with care— to echo the ache,
the softness, the want, and the weight these characters carry.
These aren't just background tracks. They're soundscapes for grief. For pleasure.
For legacy. For love that comes back full and doesn't ask for permission to stay.
You'll find warmth here. And bruises. And Black joy that dances even when it hurts.
So let the music take you there—scene by scene, kiss by kiss, root to bloom.
This is Zora's rhythm. This is Darius's steadiness. This is love, turned all the way up.
—C.M. Campbell

CBT (Cognitive Behavioral Therapy)
A structured, evidence-based form of psychotherapy that focuses on identifying and changing unhelpful thought patterns, emotional responses, and behaviors. Often used to manage anxiety,
depression, trauma responses, and more. It teaches practical tools for reframing thoughts and regulating emotions in the moment.

IEP (Individualized Education Program)
A legal document developed in U.S. public schools for K–12 students with qualifying disabilities under the Individuals with Disabilities Education Act (IDEA). It outlines specific learning goals and the
accommodations or services needed to support a student's educational success. IEPs can be powerful — but also carry stigma, especially when misunderstood or poorly implemented.

synopsis

Zora Hart has leaned to thrive on her own terms. A plant
shop owner with roots deep in Atlanta's neighborhoods, she
knows how to nurture growth—but trusting people? That's
harder. After too
many years building walls she calls independence, Zora's not
looking for anyone to save her. Not again.
Darius Lawson moves quietly through the world.
An app developer with a sharp mind and a steady hand, he
keeps his circle small and his peace closer. Love has always felt
like something loud he
didn't know how to hold—until Zora crashes into his life with
all her stubborn beauty and wild heart.
Neither of them is built for halfway.
And neither of them is used to someone staying without being
asked.
As business pressures, betrayals, and old fears surface,
Zora and
Darius must learn how to move at a rhythm neither of them
controls—a rhythm made for two.
In My Rhythm
is a soulful, slow-burn romance about tenderness without

The house was still—just the way he liked it.

Soft under lighting from the kitchen cabinets spilled across the smooth concrete floors, casting a faint glow on the walnut countertops he picked out himself. No TVs humming in the background. No voices clashing with his thoughts. Just the steady, low hum of silence.

Darius Lawson stood barefoot near the sink, sipping water, one hand braced on the counter. His fingers slid across the cool surface like a reminder—I made this. I built all of this.

The air smelled faintly of cedar, clean cotton, and the lavender oil Mama Regina insisted he keep diffusing near the vents. Said it calmed her nerves. Truth was, it calmed him too —he just wasn't the type to admit it.

He looked around. Everything in this house had intention behind it. The soft textures. The muted tones. The way natural light poured in at just the right angle during the day. No clutter. No chaos. It was a space that made sense—to him. For him.

Eight years ago, he couldn't hear himself think over the noise in his own head. The guilt. The shutdowns. The feeling that he had to perform just to be tolerated.

Now? He could hear his heartbeat.

Slow. Steady. Peaceful.

He wasn't fighting to be understood in this space. He just was. He didn't have to shrink here. Didn't have to explain. In this space, silence wasn't punishment. It was freedom.

His eyes drifted to the glass doors leading to the back porch—just past them, a soft glow from the cottage out back. Mama Regina's light was still on. That woman stayed up too damn late watching court show reruns and talking to the Lord about everybody's business but her own.

He smiled to himself. Just a little.

It was quiet now. But the road here hadn't been.

He carried his glass across the room and slid onto the stool at his built-in desk. One tap, and his laptop lit up—lines of code glowing in the dimness like a language only he could read.

Dashboard loaded: Rithm, Creator View.

Notifications rolled in—testimonials from teachers, reviews from parents, quiet messages from teenagers who said the app helped them "feel normal for once." The user count had just passed half a million.

He didn't build it off theory. He built it off survival—and therapy. Years of CBT sessions taught him how to map his thoughts instead of drowning in them. Track the moment, name the spiral, rewrite the script. The same tools that aided his nervous system now lived inside the app— only simpler. More intuitive. For kids like him who didn't need more performance. They needed permission.

Darius let the numbers settle in.

He wasn't smiling for the stats. He didn't get high off analytics. This wasn't ego. This was his purpose. Peace. Even.

He didn't build this to be seen.

He built it to survive.

He never needed to go to college. Didn't need a degree to validate the way his mind worked. While other people were chasing diplomas, he was at home learning how to breathe through overstimulation and writing code that could calm a nervous system faster than his own therapist could.

Those same tools became the foundation for Rithm. Not textbook theory—lived experience. A system built for nervous systems like his. He didn't need more reminders to behave. He needed language for what his body was saying. Rithm offered that. Quiet, intuitive structure. Less about correction. More about clarity.

He'd always known he was autistic.

Jemma made sure of that.

She didn't use the word like something sacred or clinical. She used it like a curse. Like a reason not to deal with him.

You're too much work.

You always got something wrong with you.

I swear, you don't know how to act like a normal kid. She called it honesty.

All he heard was rejection.

So, he internalized it. Carried it. Let it seep into his bones. For years, he thought being different meant being unwanted. That he had to work twice as hard just to be tolerated.

It wasn't until he was grown—on his own, paying bills, in therapy— that he started to see it clearly. He wasn't defective. He was just... wired with a different rhythm. One the world didn't know how to dance to.

So, he created his own.

The first version of Rithm was simple. No name. No direct callout. Just the kind of vague, grinning theft that made your gut knot before your brain caught up. No roadmap. Just building what he needed—what nobody had ever given him.

Eventually, someone noticed. A client at the tech repair shop he worked for caught a glimpse of the code on his second monitor.

"What's that?"

"Something I made for myself."

"No—that's something people need."

After that, it moved fast. Word of mouth. A local nonprofit

gave him a micro grant. He pitched it at a city innovation lab and got his first backer. The app took off faster than he expected—and he still wasn't chasing clout. He was chasing ease. Relief. Solutions.

I didn't build Rithm to be rich. I built it so no kid like me would have to suffer in silence.

And yet, the money came. The platform grew. Districts licensed it. Therapists incorporated it. Families sent thank-you emails and videos that Darius never responded to—but watched more times than he'd admit.

Still, some part of him believed he was just getting started.

Darius stepped onto the back porch, cool night air brushing over his skin like a familiar rhythm. Out here, things slowed down. The city was close enough to feel alive, but this space? This was his own kind of quiet.

From this angle, he could see the glow from the cottage past the treeline. The house he built for Mama Regina two years ago—brick by brick, custom everything. The whole damn thing done right.

She didn't cry when he gave her the keys. Just hugged him. Hands trembling.

That was how she said thank you.

She didn't birth him. But she raised him.

Technically, Jemma did, too. She showed up—sometimes. Paid bills when she remembered. Signed school forms. But the actual work? That fell on Saige and Ms. Regina.

Jemma found Regina when he was still a boy. Hired her as a paid caregiver to "help out."

Except that help turned into pickups, meals, IEP meetings, and silent nights full of presence when the world overwhelmed him and his body shut down. Regina didn't clock out. She stayed.

Saige, only four years older, was barely holding herself together. But she cooked. She defended him. She listened. She mothered when their actual one didn't.

And then, eight years ago, it all snapped.

Jemma came back from one of her disappearing acts, full of opinions and accusations. She sided with Trevon—Saige's ex. She told her he was a good man. That he had a right to the kids. That Saige couldn't just erase their father.

Darius had stood there, still at first. Listening. Watching.

Then, he stepped forward.

"You called him a good man," he said, voice even. Fingers tapping against his leg. "Even after everything."

"Because he is," Jemma snapped. "Just 'cause you got a new man doesn't mean you can erase him."

Saige had snapped, too. "He erased himself, Ma. You think I forgot all the nights he didn't come home? All the ways he let me struggle?"

And when Jemma crossed the line again—called Darius weak, said he was "just like his daddy"—the room went silent.

He didn't flinch. Didn't speak.

Just stared at the woman who never once stood up for him.

That's when Miss Regina slapped her across the face.

"Now, I let a whole lotta shit slide," she said, shaking her head. "But what you not about to do is disrespect that boy in this house."

Jemma's eyes went wide. Then narrow. "You think you won," she spat before storming out. "But you still got my blood in you."

That was the last time they saw her.

He didn't call Miss Regina Mama right away. That came a year later, when he was 27.

They were sitting at her kitchen table, drinking lukewarm tea. He'd been helping her organize meds, pretending not to notice her forgetting small things.

He looked up from the label in his hand and said, "Thanks, Mama."

She didn't blink. Just smiled—soft and steady.

Like she'd been waiting for him to say it on his own terms. Now, she was still Mama Regina. Always would be.

So, when her memory started to fade and her joints got stiff in the mornings, he did what needed to be done.

Built her a home.

Quiet. Close. Hers.

"She gave me a soft place to land," he murmured, watching the light flicker through her window. "So I gave her one, too."

He stayed on the porch a little longer, letting the silence fold around him.

Then turned back inside.

The thing nobody ever tells you about therapy: you don't walk out lighter. You walk out, raw.

Darius remembered his first session as if it was branded into his bones. Twenty-five. Tight jaw. Fists clenched. Sitting in a gray-walled room that smelled like old books and peppermint tea. He didn't want to talk. Hell, he barely wanted to be there.

His therapist—an older Black man with salt-and-pepper locs and quiet eyes—just sat across from him. No clipboard. No pressure.

"You don't have to explain," he said. "You just have to tell the truth."

And that was the thing.

Darius didn't know what the truth sounded like in his own voice. He'd spent so long being managed—by systems, by Saige, by silence— that when someone finally asked what he needed, it damn near broke him.

That first session, he didn't cry. He shook. Hands. Breath. Thoughts. Everything trembled from the inside out. Despite that, he came back.

Every week, like clockwork.

He learned the difference between a shutdown and a spiral. Learned how to name what his body did under pressure. Learned he could say, "I need five minutes," and not feel like a burden.

Therapy didn't turn him into a new person.

It just helped him learn who he was—underneath the masking, the shrinking, the survival.

Now, watching the room, Darius stared at the soft glow of his phone screen—Rithm still open. He'd taken the same strategies that saved him and coded them into tools other people could hold.

He'd designed it for autistic Black kids who'd never seen themselves reflected in calm spaces. Kids who didn't just stim, but shut down. Kids who got labeled "problem" when what they really needed was a quiet room, a soft voice, and some damn understanding.

I wasn't broken. I was overwhelmed.

His therapist had said that once. And it stuck.

It stuck through late-night coding sessions, breakdowns he logged as data, and the quiet victory of being able to say, "I'm not okay" out loud —and still be loved, anyway.

It stuck when Mama Regina forgot the name of the show they watched every Thursday, and he held her hand like it was the first time.

It stuck when Saige called just to check in, even though she was busy as hell, because she still worried about him slipping into silence.

I'm not broken.

Darius whispered it now, just to hear it bounce around the walls of the house he built.

He wasn't the same man who walked into that therapist's office all those years ago. But that man still lived inside him—quiet, watchful, waiting for proof that safety could last.

And maybe it could.

Maybe peace wasn't something he had to survive his way into. Maybe it was something he could live in.

And maybe, if the right person came along—Love could move to his rhythm, too.

what things fall (and start)

"LOVE'S TRAIN" BY BRUNO MARS, ANDERSON.PAKK & SILK SONIC

Zora Hart shoved the last crate of hand-mixed soil into the back of her plant truck and slammed the doors shut with more force than necessary.

"Don't start the day with violence," Keira called from the front steps, coffee in one hand, phone in the other. "Especially not truck-directed violence. You know she's sensitive."

"She deserves it," Zora muttered, brushing dirt off her high-waisted jeans. "She's been acting like she's got transmission trauma. I need her to hold on just one more week."

"You said that last week."

"I meant it then, too."

The sun was already burning high, sticking to her shoulders and catching sweat along her collarbone. The crocheted halter top she threw on—bright, loud, all orange and pink zigzags—was cute, but not built for heavy lifting.

Keira sipped her coffee and gave her a slow side-eye. You out here looking like summer and stress."

"Good. It's accurate."

Zora adjusted a trailing fern that kept sliding out of its crate, tucking it back into place like a baby's blanket. "Don't embarrass me in front of the customers," she warned it gently.

Inside the Wild Hart storefront, the air smelled like lemongrass and eucalyptus. Plants lined the front windows like gossiping aunties, their leaves already tilted toward the light. The whole place was alive. Zora's hands had made it that way —her vision, her sweat, her name painted on the wall behind the counter like a promise.

The music was low—Erykah Badu humming something wordless in the background. A diffuser puffed lemongrass into the air, blending with the damp sweetness of soil and sage. Hanging pothos framed the windows, and a monstera leaf slowly unfurled with a soft scrape, like it was stretching into the morning.

"You gonna wear yourself out, Zo."

"Not before I get this bag."

"You already got it. You need to rest in it."

"Later," Zora said, hopping down from the truck. "Right now, I got dirt to sell and peace to push."

She was exhausted. But it was working.

Wild Hart was finally gaining momentum. Her custom soil blends had started flying off shelves—blends she'd spent two years perfecting, down to the mineral balance and the way the mix held moisture without choking roots. Customers were obsessed. A few boutiques had even reached out to stock it, and she'd gotten inquiries from wellness brands about potential partnerships.

Today's pop-up was supposed to be easy. A quick setup. Meet the plant girls. Sell out of her signature blends. Smile. Bounce.

This was her proving ground. If it hit, she could pitch her mobile consulting service to that yoga studio off Auburn. Maybe even get a meeting with that slow-food collective downtown. One step closer to making Wild Hart the name on everyone's lips when they thought of roots and rest.

Easy, she told herself again, hauling into the driver's seat.

She didn't believe it.

The drive started smooth. Too smooth. Like the truck was trying to lull her into a false sense of security. The first few turns out of the neighborhood came easily, tires humming over hot pavement. But three blocks from the community park, the engine hiccuped. Once. Then again.

Zora stiffened. "Don't do this to me. Not today."

She gripped the wheel tighter, leaning forward as if her body could will the truck to keep going. "I got a table with your name on it," she whispered. "A whole corner booth in the shade. I cleaned your windshield and everything. Don't play with me now."

She eased off the gas, listening.

A clicking noise started near the front right tire. The engine's rhythm stuttered—coughing like it needed a hit of ginger tea and a prayer.

She turned down the next street, eyes scanning for a place to pull over.

That's when it gave out completely—shuddered once, wheezed loudly enough to make a couple walking past glance over, and coasted to a pitiful, steaming halt in front of a faded brick building.

Zora slammed her palm against the steering wheel.

"You raggedy, beautiful bitch."

She sat there for a beat, breathing through the frustration. She wasn't gonna cry. Not over this. Not over a damn engine. But the pop-up was supposed to be a win. A small one, yeah, but she needed it. Just one damn thing to go her way this week.

When she climbed out, sandals hitting pavement, sweat clinging to her back like stress, she glanced through the side window. Her little mobile greenhouse looked back at her— rows of baby succulents, starter kits, dewy leaves lined up like students before a test. They looked too hopeful for what was happening out here.

She rounded the front and popped the hood.

A cloud of hot steam greeted her like disrespect.

"Mother—goddamn."

She stumbled back, coughing and fanning herself.

The sign on the building read: Rithm Community Center. Kids' laughter echoed through an open window. Stevie Wonder played from somewhere inside.

Zora stared at her truck as if it had betrayed her. Because it had.

Then she heard, "Need help?"

The voice was low. Measured. Steady enough to cut through the chaos in her chest.

She turned, squinting through the shimmer rising off the sidewalk.

He was leaning against the low brick wall in front of the center. Broad shoulders. Clean-cut beard. Fire frames catching the sun just right. His button-up was soft, blue plaid, layered over a white tee, paired with khaki cargo pants and crisp Nike Dunks. A blue Louis crossbody bag rested at his side like it belonged there—like he did.

He wasn't smiling. Wasn't frowning, either. Just... watching her. Calm. Focused. Like she was a puzzle, not a problem. He didn't make direct eye contact. Not the whole time. His face shifted, sharp one moment, distant the next, as if he were tracking everything but reacting to nothing. One hand stayed tucked in his pocket, thumb rubbing a slow circle on the fabric. Not nervous. Just... managing.

Zora blinked.

He was fine. Not just attractive—but grown-ass man fine. The kind that didn't have to raise his voice to own a room. Who didn't flirt, but observed—and somehow made you feel like the only one in focus. There was something steady in the way he stood, like he chose silence over spectacle. And that silence was louder than anything else happening on the street. The kind that made you second-guess your boundaries and your taste in exes.

She blinked again. "I'm fine."

She wasn't. Her pulse had jumped the moment he spoke, and now her body was acting like she'd just run a lap around the block. Which was rude. She hadn't even seen his full smile yet.

He nodded toward the hood, where steam still curled up like attitude. "Doesn't look fine."

She crossed her arms. "She's dramatic."

"She?"

"The truck."

He nodded like that tracked. "Got it."

Silence stretched between them. Not awkward. Just unexpected. She wasn't used to strangers who let silence breathe. "You work here, or just enjoy watching women get roasted alive on sidewalks?" She asked, more bite than she meant.

He let the smallest smile tug at one corner of his mouth. "Both."

Zora's mouth twitched. She hated how curious she suddenly felt. "I'm Zora Hart. You got a name, or is 'mechanic stalker' accurate?"

"Darius Lawson."

It fit. Solid. Uncomplicated. Grounded, like someone who meant what he said.

"You got truck-fixing skills, Darius?"

"Enough to know that steam's a bad sign. I can call someone for you."

She hesitated, then nodded. "Yeah. Okay. Just—no shady referrals. I don't need a man named Scooter charging me $200 for a look."

"Noted. No Scooter."

She snorted.

There was something about the way he looked at her— like he wasn't just seeing a woman sweating through her clothes on the side of the road. He saw all of it. The fury. The fight. The piece of her trying not to unravel. And he wasn't turned off. If anything, he looked like he understood.

"You always this calm, or is it part of the 'community resource center' charm?"

He lifted a shoulder. "Depends who's asking."

And for the first time that morning, Zora almost laughed.

A tow truck rumbled up a few minutes later, and, of course, Darius had already handled everything. Quietly. Efficiently. Like this wasn't his first time showing up for somebody who didn't expecting it.

Zora stood off to the side, pretending to scroll through her phone, trying not to feel like the sidewalk had turned into a stage. Her truck was steaming. Her day was wrecked. And somehow, this man had shown up with calm and competence like it was in his job description.

He came back over, hands in his pockets, head tilted slightly.

"He'll get it hooked up. Do you have a shop you trust?"

She hesitated. "My best friend's ex. He's decent with engines and shit, but he's got a mouth on him, and Keira swore if I gave him one more dollar, she was putting sugar in his tank."

Darius pulled out a card. Clean font. No flash. No fluff. Just a number and a name.

"If you want a real one, my boy Zion runs a shop a few blocks from here. He's sharp. Doesn't play games. Doesn't overcharge."

Zora raised a brow. "Zion, like biblical Zion?"

"Zion like he'll have your truck back breathing before sundown." Their fingers brushed when she took the card. Just long enough to be something.

Zora turned the card over. "You just carry these around?"

"I carry tools," he said. "This one's just printed."

Zora almost smiled. Again. This man was a walking quote board.

"I'll keep it in my back pocket," she said.

His gaze shifted to the Wild Hart Botanical logo on the side of the truck. "That yours?"

"Yeah." She nodded. "Brick-and-mortar in Grant Park. This"—she gestured to the truck—"is the mobile version. I do pop-ups, workshops, custom blends. Grew it from nothing."

He looked at the truck like it had history. Like he understood. "That's yours," he said. "You built that."

It wasn't a question. And it made her chest tighten in a way she wasn't ready to name.

"Yep. That explains the pride," he added. "And the cursing."

Zora huffed a laugh. "You're not wrong."

There was a pause. Then he said it—simple, no pressure. "You ever need help staying organized? I build systems. And I listen well."

She didn't answer right away.

It wasn't a pickup line. It was an offering. A window. And something in her wanted to climb through it. The driver waved her over, ready to go.

Zora looked back at Darius. "Thanks. For... all this. Here's my card if you ever need some plants to help your space."

"I didn't save you," he said. "You had it. I just added structure." She climbed into the passenger seat and shut the door.

Didn't look back.

But she held onto the card.

And for some reason, that one sentence wouldn't leave her alone.

I just added structure.

the quiet pull

"THE RECIPE" BY SIR

The tow truck had rolled away ten, maybe fifteen, minutes ago, but Darius hadn't moved from his spot behind the desk.

His computer screen glowed in front of him, lines of half-written code sitting idle. His fingers rested on the keyboard, still—as if they didn't know what came next.

He slid one loop earplug into his right ear. Just one. Enough to dull the edge of hallway noise bleeding into his space. The soft whir of the HVAC. The uneven cadence of footsteps from the teen group down the hall. None of it was new.

But today, everything felt... off.

He tapped his thigh in a slow rhythm. Four counts. Pause. Four counts. Pause.

It usually helped.

Not today.

His gaze shifted to the edge of the desk before pulling out her business card from his pocket. Zora Hart there in golden embossed letters. Her personal phone number was there too. He quickly programmed it into his phone. Zora Hart

Darius leaned back in his chair and closed his eyes.

He should be fine. This wasn't new. Unexpected noise. Bright energy.

People with too much presence. He'd learned how to buffer himself against that—years of grounding, breath work, focus strategies. His therapist had helped him name his thresholds, build internal walls so nothing got in too deep.

But Zora hadn't gotten in like that. She walked in like the door was already open.

And what bothered him most... was that it hadn't felt invasive.

She hadn't overwhelmed his senses. Not exactly. She'd stimulated them.

Her voice had texture. Her body language was loud, but anchored. She cursed with intention. Pivoted fast when her truck failed her.

Didn't shrink. She adapted. Shifted.

He respected that. Easily.

But respect didn't explain the static still humming in the back of his skull, or the way his heartbeat had taken on a new tempo the second she turned to face him.

His therapist would've called it activation—not anxiety. A shift in sensory input. Something new, not something wrong. The kind of energy he didn't need to fight—just notice.

I didn't save you. You had it. I just added structure.

The words had come out before he could second-guess them.

And for once, they felt right.

His shoulders dropped a fraction. He didn't smile. But something inside him... loosened.

Still, his rhythm was off. And he hated that.

He was used to knowing the layout. Used to reading people.

Absorbing without letting them sink in. He moved through the world with distance—not coldness, just enough grace to keep from losing himself.

But she didn't let him stay distant.

Not in a pushy way.

Just by existing in her full self, unedited.

And somehow, that made space for him too.

He opened his eyes, exhaled, and looked back at the card.

It was still there.

And he wasn't ready to put it away.

A soft knock landed on the door. Once. Then silence.

Darius didn't respond. Not out of defiance…he just didn't rush to fill quiet space. The people who mattered understood that.

The door cracked open.

Saige peeked in, holding a to-go cup with his name half-faded on the side. She set it on the edge of his desk, then leaned against the cabinet like she had nowhere else to be.

He tapped the desk once in thanks. No words yet. Still calibrating.

"It's oat milk this time," she said. "So you can't say I'm trying to throw off your whole routine."

Darius raised a brow. Just barely. "You used to."

"Yeah," she said, smirking. "Back when I still wanted to see you react."

He took the drink and sipped once, settling deeper into his chair. "You don't now?"

"I still do," she said. "But I don't need it like I used to. You've grown. You're good."

Darius nodded once.

That was their version of I love you.

"You've been quiet all morning," she said. Easy tone. "Open for you."

"I'm thinking."

Saige tilted her head, watching him. "About the woman I saw you helping on the street?"

He didn't look at her. Just kept his eyes on the rim of his cup. "I noticed her. Yeah."

"Mmm." Saige crossed her arms. "She had that kind of

energy that doesn't wait for permission. But it didn't feel messy."

"No," Darius said, voice steady. "It felt real."

That made her pause.

He leaned forward slightly now, elbows resting on his knees. "She didn't try to be anything. Just was. Most people perform. She wasn't."

Saige studied him for a second. "You don't usually notice that kind of thing."

"I do," he corrected. "I just don't usually care."

A small smile curled her mouth. "You think she noticed you?"

He finally looked at her. "She saw me. She didn't flinch."

Saige whistled under her breath. "Well damn. Okay." She pushed off the cabinet, walking toward the door. "I ain't gonna say more. You already sound like you know what's what."

Before leaving, she paused.

"Just remember, not everybody can carry you the way you need, D. But some people? Some people get it. And from where I'm standing... she might."

He didn't answer.

Didn't need to.

When the door clicked shut behind her, Darius sat still.

Then reached for his phone.

He tapped Zion's name, thumb hovering for a moment before he pressed Call. It rang once.

"Yo," Zion answered.

"Got somebody bringing her truck in," Darius said. "Name's Zora Hart."

"You vouching?"

"Yeah."

A pause. Then, "Bet. I'll be here."

Darius ended the call and set the phone face-down.

No need for a long conversation. Zion understood—Darius didn't say people's names lightly.

He looked back at the card again.

He didn't feel rushed.

And for once, it didn't feel like time was on his side.

The hallway was louder than it should've been.

After Saige left, Darius gave himself two full minutes.

Finished his drink.

Let the weight of her words settle—quiet, but heavy in the way only truth could be.

Then he stood, slid his phone into his pocket, and stepped out of the office.

The center buzzed around him—kids running, two staff members talking too close to the vending machine, the printer coughing out flyers someone would forget to pick up.

On any other day, he'd have slid his earplugs in without thinking. But today, he didn't.

He moved past the front desk and pushed through the double doors. The second they closed behind him, the heat glazed his skin like a weight—thick, sticky, personal.

Atlanta heat in late spring didn't ask permission.

But today, it grounded him.

The weight of it. The honesty of it.

No artificial buffer. Just the world, loud and real.

He didn't decide to walk.

His feet did.

Past the row of uneven sidewalk squares. Past the mural of Black girls planting seeds, paint flaking at the edges. He didn't have a destination, but he wasn't wandering either.

He never did anything aimless.

Open now, his steps moved to a beat he didn't fully recognize—but didn't fight.

Three blocks down, he slowed.

The lot sat empty. The old Saturday market spot—graveled, cracked pavement, a chain-link fence hugging the perimeter like a tired apology. He hadn't thought about this place in months.

But Saige had mentioned it last year.

A rusted planter leaned against the back corner, half its frame glistening. Mint leaves still popped up from the soil, unruly but determined. He didn't know much about plants.

But he knew survival.

And that mint? That was a declaration.

He stepped closer.

A torn flyer clung to the fence, weather-worn and faded. He couldn't make out the words, but he saw the colors—green and bold. Vibrant.

Intentional.

A Zora kind of palette.

His hand drifted to his pocket, where his trust metal fidget cube sat.

He didn't pull it out.

Just let his fingers trace the corner.

Enough to ground his racing thoughts that he hadn't make Zora up. She was real. That the static still lingering in his chest had a source.

She stayed grounded. Even when her truck hissed smoke. Even when she caught him watching. Even when she talked about what she built from scratch. She was solid.

She hadn't flinched.

He took a breath.

In through his nose.

Out through his mouth.

He didn't have a plan. And that used to bother him. But today?

Today, it didn't feel like a threat.

It felt like permission.

He looked down the street—past the cars and cracked pavement, past the people moving through their own rhythms. Some fast, some messy, none of them touching his.

Everything looked the same.

Same houses with paint peeling at the corners.

Same power lines drooping across the sky.

Same sun sinking lower, turning the sidewalks gold.

But he didn't feel the same.

There was a different cadence in his chest. A slight lean forward.

Like something in him had tilted—quiet, but sure.

He hadn't planned to meet her. Hadn't expected to think about her this long after she pulled off. But he was.

Not obsessively.

Just consistently.

Her voice. The weight of her presence. The way she looked him in the eye without flinching.

Zora had entered his world like she belonged there.

And somehow, that didn't feel like an intrusion.

It felt like an alignment.

He didn't know what that meant yet.

Didn't know what he was supposed to do about it.

For once, he didn't feel the urge to pull back.

Didn't feel like explaining himself or bracing for the fallout of being misunderstood.

He just wanted more. Of that presence. That came with her chaos. That noise that didn't hurt.

His fingers brushed the card again. He hadn't made a move.

But he would.

Soon.

back in the dirt

"GOOD MOURNING" BY INDIE.ARIE

The ride to the mechanic was quiet, but not peaceful.

Zora sat stiff in the passenger seat of the tow truck, thighs sticking to the cracked leather, sweat clinging to her lower back like betrayal. The A/C blew air that technically counted as cool, but it didn't touch the heat in her face. Or the flush she'd been trying to will away ever since she walked out of that damn community center.

The driver glanced her way. "Your friend said he called ahead."

Zora blinked, surprised. "He's not—" She stopped. Sighed. "Yeah. He did."

Friend. That was generous. She didn't even know him.

But she knew his voice. The way it settled over her like weighted velvet. The way it slipped under her skin without asking. Like they'd known each other forever.

"Lord have mercy," she muttered, pressing her forehead to the window.

"Everything okay?" the driver asked.

"Just re-evaluating my emotional boundaries."

They pulled up to the shop—a clean, organized garage with no loud music and no men lingering in the lot pretending not to stare. Just real work being done.

A tall man stepped out of the bay, wiping his hands on a red shop rag. Tattoos climbed his forearms, and his expression was unreadable. He moved like he didn't waste words—or time.

"You Zora?" he asked as she stepped down from the truck.

"That's me," she said. "Darius said he'd call."

Zion nodded once. "He did."

No surprise. No extra talk. Just confirmation.

"He doesn't usually put his name on things unless he means it," he added.

Zora paused at that. It landed heavier than she expected. "Yeah," she said. "I'm starting to pick up on that."

Zion circled the truck with quiet efficiency, eyes scanning the frame like he was already diagnosing it in his head.

"She died on me real boldly. Smoked up the entire block," Zora said, crossing her arms. "Whole neighborhood got to witness me unravel in public."

"Did the engine turn over at all?"

"Barely. She coughed twice, then gave up on life."

Zion crouched, checked something near the wheel. "Transmission?"

"She's been jerky. I've been ignoring it."

He stood and looked her in the eye. "I'll need your number to let you know when she's done. You want a call before any big decisions are made?"

"Yes, please. My wallet's got boundaries."

He held out his hand. "Zion."

She shook it. "Thanks for fitting me in."

"I trust Darius," he said simply. "So you're covered."

Zora nodded, handed off her number, and turned to leave before her face could betray anything.

She pulled out her phone to call the organizer of the event to fill them in on what was happening.

Half a block away, she pulled out her phone and hit Keira's name. As it rang, she muttered to herself, "I really let a man with good arms and a cute smile rearrange my central nervous system."

By the time Zora reached Wild Hart, she'd talked herself into five different reasons why today was not about a man.

It was about the truck. The damn humidity. Mercury probably being in Gatorade. Maybe low blood sugar.

But not Darius.

Definitely not him.

The bell above the door chimed as she stepped into her store, the scent of basil, soil, and eucalyptus wrapping around her like a weighted blanket. The air was cooler in here. Softer. Safer. Home.

She exhaled slowly, letting the smell ground her.

Plants lined the windows, the floor, and most of the walls —hanging baskets, potted snake plants, trailing pothos. Her whole life in green. Everything in its place.

She dropped her tote behind the register and got to moving.

Lights on. Sage lit. Fans rotated to wake up the air. Her playlist kicked in—Anderson.Paak and Ari Lennox floating through the speakers like ease.

It helped. Not a lot, but enough.

Zora moved to the back counter, already tying her locs up tighter. Her phone buzzed—three Shopify notifications and a new DM request.

She ignored the DM. Clicked the orders. Signature Soil Blend—3-pack. Custom Blend: Lavender + Peppercorn + Loam. Local pickup scheduled for Friday.

Her chest lifted a little.

The blend was catching on fast. She'd developed it herself —moisture- balanced, nutrient-dense, with a deep brown base that smelled like rain. No filler, no bullshit. Just good dirt that helped things grow.

And people were eating it up.

She walked to the back storage shelf and pulled a fresh bag from the bin, slipping into her gloves as she prepped the mix.

Her hands knew the rhythm. Scoop, pour, stir, weigh, seal. Reseal. Tag with her stamp. Move to the bin.

No thinking. Just motion. Just control.

She didn't want to admit how much she needed that.

Her phone buzzed again.

She didn't check it this time. She just flipped it face down.

Then flipped it back over two seconds later, just to see.

It wasn't him.

Of course not.

He didn't seem like the type to text right away. Probably had boundaries and balance and a damn meditation schedule. Still.

She set the phone down again and moved back to the mix.

Five minutes later, she was labeling another order when her thumb slipped, and the label stuck crooked.

She tried to fix it. Peeled it up, laid it down again.

Still off.

The whole thing felt off now.

Zora ripped the label off and cussed under her breath.

Her gaze drifted toward the shelf in the corner where the last sample of her Signature Blend sat. The bag looked off somehow. Tilted. Like someone had picked it up, maybe even opened it, then put it back slightly wrong.

She walked over, straightened it, checked the seal. Intact.

But something in her gut twisted, anyway.

She didn't know why it made her think of her.

But it did.

That slick smile. That fake "I love what you're doing here" tone. The way she'd lingered just a second too long at the last market. Asking what Zora used for her drainage base. Asking what type of mulch she preferred. Smiling like they were peers when Zora had taught her the basics.

She hadn't seen her in a few weeks.

But her name had popped up in Zora's tagged photos recently— under a new page.

A new blend. Same packaging style. Same color palette. Same earthy font.

Zora hadn't said anything.

Not yet.

But she'd been watching.

And now she couldn't shake the feeling that somebody was watching her back.

The bell above the door jingled again.

Zora was behind the counter, labeling a new batch of soil blend, pretending she was fine. Pretending the crooked label from earlier didn't still haunt her spirit.

She didn't look up. "We're closed."

"Oh," Keira said, voice already full of attitude. "So, this is how you greet the friend who brings snacks?"

Zora exhaled and looked up. "Do you have plantain chips?"

"Of course I do." Keira held up the brown paper bag like an offering. "And a lemon water because you're dramatic and dehydrated."

Zora cracked a smile and took the bag as Keira walked around the counter like she owned the place. She hopped up to sit on the edge, crossing one leg over the other.

"Your energy's weird," she said without preamble.

Zora rolled her eyes. "That's your opener?"

"Yup." Keira peeled open a second bag of chips for herself. "You been acting off all week, but today? You're real quiet. Real... centered in a way that feels fake."

"I'm just working."

"You're working in silence. That's unnatural."

Zora didn't respond. She pressed a fresh label onto the next soil bag and lined it up perfectly on the shelf.

Keira watched her. Didn't push. Just let the room breathe for a second.

Then, softly: "Truck break down?"

Zora froze.

Not dramatically. Not visibly.

But enough.

"Yeah," she said after a beat. "She died in front of a damn community center."

Keira winced. "Ugh. That's disrespectful."

"Fully. She picked the busiest block on the hottest day of the week."

"Did you call Triple A or scream into the void?"

Zora huffed. "Neither. A man helped me."

Keira blinked, then turned to look at her fully. "A man?"

Zora was already regretting this. "It wasn't a moment."

Keira said nothing.

Just waited.

Zora gave in with a sigh. "He works at the center. Helped me call the tow. Calm. Quiet. Very... grounded."

Keira didn't blink. "Fine?"

Zora glared.

Keira grinned. "So, yes."

Zora tossed a chip at her. "It wasn't like that."

"Did you make a fool of yourself?"

"I was hot. Flustered. Loud. In full Zora mode." "So, yourself."

Zora rolled her eyes again, but this time with less fight. Keira's grin softened. "So why you acting like this?" "Because he didn't flinch," Zora said quietly.

Keira tilted her head.

"I'm used to being too much. He just... absorbed it. Balanced it."

They let that sit.

Then, Keira nudged her with a foot. "You want me to say something reckless, or something true?"

"Truth. Soft, though."

"Alright," Keira said, her tone gentle now. "Maybe it ain't about if he saw you. Maybe it's about the fact that—for once —you didn't shrink."

Zora stared at the bag in her hand. Then nodded.

Keira slid off the counter, brushing crumbs off her leggings. "Alright. I'm heading out before you talk me into alphabetizing your fertilizer bins again."

Zora cracked a tired smile. "You loved that, and you know it."

"Mmhmm." Keira picked up her tote, then paused near the crate by the back door. "You still want this dropped at Bliss Botanicals?"

Zora blinked. "You serious?"

Keira shot her a look. "Girl. You think I'm letting your hard-earned signature blend sit here pouting like it didn't get invited to the pop-up?"

Zora hesitated. "It's already late."

"And?"

Zora almost said no. Almost reached for the crate herself out of reflex. But then—she didn't.

"Yeah," she whispered. "If you don't mind."

Keira winked. "I got you. Besides, I look way better doing deliveries than you do when you're this stressed."

"Wow. And yet I'm trusting you with my soil."

"Because you know I'm loyal," Keira called over her shoulder, already heading out with the crate like it weighed nothing. "And your shit smells like money."

The door swung shut behind her, and Zora stood in the quiet, a little lighter than before.

By the time Keira left, the sun had dipped just enough to throw gold across the front windows of Wild Hart.

Zora stood alone in the quiet shop, the last bits of lavender incense curling up toward the ceiling like exhaled breath.

She locked the front door, flipped the sign to CLOSED, and leaned her forehead against the cool glass for a few seconds before turning the lights down low.

It had been a long day. And not because of the heat, or the truck, or the orders.

Because of him.

And the part of her that didn't know what to do with being seen. She moved slowly now—sweeping near the entry, wiping down surfaces, checking that every plant had what it needed.

The motions soothed her, even when the thoughts didn't.

In the back, she opened the cooler and pulled out a half-bottle of hibiscus tea. Sipped. Let it sit on her tongue before swallowing.

She could hear Keira's voice in her head already: That man got you drinking floral and contemplative.

Zora rolled her eyes and smirked, just a little.

She walked back to the front counter, phone already in hand. No notifications. No messages.

She told herself she didn't care.

Then, as if summoned by contradiction, her screen lit up.

Unknown Number:

Your truck folded under pressure. You didn't.

Zora blinked. Stared.

The smallest laugh slipped from her mouth—barely there, but real.

He remembered her. He followed up.

And somehow, even through text, his tone was exactly the same tone: calm, dry, and intentional.

And somehow, even through a text, his tone was exactly the same:

No emoji. No weird punctuation. No pressure. She didn't reply.

Just presence.

Not yet. response, then backspacing it into silence.

Her fingers hovered over the screen, thumbs tapping out a half-response wasn't sure she could walk through.

She didn't want to seem eager. Didn't want to open a door she But her heart was pacing like her body already had.

She saved the number. Just his name.

No emoji.

Darius

Then set the phone down on the counter, placed her palm on the nearest soil blend bag. The quiet wrapped around her like the end of a song.

Not finished.

Just... pausing.

something to offer

"LET ME IN" BY H.E.R

Darius crouched beside the robotics table, watching Roman fumble with the drone casing for the third time. The kid's brows were furrowed, lips pressed tight in frustration, but his hands? Steady now— irritated, yeah, but focused. Darius didn't speak. Just leaned in close enough to offer presence without pressure.

He'd learned a long time ago that kids—especially his family—didn't respond to force. They responded to consistency. To stillness that didn't feel like surveillance. To a structure that didn't assume it knew better.

He offered that. The same way he wished someone had offered it to him when he was younger.

Roman grunted, finally clicking the shell back into place.

"Thought I broke it."

"You didn't," Darius said simply, standing. "You were just trying too hard to control it."

Roman side-eyed him, the ghost of a smirk tugging at his mouth.

"Ma said you'd be all extra about this drone."

Darius arched a brow, but let it slide.

"You eat?" he asked, eyes scanning the rest of the table.

"Ma made me," Roman muttered, straightening up.

Darius nodded once. That tracked.

He moved toward the back wall, gaze catching on the mural Saige helped him paint that first summer—Black kids in wild colors, arms outstretched, mid-motion, unbothered. He let it hold him for a second.

It hadn't always looked like this.

This building used to be a half-gutted tutoring center with water damage, bad wiring, and city officials who side-eyed his grant applications like he was asking for too much.

He remembered the zoning fight.

The contractors who ghosted.

The all-white grant panel that told him his mission sounded "ambitious" when all he said was that Black kids deserved quiet without consequence.

There were nights he'd sat in his dark kitchen, too overwhelmed to speak. Just pressing his fingertips to the tile floor to ground himself, trying not to let the noise of doubt spiral too loudly in his head.

But he kept going.

Saige cussed on his behalf when he couldn't.

Mama Regina kept praying like the permits would come through on faith alone.

And somehow? They did.

Now, Roman was here—his nephew, dropping drone parts and picking them back up, learning how to be still without being silent. Other kids were too—bouncing off walls, curled up in quiet rooms, unraveling safely.

This place wasn't perfect. But it was theirs.

He let his hand brush the edge of the robotics table. Roman was stuffing tools back into the bin, grumbling under his breath but focused. At home here.

Yeah. This was worth every fight.

Darius crossed to the windows and scanned the rest of the center—two kids playing chess near the snack bar, one teen crashed on the couch, hoodie up and headphones in, blocking out the world.

The hum of the center settled in his bones like a song—low, steady, exactly the tempo he'd spent years fighting to find.

He made a quick note in his phone to restock soldering wire, checked the goggles bin one last time, and stepped into the hallway just as his phone buzzed.

Short. Soft. Familiar.

Zora.

He didn't check it right away. Just breathed in, slow and deep, fingertips brushing his pocket. Grounded.

Ready.

> So you always this when people unravel in
> front of you?

He didn't laugh. But it sat with him—sharp, a little self-conscious, wrapped in humor. Exactly the way she probably intended.

His thumb hovered. Not anxious. Just alert. This wasn't dysregulation —it was anticipation. Another thing CBT helped him recognize: not every flicker meant fallout.

He typed slowly, deliberately. No performance. Just presence.

> You moved like you needed stillness.

I know how to be that.

He paused. Considered. Then added:

> You ever bring plants into schools?

The center could use some green. A beat. And then:

> Kids run the place like it's chaos and
> potential. You'd fit right in.

He hit send, slipped his phone back into his pocket, and let the rhythm of his steps pull him down the hall.

IN MY *Rhythm*

Outside the main office window, he glanced at the lot. It was cracked at the edges, paint faded. Not much to look at. But he pictured her truck anyway—maybe not fully fixed, maybe still protesting in the mornings, but pulling up like it belonged there. He didn't imagine a flawless arrival. He imagined something persistent. Intentional. A little uneven, but still. Like her.

That's how his therapist had described progress once—loud and unpolished, but still yours.

She'd probably complain about the broken curb. Tell him this place needed real landscaping. Then step out of her truck in those loud colors and gold hoops and that voice that didn't ask for permission before taking up space.

He passed the quiet room, opened the door, and looked around. Bare walls. White noise machine was still running. The light in here was soft —filtered through sheer curtains, no overhead glare. The kind that made overstimulation easier to manage. He'd helped design it that way. Routine, structure, low-sensory input. Peace that didn't demand stillness —just offered it.

His gaze drifted to the back wall—bare. Empty.

He imagined a tall plant there. Something grounded. Something with presence.

A fiddle-leaf fig? No. Too finicky.

Maybe a monstera. Broad leaves. Lush but low-maintenance.

He made a mental note to mention it to her—if she showed up. But truthfully, he wasn't worried.

He hadn't offered an invitation for the sake of it. And he hadn't offered it lightly.

He wasn't trying to impress her.

He wanted her to see him there.

Not the polished version. Not the man who could text a clean sentence and sit in silence without flinching.

The man who built something and left a space in it—just in case someone like her came along and decided to stay.

The center was settling. Robotics kids, done for the day. The halls was quiet except for the occasional sneaker squeak or crinkling snack wrapper. Darius stood in the main office, sorting flyers that didn't need to be sorted, phone on the desk beside him, screen off.

He hadn't been watching it. Not exactly. But his body clock had already started syncing to hers.

CBT had taught him how to notice emotional shifts without labeling them emergencies. This wasn't a spiral. Just motion. Alignment.

It buzzed once—short and direct. Just like her. He picked it up.

> What's your budget? I don't do pity plants—
> but I might make an exception.

He stared at it for a beat. Let the words settle.

She said yes. Wrapped in fire, dressed like a maybe—but make no mistake, it was yes.

He could see the layers in it. The tease, the test, the tug-of-war between curiosity and control. But buried underneath the shade was her decision. She was coming.

The corner of his mouth curved—subtle, slow. Not smug. Just satisfied.

Zora didn't bend easily. He could tell. She moved like someone who'd been dropped before. Someone who built her own world, so she never had to need anyone else again. And now she was about to bring that world—her world—into his.

Not because he convinced her.

Because she chose to.

He locked the screen and slid the phone into his back pocket, the reply already forming in his mind. He didn't rush to send it. He moved through the back hallway, checking the community room. He didn't need a clipboard to take inventory, but sometimes he carried one anyway —routine soothed the kids, and, if he was honest, it grounded him, too.

The big windows in the front still needed to be cleaned. He made a note to clear the lot in the morning—move the folding sign, fix the sagging chain link.

When he sat at his desk again, he pulled out his phone and typed slowly, each word deliberate.

> See you Thursday. I'll clear the front windows. You'll know where to park.

He paused. Then added:

> I'll have coffee. You bring the green.

He hit send. Sat back. And exhaled—not because he'd been holding his breath, but because something in him had started adjusting. Realigning.

This wasn't just a text exchange anymore. This was motion.

And Zora was moving toward him.

Darius moved through the center in rhythm. No rush. No noise. Just motion with purpose.

He shifted two tables near the front windows and opened the blinds halfway to let the light fall where he wanted it. He rarely bothered with this much—most of the space stayed exactly how it needed to be. But today, he made room. Not because it had to be done. Because she was coming.

He didn't need perfection. Just intentional.

The air smelled faintly of lemon cleaner and warm dust from the vents kicking on. He walked to the sensory shelf and moved a bin out of the main path, checking it without thinking. Everything in is place.

His phone buzzed on the desk once, screen lighting up with her name, but he didn't reach for it yet.

The door opened behind him with that soft groan it always made when the weather turned.

"Yo," Zion called, stepping inside with a laptop bag slung over one shoulder and a box under one arm. "Dropped off those extra chargers. Roman's crew was out here using duct tape like it's insulation."

Darius looked over, took the box from him with a nod. "Appreciate it."

Zion set his bag on a chair and looked around. His eyes landed on the cleared corner near the window. "You redecorating now, or just restless?"

"Rearranging," Darius said.

Zion raised a brow but didn't say anything for a second. Then, casually, "That woman you sent to the shop. Zora. She good?"

Darius nodded once. "Handled herself."

"She did," Zion said. "Truck didn't, but she wasn't pressed. Said what she needed, kept it cool."

Darius didn't speak. Just folded the towel in his hand and kept wiping the last fingerprint off the desk.

Zion took a sip from the bottle he pulled out of his bag, still watching him. "You checkin' in on her later?"

Darius glanced at the clock, then at the lot outside. "She's stopping by."

Zion tilted his head like that confirmed something he already suspected. "Cool," he said. "She had a solid presence. Felt grounded."

"Yeah."

"Good energy," Zion added, and left it there.

Darius gave a small nod, subtle but sure. "That's what caught me."

Zion picked up his bag and headed for the door. "Aight. I'll let you get back to your—rearranging."

Darius cracked the faintest smile. "It's called preparation."

Zion smirked. "Whatever helps you sleep, man."

Then, he was gone.

Darius stood there a moment longer, letting the quiet settle around him again.

Everything was in place. Nothing extra.

Just space—intentional, open. Structured enough for calm, flexible enough to let someone else move through it.

Ready.

CHAPTER FIVE

don't play with me

"SWEETER" BY LEON BRIDGES FT
TERRANCE MARTAN

Zora knew peace wasn't supposed to feel suspicious.

But that's exactly what it felt like—this quiet, steady rhythm Darius had slipped into without warning.

Three days since she delivered the plants to the center. Three days of phone calls. Not daily check-ins or long deep talks, but just enough for the silence not to swallow her.

Sometimes they talked about nothing. Sometimes about soil and sensory bins. Once, she told him about a plant called "goldfish vine" that didn't smell like anything but bloomed like drama, and he'd said, deadpan, "Seems like your kind of flower."

She'd laughed harder than she meant to.

And that, right there—that ease—was the problem.

Because Zora didn't do easy. She did plans. She did systems. She did energy exchanges that made sense. But now she was standing in her own damn store with her chest feeling too open and her hands too empty.

She adjusted the snake plant near the register, then adjusted it again, even though it wasn't crooked. The playlist was on low—instrumental jazz, heavy on keys. It let her move in rhythm. Or, more accurately, let her spiral in silence.

Not about him.

About herself.

Because she wasn't used to someone following up without being asked.

She wasn't used to saying yes to a man and having him not push or flinch, or fumble the space between them. She wasn't used to someone keeping his word and still leaving her this... still.

Three days wasn't long. But that didn't matter.

Back in foster care, silence had always meant something was about to go left. Social workers coming. Another trash bag packed with her life in it.

A locked door or a new "auntie" who wanted obedience but not presence. She'd learned early to make noise first. Be useful. Be hard to forget. The girls who were too quiet got left behind.

But Darius didn't make her work for his attention.

He just gave it. Even when he didn't say much. Especially when he didn't say much.

And somehow, that felt louder than anything.

IN MY *Rhythm*

Zora stepped behind the counter, picked up her phone, and checked it like she hadn't just talked to him last night. No messages. Not yet. She set it back down and shook her head at herself.

She grabbed the watering can instead. Something to do. Something grounded.

She was halfway through misting the ferns when Mr. Kenneth walked in. Regular. Retired. Always wore too much cologne and acted like his pothos could sing if he talked sweetly enough.

"Afternoon, Ms. Zora," he called, with that extra bass he used every time. "That tall plant in the window still single?"

Zora grinned before she turned around. "Depends—she's got commitment issues, but she thrives under gentle care."

"Mmm. Sounds familiar," he said, patting his chest. "I'll take her. And one of those three-pack blends, the good dirt. You know the one."

"Signature's ready in the back," she said, already moving.

That helped. For a minute. The rhythm. The motion. Her body remembering how to feel solid.

She was restocking the shelf, breathing deeper, when her phone buzzed again.

She let it sit for a beat. Finished the line of blend bags. Then walked over, calm.

It was a tag.

She tapped it open.

A boutique she barely followed had posted a carousel of "inspired soil blends." Polished photos. Warm tones. Clean branding.

Zora might've been impressed—if it hadn't been for one photo dead in the center of the swipe.

Her blend. Not a copy. But close enough. Off by just enough to claim difference. The caption sealed it.

"Tried a mix inspired by a friend's formula. Ours has more texture—plus a little secret ingredient 🤍😌"

Her jaw tightened.

No name. No direct reference. Just the kind of vague, smirking theft that made your gut clench before your mind caught up.

She zoomed in on the packaging. No wild accusations to be made. Just a very familiar layout. Too familiar. Even the font was damn near her custom one.

She closed the post. Then paused.

Someone she followed had liked it. Not a bestie. Not a hater. Just...someone who saw it. Someone watching.

Zora's stomach flipped.

Not from panic. From rage that came dressed like a question.

She didn't open the comments. Didn't go looking. That's how people spiraled.

Instead, she set the phone down face-first and pressed her palms to the counter.

The soil in her mix bin was still damp from this morning's batch. She reached for it, ran her fingers through it slowly—thumb to forefinger, wrist to wrist. Loam, compost, perlite. Her blend. Her rhythm.

She needed that texture to remind her she was still here. Still rooted.

Then, she picked up the watering can and moved to the next shelf. Her motions were calm, but her grip was tight.

Zora didn't do silence well. But she did stillness.

And sometimes, that was enough.

The bell above the door jingled, and Zora didn't look up.

"I come in peace," Keira called, "but I'm not above stirring something if needed."

Zora didn't flinch. Just kept rotating the monstera on the front display stand. "I didn't ask for peace. Or company."

"You're getting both," Keira said, strutting in like she paid bills here.

"Also, snacks. And unsolicited opinions."

She dropped a brown bag on the counter and slid behind it like she hadn't just broken every boundary Zora never gave her. The scent of plantain chips and lemon water followed her, softening the edge of her entrance.

Zora gave her a sideways glance. "You always bring snacks like it's an apology for the chaos you're about to cause?"

"Exactly," Keira said. "Now why your jaw tight and your shoulders higher than the price of rent?"

Zora didn't answer. Just moved a little slower than usual behind the register.

Keira pulled out a chip and crunched into it. "So this about a man or a petty tag?"

Zora blinked. "You saw it?"

Keira nodded. "Didn't even follow them, and it showed up

on my explore page. That's how you know the algorithm got beef."

Zora sighed. "Didn't credit me. Just a wink and 'inspired.' Like I'm supposed to be flattered."

"People be remixing your work like it's a Cirqle trend," Keira muttered. "But you already knew that was coming. Your blend too solid not to get jacked."

Zora leaned back against the counter, arms folded. "I know. It's not even about the post."

Keira popped another chip and waited.

"It's about how it still gets to me," Zora finally admitted. "Like I haven't done enough to feel steady."

"You have done enough," Keira said. "You just haven't had enough people protect it the way you do."

Zora looked away.

"And maybe," Keira added, quieter now, "you're getting used to somebody who does."

Zora didn't speak.

Three days. Three calls. Three conversations that didn't ask for anything, just offered presence. She hadn't told Keira about the way Darius let her ramble about pH levels like it was poetry. Or how he paused when she spoke, like he didn't want to miss anything.

She hadn't said it out loud because she didn't know what it meant. "You talked to him today?" Keira asked, casually, but not really.

Zora nodded. "This morning. He was headed into a meeting."

Keira raised an eyebrow. "And?"

"He said he'd call after. No pressure. Just said it."

Keira stared at her. "Girl, you're being courted."

Zora rolled her eyes, but her face betrayed her. "It's not like that."

"No, it is," Keira said. "You're just not used to it."

Zora swallowed hard, heat rising in her chest.

"I'm not saying trust it right away," Keira continued. "I'm saying don't flinch from it before it has a chance to be real."

Zora looked at the plants she'd just watered. Every one of them thriving under consistency. Not over watering. No pressure. Just presence. Stillness.

She let that thought sit.

Then picked up the bag of chips and took one without asking.

Keira grinned as if she'd won.

Keira was mid-rant about comment section etiquette—"If you gonna be shady, at least be clever"—when the bell over the door jingled again.

Zora looked up, expecting a customer.

She wasn't ready for him.

Darius stepped into the shop like it weren't a surprise visit. Like this was just what people did on a Wednesday afternoon —show up. Quiet. Solid. No fanfare.

He had on a black crewneck, soft-washed jeans, and that same unbothered calm he wore like skin. His gaze found hers instantly. Steady. Focused. Present.

Zora's throat went dry for half a second.

Keira froze mid-chip. "Oh."

Darius gave her a nod, polite but not performative. "Afternoon."

"You're real," Keira whispered under her breath, like she'd spotted a unicorn.

Zora shot her a look.

Darius walked closer, pace even. He didn't crowd the counter. Didn't reach for anything. Just stood where he was, a few feet away, eyes only on her.

"I was in the area," he said. "Thought I'd stop by."

Zora tilted her head, skeptical. "You were in this area?"

His mouth twitched—barely a smile. "Felt like the right direction." Something inside her unraveled and snapped into place at the same time.

She set down the clipboard in her hand and crossed her

arms—not defensively, just grounding herself. "You just out here popping up on people now?"

"You said this was your day off. I figured I might catch you here working anyways."

"And if I wasn't?"

"Then I'd try again."

That quiet confidence hit her low. No pressure. No pretense. Just Darius, being Darius.

Keira cleared her throat dramatically and stood up from behind the counter. "I'm gonna go... pretend to be somewhere else."

Zora didn't stop her.

Darius waited until Keira was out the door before he spoke again.

"You good?"

Zora nodded. "Working on it."

He looked around. "It smells like basil and honesty in here."

Zora smiled for real then. "I think that's the sage and judgment."

Darius let out a low breath that could've been a laugh. "Fair enough."

She walked around the counter and stood in front of him, still not too close. Still giving herself space to feel it all.

"I wasn't expecting you."

"I know."

She met his eyes. "But I'm not mad about it."

That was enough for now.

Darius let a beat pass. Let the silence stretch, not heavy, but meaningful. Then he said, "Tomorrow night."

Zora raised an eyebrow. "Tomorrow night, what?"

"I'm picking you up," he said, voice low but certain. "Seven-thirty. Dress comfortable."

Her mouth opened. Closed. "You already planned it?"

"I don't offer things I'm not ready to follow through on."

Zora blinked once. She wasn't used to that kind of clarity. It didn't feel like pressure. It felt like structure.

Safe. Intentional.

She tilted her head. "You always move like this?"

"I move when I mean it."

Zora looked down at her hands, then back at him. "You know that's not normal, right?"

"Good," he said. "I'm not trying to be."

She hated how fast her stomach flipped at that.

But she didn't show it. Just nodded. "Alright. Tomorrow then."

Darius gave her one last look that lingered without hovering, then nodded once and turned to leave.

The door closed behind him with the softest click.

And somehow, the shop felt warmer.

comfortable isn't easy

"THE LINE" BY DVSN

Darius leaned back on his couch, Cirqle app open, scrolling slow. He wasn't the snooping type—but tonight? He made an exception.

Zora's Wild Hart page was easy to find—clean branding, rich greens, full of customer posts and workshop shots. He scrolled back a bit until he hit one of the pop-up event posts, a group pic with three women grinning behind a table of plants and soil bags.

He tapped the tags. @plantbae.keira. Loud captions, bold energy. Yeah. That was her.

He hesitated for half a second, then hit Message.

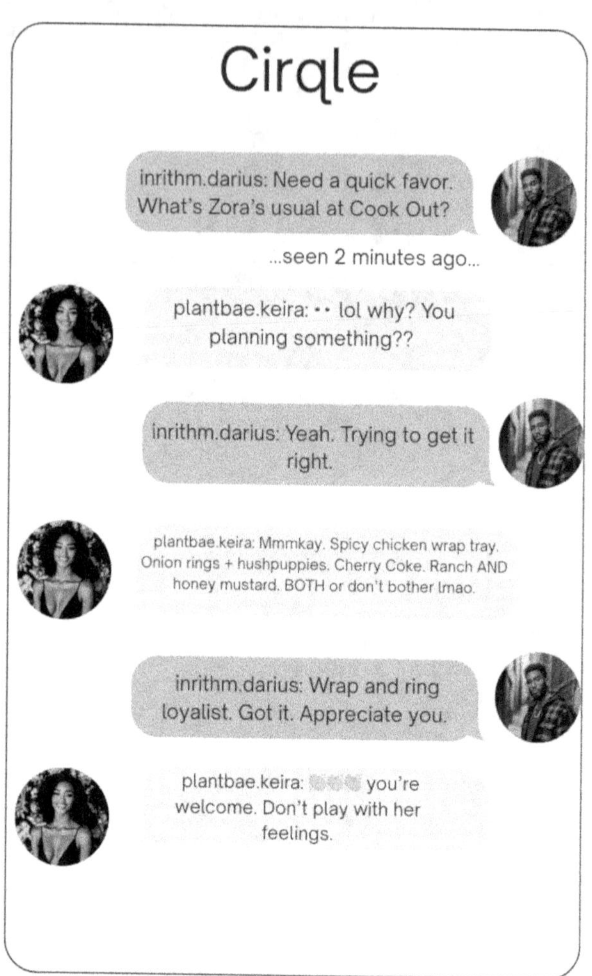

Darius smirked, locked his phone, and stood—grabbing his keys from the counter like the next move had already decided itself. Plan secured.

IN MY *Rhythm*

Darius pulled into the lot in front of Wild Hart at exactly 7:28. He didn't do late. Not for people. Not for plans. And definitely not for her.

He let the engine hum for a moment, watching the last of the sunlight streak the front windows. Then he shut it off, climbed out, and headed to the door. No honk. No text. Just steps measured and full of intention.

The door opened before he even reached it.

Zora stepped out, locking up behind her with a flick of her wrist. When she turned, he saw her fully—and for a second, he just stood there.

Her outfit did the most—without even trying. That brown crochet set hugged her hips like it had grown onto her skin, the top snug against her chest, little flowers stitched into the fabric like they bloomed on cue. Her locs were down, thick and wrapped with just enough copper thread to catch the light. Gold hoops. Glossed lips. Waistline soft and loud at the same time.

She looked like warmth and fire—something alive, buzzing just beneath the surface.

"Damn," Darius said, voice low. "You look gorgeous."

Zora tilted her head, a slow smile threatening. "You practicing compliments now?"

"No," he said, calmly and steadily. "Just calling it like I see it."

She didn't say thank you. Just walked past him to the truck, hips loose, fully aware he was watching.

He followed, opened the passenger door for her, and helped her in. She settled in easily, one leg crossed, hands smoothing over her thighs like she was grounding herself. He walked around the front, got in, and let the truck warm back up with the soft hum of Daniel Caesar's "Get You" spilling from the speakers.

They rode in silence for the first few blocks—comfortable, but present. Darius felt the edge of it—and leaned in.

"You nervous?" he asked.

Zora glanced over, amused. "About what?"

"Dates. Letting somebody else lead."

She smirked, one brow rising. "You assuming I don't date?"

"Nah, I'm saying you don't follow."

That pulled a small laugh from her—real and quick. "You really think you know me already?"

"I think you know how to stay in control. And I respect it."

Zora didn't respond at first. Just looked out the window, the city lights catching the edge of her profile.

"Okay," she said eventually. "Maybe I'm a little nervous."

"So am I."

She turned, surprised. "You don't look it."

"That's 'cause I planned this for you. Not for me."

The look she gave him then held a little more weight than the smile behind it.

And just like that, the quiet between them wasn't empty anymore.

It was anticipation.

The Cook Out lot was buzzing, even for a weeknight. Cars lined up in both lanes, music bumping from somewhere near the back. Darius eased the truck forward, calm, one hand resting on the wheel while the other tapped a slow rhythm on his thigh.

Zora glanced out the window, then back at him. "You really brought me to Cook Out... on a date?"

He raised a brow. "You disappointed?"

"No," she said. "Just making sure I'm not dreaming."

He smirked, but didn't take the bait. She was already smiling, so he didn't have to say much else.

The truck rolled up to the speaker. The voice on the other end cracked through. "Welcome to Cook Out. Go ahead when you're ready."

"Spicy chicken wrap tray," Darius said, smoothly and without hesitation. "Onion rings. Hushpuppies. Cherry Coke. Ranch and honey mustard. Please don't make me have to come inside over some sauce because my girl ain't get her sauce."

Zora turned to him fast, eyes wide. "How'd you——"

He kept going. "And one Cajun chicken tray. Double fries. Sweet tea." The speaker crackled again. "Anything else?"

"We're good," he said, and pulled up.

Zora stared. "You really ordered my tray like you've been memorizing it."

"I have good intel."

She narrowed her eyes. "Keira."

"She made it sound like if I got the sauces wrong, she'd personally slash my tires."

Zora laughed, for real this time. "Sounds about right."

"She also called you a wrap-and-ring loyalist."

"That woman talks too much," she muttered, biting back another grin.

Darius handed over a bill at the window, tipped the teen who handed him their food, and passed Zora her tray with care. She peeked inside, saw everything was dead-on, and leaned back—finally, her shoulders loosening like she could trust it now.

"You really did your homework," she said, pulling a hush puppy apart like it owed her answers.

"I listen," Darius said simply.

"Not everybody does."

"I'm not everybody."

Zora didn't respond right away. Just dipped the hush-puppy, popped it in her mouth, and chewed slowly. Like, maybe she was still deciding if that was a compliment or a threat to her emotional equilibrium.

They rode in silence for a minute, windows cracked, music still playing low from the speakers. Daniel Caesar had faded out, replaced by a mellow groove with just enough bass to keep her tapping her finger against the cupholder.

"Where we going?" she asked eventually. "You'll see."

"You always this vague?"

"Only when I've got a plan."

"And you do?"

Darius nodded, keeping his eyes on the road. "You'll know when we get there."

Zora unwrapped her straw, took a sip, and watched him for a moment longer.

Then she smiled again, soft this time. "You're lucky I'm into mystery."

He didn't say anything.

But he noticed the way she settled deeper into the seat after that.

IN MY *Rhythm*

They pulled into the drive-in just after sunset, the sky still holding onto streaks of gold and plum. Darius rolled to a stop in the far row, tucked in under one of the older screen towers, just out of reach of the main crowd.

Zora climbed up into the bed of the truck like she belonged there, kicked her shoes off, and leaned back on the pillows like her body knew it before her brain caught up. A few cars away, someone turned up their radio a little too loud, and the sound of opening credits filtered across the lot. The sky above the screen glowed silver-blue, and the opening scene lit up the gravel around them like a pulse.

She looked up once, then back at Darius. The movie was starting. But this? This was the main event.

Darius joined her, sitting beside her without touching, just breathing in the moment. As the movie previews started and the lot filled with more chatter, more revving engines and speaker crackle, Darius reached into his pocket and pulled out his loop earplugs.

Zora noticed. Her brow lifted slightly, not judging, just curious.

He slid them into place, slow and practiced, then turned to her.

"Too much sound out here, "he said." I'm blocking out everything that don't matter."

Then he looked at her, dead center.

"This? This matters."Z

ora didn't blink. Didn't smirk. Just looked at him maybe she believed him more than she wanted to admit.

She turned back to the screen, quieter now.

Blikcher body was a little closer than it had been.

The movie played on, but Darius wasn't watching. Zora sat beside him, settled now, but still holding that settled now, but still holding that charge in her body. Her thigh pressed into his, her fingers grazing his every time she reached for the kettle corn. She didn't apologize. Didn't pull back. Just kept shifting closer in that slow, natural way that didn't ask for permission.

She was so close he could smell her. Something citrusy and warm, probably from the oil in her locs, mixed with popcorn salt and cherry Coke. He hadn't planned on memorizing it— but it was already there.

Every few minutes, she'd glance at him like she wasn't trying to, then turn her head like she hadn't been caught.

He let her have that. Let her pretend.

But he wasn't pretending.

Zora adjusted the blanket in her lap and leaned just slightly in his direction, her voice low, steady. "You always this quiet when you're about to make a move?"

Darius didn't answer right away. He turned his head and looked at her—eyes tracing the curve of her cheek, the gold glint in her hoops, the softness sitting in her mouth like it hadn't decided if it wanted to smile or speak.

He held her gaze. "No," he said. "Just don't like wasting words when action speaks clearer."

And then he leaned in—slow, steady—and kissed her.

Her lips met his without hesitation, but the way her hand curled into his shirt said she hadn't been expecting it. Her other hand slid up, fingers brushing the side of his neck like she was checking if he was real.

His palm found her thigh, slow and grounding, not grabbing— holding.

She tasted like cherry Coke and something warm he couldn't name—but already wanted more of.

He didn't rush it. Didn't deepen it.

He just kissed her like he meant it.

When he finally pulled back, her hand stayed on his chest, fingers still curled in fabric like she hadn't quite decided to let go.

Zora blinked once, her eyes still on his mouth. "That wasn't subtle."

His thumb brushed the side of her thigh. "Didn't feel like tonight called for subtle."

She didn't say anything. Just stared at him for another second—long enough for him to see it in her face: this changed something.

Then, slow and quiet, she leaned in and kissed him again.

This time deeper. This time with a little more breath in it. A little more weight.

And when they broke apart again, she didn't move away. Just let her body lean into his like her decision had already been made.

Darius stayed still. Arm around her now. Her head was just barely resting near his shoulder.

The movie blurred into the background, just light and movement playing across the screen. Neither of them was watching anymore.

Zora's body was curled toward his now, blanket pulled up to her waist, head resting near his shoulder. Her fingers toyed absently with the seam of his shirt, like muscle memory she didn't clock.

Darius didn't speak at first. He didn't need to fill the quiet. But this wasn't just silence. It was space. A soft pocket between moments, and he didn't want it to close without meaning something.

So he spoke—low, careful. "I don't do crowds well," he said. "Too much sound. Too many people moving at the same time. My brain don't like it."

Zora didn't lift her head, but her hand stilled.

"I'm autistic," he added. "Level one. I've always knew that I was different from other kids. My mom made sure I knew."

Her voice was soft. "You don't seem like you let people talk over you."

"Not anymore," he said.

Zora was quiet for a long moment. Then, she shifted, just enough to lay her head against his chest, fingers still resting near his ribs.

"I grew up in the system," she said, just as quietly. "Foster homes. Five of them. Some better than others. All temporary."

Darius's hand moved from her thigh to her waist, settling there, warm and anchoring.

"I learned not to need people," she said. "Didn't mean I stopped wanting to."

He didn't respond right away. Just rubbed his thumb in a slow circle against her side.

"You don't have to need me," he said. "But if you want me here, I'll stay."

Zora didn't answer with words. She just curled in—slow, certain—as if her body had made the decision before her mind caught up.

almost

"MY AFFECTION" BY SUMMER WALKER FT. PARTYNEXTDOOR

Zora had repotted the same snake plant three times. Not because it needed it.

Just because it gave her hands something to do.

The shop was quiet—too quiet. Keira wasn't in yet. No playlist was running. The sage she normally lit every morning sat untouched on the windowsill. The scent of eucalyptus lingered faintly from yesterday, but even that felt like a memory trying too hard to stay relevant.

She swept soil into a bin, wiped the same counter she'd already cleaned, adjusted the placement of a pothos that didn't need adjusting. None of it helped.

It had been three days.

Three days since the drive-in.

Three days since Darius kissed her like he meant every second of it. Three days since he looked her in the eye and said she didn't have to need him—but he'd stay if she wanted him. And she hadn't texted him once.

Not because she didn't want to.

But because she did.

Too much.

Too fast.

Too loud, and she didn't know how to quiet that kind of wanting without pushing it away.

Her stomach flipped just thinking about how steady he was. How he'd sat beside her like the world didn't need anything but that moment. How his thumb traced lazy circles into her thigh, like her body was a thing to study, not control. Like he was trying to understand her before touching anything else.

But soft didn't mean safe. She knew that.

Her parents were soft—warm, full of music and plants and Sunday dinners. But they were gone. She was eight. It was supposed to be a regular night—her mom in the kitchen humming to Anita Baker, her dad fixing the wonky porch light that never stayed lit. They left to pick up takeout, promised they'd be back before her bedtime. Zora remembered the way her mom kissed her forehead and said, "Be good, baby. We'll be right back."

But they didn't come back.

It happened fast, the cop said. A truck ran a red light. Hit them on the driver's side. Her dad died at the scene. Her mom made it to the hospital, but not through the night.

Zora hadn't even finished her homework when the knock came at the door. A cop's face, tired and grim. Words that didn't sound real at first. A woman from child services already waiting in the hall.

The rest blurred. Their house emptied out. Clothes in boxes. Toys she didn't remember packing. The smell of her mom's perfume fading off her pillowcase. By the end of the week, she was sleeping in a stranger's guest room with a nightlight she didn't recognize and a silence too big to crawl out of.

That's when she learned: Love could be soft. It could be everything. And it could vanish in a blink.

After that, soft stopped showing up.

Foster care taught her how to keep her hands busy and her face unreadable. How to say thank you without trusting what came next... How to survive being passed around like paperwork and smiled at like a performance.

She'd had one woman slap her for crying too loudly.

Another who made her sleep on the floor "until she earned the bed." And then there was the last one—the one who smiled sweetly and let Zora call her "Auntie," right until she packed Zora's things in silence and said, "You don't fit here anymore."

She never begged again after that.

Then came Montgomery.

The relationship that felt like home until it started feeling like a hallway—long, echoing, and cold.

He never yelled. Never hit. Never even left dramatically. But he made her feel like too much and not enough in the same breath. Called her passionate one day and difficult the next. Said she was "emotionally high-maintenance" when she asked for clarity. Said he needed space, then acted like she'd taken something from him by letting him go.

So yeah—Zora knew what "too good" felt like.

It felt like being reminded of everything she'd ever lost.

Which is why, even now, three days after a kiss that still buzzed through her skin like electricity, she hadn't texted back.

Because silence meant control.

And control? That was how she survived.

Zora grabbed the watering can again and started her loop, even though the plants didn't need it. She needed it. Something steady. Something predictable.

She just needed to stay busy enough to forget how much she wanted him to reach out again.

IN MY *Rhythm*

The bell over the door jingled, and Zora didn't bother looking up. She already knew.

Keira moved like she had a key even when she didn't.

Loud steps. Intentional attitude. That energy that always entered a room three seconds before her body did.

"You been up in here rearranging the same three plants since nine a.m.?" Keira asked, setting her tote on the counter.

"Morning to you too," Zora mumbled.

Keira looked around—scanned the space like it had secrets. "You swept already?"

"Twice."

"The pothos shelf?"

"Three times."

Keira narrowed her eyes. "Zora."

Zora grabbed a pair of gloves and turned her back. "I'm just getting ahead for the week."

"You mean running from something."

Zora didn't answer.

Keira stepped around the counter, folded her arms, and leaned against the edge like she was about to preach. "You ain't said his name once. Not since that date. And don't think I didn't notice."

Zora pulled a soil bin down with a little more force than necessary. "It was just a date."

"That ended in two kisses, a blanket setup, and a man telling you he'll stay if you want him to."

Zora looked up, sharp. "Why you bringing that up?"

"Because you acting like it didn't happen."

Zora set the bin down and rested her hands on the edge, breathing slow. "I don't know what you want me to say."

"I want you to admit you're scared as hell."

Zora didn't move. Didn't blink.

Keira's voice softened, but only a little. "You do this every time, Zo. You pull back the second someone feels good."

"Because good don't last."

"Not when you keep ghosting it before it gets the chance to stay." Zora's throat tightened.

Keira stepped closer. "You're not the girl on the floor anymore. You're not the 'too much' girlfriend or the foster kid with a timer on her bed. You're not waiting to be dropped. You're choosing to disappear."

That landed.

Hard.

Zora turned away like she needed something to clean, but her hands stayed frozen in place.

Keira softened fully now. "You want love, Zo. Real love. But you act like you gotta earn it every damn time."

Zora whispered, "What if I'm not built for it?"

Keira didn't hesitate. "Then why do you keep planting things that need time to grow?"

Zora looked down, the gloves in her hands suddenly feeling like armor she didn't ask for.

Silence filled the shop again—but this time, Zora felt seen inside it.

IN MY *Rhythm*

Keira had left over an hour ago, but her words still lingered in the air like incense smoke—visible in the light, impossible to shake. Zora sat behind the register with her knees pulled to her chest and a half-empty bottle of lemon water sweating on the counter. The shop was still, too still. She hadn't turned on music. The sage bundle sat untouched. Every shelf had been wiped twice, every plant checked and watered. She couldn't pretend there was anything left to do.

She'd checked her phone five times—quick glances, scrolling like it meant nothing. Just the lock screen. Just enough to pretend she wasn't waiting for his name.

Then it buzzed—once. No sound. Just that quiet little vibration that somehow landed loud as hell.

His name lit the screen.

Darius.

One message. Longer than usual. It started simple, but it didn't end like that.

Zora stared at the pop up on the screen. Her throat tightened.

She could almost hear the way he would've said it—calm, sure, low enough that it landed somewhere beneath her ribs instead of in her ears. Not performative. Not needy. Just solid.

It wasn't what she expected.

And that was the problem.

People had asked her if she was "okay" her whole life. But they didn't mean it. Not the case workers. Not the teachers. Not Montgomery, who only asked when it suited him. They wanted the lie. Wanted her to say yes so they could move on.

But Darius didn't feel like that.

She tapped the thread open. Typed, "I'm good." Stared at it. Deleted it.

Tried again: "I'm fine. Just been busy." Deleted that too.

Her thumbs hovered over the keyboard like the wrong word might shatter something. Like saying too much—or not enough—might send him retreating into the quiet she'd created.

She hated how vulnerable it made her feel. Hated more that she wanted to reply.

She locked the screen. Then, unlocked it again. The message sat there. Waiting. Like him.

She didn't text back.

Not yet.

But she didn't turn her phone over this time.

She left it face up on the counter, like maybe that was her way of keeping the door cracked open.

Because even if she couldn't say it yet, she wanted him there.

Zora stood in the back room of Wild Hart, scooping soil into kraft paper bags like she hadn't just spent half the day pretending her phone wasn't whispering at her from the front counter.

The scoop-shake-seal rhythm was usually meditative. Therapeutic even. But today, it just felt loud. Every motion made her think about him.

She packed three bags of her signature blend—moisture-balanced, good for indoor tropicals—and labeled each with her initials and a thin strip of Washi tape. Normally, she reserved these for her best pickup clients. But today, they were going in the cooler, headed to the community center.

Because someone at the center had mentioned wanting starter soil. And because it made sense to send it.

Business move. Nothing more.

Except that she was also packing lemon cookies.

Two of the soft kind from the bakery on her block. The ones she'd claimed were "too sweet" the first time Keira brought them over. The ones she'd eaten four of after the drive-in, while pretending not to replay the feel of Darius's hand on her thigh.

She sealed them in a small container and tucked them into the corner of the delivery crate, beneath the edge of a cloth so they wouldn't be the first thing anyone saw.

Not that it mattered.

It wasn't for everyone.

It was for him.

Zora stood back and looked at the crate. Perfectly packed. Neat. Like everything, she wished her mind felt like.

She told herself she was too busy to drop it off herself. That she'd have a delivery driver swing by tomorrow. Maybe even Keira. But then she grabbed her keys off the hook, anyway. Because sometimes the motion came before the courage. And today, her hands were braver than her heart.

And sometimes, maybe, she didn't need a reason to show up.

She walked out of Wild Hart as the sun started to drop behind the neighboring buildings, casting long shadows across the sidewalk. The crate sat snug in the backseat of her car, like it belonged there.

Zora climbed in and closed the door. Sat for a second.

The quiet filled up the space quickly, pressing at the edges of her chest. She reached into her bag and pulled out her phone.

The message from Darius was still there.

Unread. Still patient.

Her thumb hovered over it, but she didn't open it. Not yet.

Instead, she placed the phone in the cupholder—face-up—and started the engine.

She didn't know what she was walking into. But this time, she wasn't running.

show up anyway

"AFENI" BY RAPSODY FT. PJ MORTON

It had been two days since he sent the massage.

I know we haven't talked the last few days. Just checking in. You don't have to say much. Just let me know you're okay.

Zora read it. No reply.

Darius didn't follow up. No second message. No emojis or half-joke. He'd said what he meant, and meant what he said.

But silence had a weight, even when you didn't try to carry it.

He kept his hands busy—something Mama Regina had taught him a long time ago. Idle hands leave space for noise. So, he stayed moving. Finished client work. Rewired a tablet for the center. Even mopped the hallway by the back door. The floors didn't need it. But sometimes the motion mattered more than the reason.

Still, her quiet lingered—different. Not harsh, no careless.

Zora's silence didn't feel like avoidance. It felt like a door cracked open with the lights still on inside. Like something was happening just out of view, but she wasn't ready to let him see it yet.

He understood that kind of quiet. He used to live in it.

His phone buzzed from the windowsill just as he finished

folding the dish towel. He dried his hands and walked over slowly, not rushing. He already knew who it was.

Saige:

No greeting. No buildup. Just straight to it.

He smiled to himself and turned the screen off.

She texted again almost immediately.

That one made his chest pause—not tighten. Just... still.

Mama Regina didn't ask things she didn't already have feelings about. If she was asking about Zora, that meant she'd already felt the shift. Picked up on the way Darius had moved differently the last time they spoke. The slight tilt in his rhythm. That was how she worked— intuition over explanation.

He didn't respond.

He walked back to the sink and stared at the clean counter. His place smelled like lemon oil and dryer sheets. The soft hum of the fridge was the only sound in the house. Even the air felt still.

He glanced at the chair across from the counter—the one Zora hadn't sat in yet, but he'd looked at differently ever since the drive-in.

She wasn't here. But the idea of her had stayed.

He let the quiet hang for a few more seconds. Checked the clock. 2:12.

Still time.

He didn't text Saige back. Didn't type "on the way."

He just grabbed his keys, slid on his sneakers, and locked the door behind him.

Sometimes, showing up didn't need permission. It just needed presence.

IN MY *Rhythm*

The smell hit before Darius even stepped out of the truck—grilled ribs, smoked sausage, onions burning just enough to be perfect. Somebody had music going, old R&B with enough bass to hum under the conversation and the shuffle of lawn chairs. That was the rhythm of summer over here. Regular. Loud in the right places. Soft on the ones that mattered.

He parked in the grass like he always did, near the edge of the driveway, and stepped out into the kind of heat that didn't ask for attention—it just showed up. The backyard was already full.

Kids darted between tables, chasing footballs and swatting at bubbles. Aunties in sundresses sat under shade tents, fanning themselves between gossiping. Saige stood by the grill, wearing a Rithm Community Center tee and holding court with a spatula like it was a microphone. Mari was next to her, laughing low at something Roman had said, holding the tongs like backup vocals.

Darius stepped through the gate. He didn't have to announce himself.

Saige saw him first.

"Well, damn," she called out. "He lives."

"I'm not late," he said, calm.

"Mm," she said, flipping a sausage like it owed her money. "I sent that text three hours ago."

"And I showed up."

"You showed up empty-handed."

Darius smirked. "Didn't say I came to contribute. I came to eat."

"Boy, go fix a plate before I put you on grill duty."

He nodded and made his way to the food table, passing the spot where Mama Regina always sat—shaded, posted with her soft blanket across her lap and a church fan working like clockwork. She gave him a slow nod when he passed, like she already knew what kind of mood he was carrying.

But before he could say a word, a familiar voice beat him to it.

"There he go," Mr. Hayes said, raising his drink like it was part of the welcome. "You know we were about ten minutes away from talkin' bad about you."

Beside him, Mrs. Hayes sat in her wheelchair under the biggest umbrella in the yard. The heat never bothered her much, but the shade helped. MS might've slowed her physically, but her eyes were just as sharp as they'd been the first time she met him.

"Darius," she said with a smile that held nothing but curiosity, "how's your heart today?"

He nodded once, subtly. "Still beating."

She tapped her nails against the armrest of her chair. "Good. 'Cause Saige's been runnin' her mouth, and now I'm curious."

Mr. Hayes leaned forward. "You got company coming? Or you just movin' like a man who needs a date?"

Darius kept his focus on his plate. "Depends who you ask."

"Well," Mrs. Hayes said gently, "if she's someone worth showing up for, you make sure she knows there's room."

Darius looked up and met her gaze. There was no push in it. Just presence. The same way Mama Regina loved—without pressure.

He nodded. "She's worth it."

Mr. Hayes grinned widely. "That's what I'm talkin' about. I like this one already."

Mrs. Hayes smirked. "We'll hold her a plate. And I'll save her this spot next to me."

He fixed a plate—potato salad, deviled eggs, two ribs, and

a link— and walked toward the back corner of the yard where the breeze could find him. The music blended with laughter. The kids were loud. The space was full.

Even so, he checked his phone.

No response.

The message was still sitting there—read, but quiet. No reply. No new texts. Just space.

Zora wasn't here.

Not unless he went to get her. So that's exactly what he did.

IN MY *Rhythm*

Wild Hart was quiet when he pulled up. The sign still said OPEN, but it didn't look like she'd had customers in a while. He parked out front like he had before, stepped out, and stood there for a second.

He'd been inside once. Long enough to know the scent of eucalyptus would hit first, then the basil, then something earthy she probably wouldn't name unless you were paying attention. He remembered it because Zora didn't do anything halfway—not even her air.

He didn't text. Didn't knock.

Just opened the door and walked in like he belonged.

The bell over the door chimed. Zora looked up fast, then blinked like she wasn't sure if he was real or just a thought that he showed up early.

Her arms folded automatically, the kind of defensive posture that had nothing to do with him and everything to do with not knowing what came next.

Darius didn't move further. Just stood still and let the silence settle between them.

"I'm not staying," he said, voice low and even. "Just came to get you."

Zora blinked. "Get me?"

"There's food on the grill. People I care about. It'd mean something if you came."

She crossed her arms, but slower this time. Her chin tilted, guarded, but not cold. "You pulled up without even knowing if I'd say yes?"

"I figured if I didn't ask," he said, "you'd take that as proof you weren't wanted."

That line landed. Not dramatic. Just matter-of-fact. But it curled under her skin, anyway.

Her arms stayed crossed, but her stance shifted—like her body was having a different conversation than her mouth.

"You could've texted," she said.

He nodded once, but his gaze stayed on her. "And given you space to back out? Probably. But I didn't want you giving yourself another reason to stay in this shop like it's the only safe place on Earth."

That pulled something deeper from her. Her jaw clenched, just a little. He saw her eyes flick to the table behind her, to the back door, like escape routes she wouldn't take.

"I'm not trying to rush you," he added, voice softer now. "I just didn't want to leave the door cracked and pretend I wasn't hoping you'd walk through it."

Zora didn't speak right away. Her fingers tapped once against her arm. That familiar rhythm she used when she was thinking—fast and hard but quiet on the outside.

"You don't even know what I'd be walking into," she said, almost like a dare.

He shrugged, just barely. "Neither do you. But I'll be there. That's the difference."

The silence that followed wasn't tense. It was thick. Real. One of those rare pauses where two people were deciding what kind of story they were stepping into.

Zora broke it first.

She turned without a word, went into the back, and came out with her bag and a large, sealed container of banana pudding that she had made to give Keria but she'd just make her another batch.

Didn't explain herself. Didn't promise anything. But she walked toward him instead of away. And that was enough.

The minute they pulled up, Zora felt the shift.

The music hit first—old-school and bass-heavy, the kind that settled into your bones. Then the smoke—grilled meat, char, something sweet cooling in foil trays. It smelled like comfort she hadn't earned yet.

She glanced down at the glass dish on her lap—banana pudding, thick with extra wafers . Her safety move. Her "if all else fails, at least I brought dessert" fallback. But sitting here with it heavy in her arms, the air buzzing ahead of her, she almost stayed in the truck.

Then, Darius opened her door, quiet and easily, and waited.

No words. No pressure. Just him, steadily.

She stepped out, tugging at her shirt like it could settle her nerves, and followed him through the open gate, clutching the pudding like armor.

The yard was full and lived-in—people stacked up near folding tables, aunties in sundresses laughing with their heads tipped back, uncles fanning themselves with paper plates while watching the grill. Kids shot across the grass, wild with energy, and the smell of ribs and jerk chicken hung thick in the heat.

A few eyes tracked them as they moved through—curious, but not cold. A man by the grill gave Darius a chin lift. Two women near the drinks cooler whispered fast behind their cups, smiling like they already knew what was up.

Then younger woman stepped out from the cluster of people near the folding chairs, dish towel tossed over her shoulder, eyes sharp and shining. She clocked Zora instantly, lips curling into a slow smile.

"Well, damn," Saige said, her tone all teasing warmth. "I thought you looked familiar."

Zora blinked, caught a little off guard. "Community center," she said, pausing.

"Mm-hmm," Saige grinned. "I knew I wasn't imagining things. Nice to meet you for real this time."

"Zora," she offered, adjusting the pudding. "Sorry for popping up all messy that day. I brought banana pudding."

Saige waved that off like it was nothing. "I'm Saige, girl, please. You showed up real, and now you're here with banana pudding? You're already ahead of the game."

Zora laughed, the tension cracking just a little. "It's my go-to."

"Oh, she a smart one," Saige said, grinning at Darius. "No wonder you been walking around looking... suspiciously happy."

"Alright now," Darius muttered, side-eyeing her with a smirk.

Before Zora could respond, Mari came strolling over, plate in hand, eyes twinkling. "So this is the famous Zora. Finally."

Zora smiled, a little shy but holding her own. "Famous?"

Mari bumped her fist lightly. "You brought puddin', you famous today. Mari—Saige's other half and, unfortunately, tied to Darius for life."

She laughed and returned the fist bump, warmth spreading through her chest.

Mari leaned in, stage-whispering, "Listen, we've been waiting for him to bring somebody around for years. We were starting to think he was imaginary-dating."

"Man, can y'all chill?" Darius said, shaking his head but grinning. "Not a chance," Saige fired back, laughing.

Just then, a deeper voice cut through the buzz of conversation. "Ain't nobody gonna introduce us?"

Zora turned to see an older man working his way over from the patio, walking stick in one hand, eyes bright. Beside him, a woman in a wheelchair—dignified, sharp-eyed, but smiling—was already watching Zora like she'd been waiting her turn.

"Zora," Darius said, sliding a hand across her back as he took the dish from her arms. "These are Mari's parents—Mr. and Mrs. Hayes."

"Ahhh," Mr. Hayes said, dragging out the word like he was savoring it. "So you're the reason this one's been acting brand new."

Mrs. Hayes grinned, eyes sparkling. "Welcome, baby. I'm Mrs. Hayes—but you can call me Mama H if you're feeling friendly."

Zora stepped forward, warmth in her voice. "It's really nice to meet you both."

"And she's polite, too," Mr. Hayes said with a deep chuckle. "Plus, banana pudding? You're already a favorite."

Mrs. Hayes leaned in, mock-serious. "Now, don't let these folks fool you, baby. If your pudding tastes better than mine, we're throwing hands."

That cracked everyone up, even Zora, who found herself relaxing without meaning to. "No competition," she promised. "Mine's got nothing on yours, I'm sure."

"Mmhm," Mrs. Hayes said with a wink. "We'll let the taste buds decide."

The laughter rolled easily between them, warm and genuine, and Darius squeezed Zora's waist lightly, murmuring, "Come on, let's get you a plate."

As they started to move toward the tables, Zora caught sight of another woman seated beneath a wide umbrella—older, with salt-and- pepper braids tucked back, a soft smile playing at her lips as she watched the scene unfold. There was no rush in her eyes, just that patient kind of calm, like she'd already seen this story play out a hundred times.

Darius nodded toward her with a little lift of his chin. "And that's Mama Regina."

Zora blinked. "Mama Regina?"

"Yeah," Darius said, voice warm. "She's my peace."

Zora stepped a little closer, offering a small smile. "Hi, it's nice to meet you."

Mama Regina didn't move at first—just gave Zora a long, measured once-over, eyes crinkling at the edges. Then, she nodded slowly, approving. "Welcome, baby," she said, voice deep and smooth. "You just bring yourself and that good energy. That's all we ask."

Zora exhaled, the knot in her chest loosening more than she expected. "Thank you," she said, and meant it.

Mama Regina's smile tugged a little wider. "We been waiting on you."

As they turned toward the food tables, Zora felt it—real and deep this time.

She belonged here. Or at least, she could. And damn if that didn't feel good.

where i belong

"FOREVER DON'T LAST" BY JAZMINE SULLIVAN

Zora sat with her plate balanced on her knees, the hum of the cookout folding around her like warm air.

She hadn't said much since she and Darius walked in—not nerves exactly, just that weighty hush that comes when you step into a space built on history. This wasn't just food and music; it was legacy, the kind of bond that moved like muscle memory. Folks knew each other here. Moved like they belonged. That kind of closeness pressed in, heavy and unspoken.

Darius had kept his hand on the small of her back while they settled in, a grounding touch that said I got you, even when the noise swelled. But now he'd drifted over by the grill, laughing with Mari and a couple of uncles, and the space around Zora felt a little quieter, even with the party still rolling.

Across from her, Mama Regina sat back easy, a paper fan flicking slow across her lap, eyes shaded but sharp. She hadn't peppered Zora with questions—just pulled her in for a hug when they arrived, her voice low and certain: "We been waiting on you, baby."

That hug was still sitting with Zora, warm in her chest,

when she noticed movement out the corner of her eye—a trio making their way over like they had a mission.

Ariyah led the charge, 18 and unbothered, braids gleaming in the sun, ripped jeans, and a too-grown confidence that Zora immediately respected. Roman trailed right behind her, lanky and grinning like he was waiting to cause trouble, and Willow bounced up last, curls wild and eyes bright, juice box in hand.

Ariyah stopped in front of Zora first, arms crossed, chin tipped just enough to say I'm watching.

"So," she said, tone casual but laced with meaning, "you hanging around for good, or just testing the waters?"

Zora smirked, setting her fork down. "I'm here enjoying the food... for now."

Ariyah's eyes narrowed in a playful challenge. "You know he doesn't bring just anybody here."

Zora held her gaze steady. "Good thing I'm not just anybody."

That landed. Ariyah's lips twitched, then she nodded—slow, approving—even if she wasn't ready to say it all out loud yet.

Roman slid in right after, plopping down with the little brother energy he embodied, licking barbecue sauce off his thumb and squinting at Zora.

"Ayo," he said, grinning, "you hoop? 'Cause if you dating my uncle, you gotta at least try to keep up."

Zora laughed, shaking her head. "I got a shot, but I don't mess up my nails for defense. That cool?"

Roman grinned wider, nodding like she passed some secret test. "Aight, long as you honest. You in if we run a Hayes game?"

"I'll keep sneakers in the car," Zora promised, her smile loosening for real now.

And then, Willow slid right up, no hesitation, planting herself next to Zora like she'd claimed her. "Hi, Miss Zora," she chirped. "Your hair's pretty."

Zora melted, leaning down. "Thank you, baby. I love your puff—you look like a whole princess!"

Willow beamed. "Can you braid? 'Cause Mommy be busy, and Ariyah says she's too grown now."

Zora chuckled, brushing her fingers through Willow's curls. "Oh, I got you. Beads too."

Willow gasped like she'd been handed treasure. "You gotta stay, then."

From across the yard, Saige—ever-watchful—raised her glass with a knowing smile, eyes locking with Zora's like: Mmhmm, I see you earning them stripes.

Roman leaned back with a smirk. "You almost part of the family now."

Ariyah gave him a look. "Boy, hush. She's doing just fine."

Zora shook her head, laughing, her chest light and loose now as the kids melted back into the fold—Roman tossing a playful wink, Willow skipping ahead, and Ariyah casting one last lingering glance, her approval quiet but solid.

Darius caught it all from the grill, his eyes on Zora, a smile playing at the corners of his mouth, like, yeah, you're good.

Zora smiled back, her heart lifting, the noise around her shifting from background static to something deeper.

She was in it now. Not just visiting—but becoming. And for the first time all day, she let herself believe it.

From behind her, the voice came.

"You gon' sit there and hold it all in, or you wanna come breathe where the air's cooler?"

Zora turned.

Mama Regina tilted her fan toward the shaded side of the porch—a simple gesture, but one Zora felt in her chest.

She stood, glanced toward Darius—still laughing with Mari, glancing her way between sentences.

And then she moved.

She didn't need distance.

But she needed breath.

The shade felt like a blessing.

Zora settled into the chair beside Mama Regina, her breath catching a little as she sat. The porch creaked beneath them, each breeze tugging at the edge of a paper plate or the hem of someone's dress. The hum of the cookout pulsed behind them—spoons clinking, dominoes slamming, and someone laughing from deep in their cut!

But here, it was still.

Zora didn't speak at first. Just folded her arms loosely and let the silence breathe.

Mama Regina fanned herself slow, the motion say and rhythmic.

"You look like someone who's been holding her breath all day," she said without turning her head.

Zora gave a half-laugh. "I probably have."

"Let it out."

Zora tried.

It came out shaky.

"It's a good party," she said.

"Mmhmm."

"They're a lot. In a good way. But still... a lot."

Mama Regina didn't respond right away. Just shifted in her seat. "That's what love looks like when it's been practiced."

Zora nodded. Her throat felt thick. "I can't tell if I passed or failed." "You didn't come here for that."

"I kind of did."

Mama Regina turned to face her fully now. "You didn't come here to be tested, baby. You came here to be seen."

Zora's breath stuttered.

"Only reason that feels the same is because you've spent your whole life performing. Trying to make sure nobody walks away."

Zora's eyes stung.

She didn't want them to.

She bit the inside of her cheek. Looked away. Nodded like she could nod the feeling back down.

"It's okay," Mama Regina said. Not softly. Just true. "You can break a little here."

That did it.

Zora turned her face to the side and covered her eyes with her hand. The tears came quiet. No shaking. Just release. Like a leak from somewhere deep inside that had never been patched.

Mama Regina didn't reach for her. Didn't fuss.

She just kept fanning.

The silence held.

Zora wiped at her cheek, shame creeping in before she could stop it.

"I'm sorry."

Mama Regina's fan stilled for half a second. "Don't you dare."

Zora let out a sound between a laugh and a sob. "Only other person I've cried in front of is Keira. She's my... she's it. My entire team."

Mama Regina nodded. "Good people?"

"The best."

"Then let her stay that. But don't make her do it alone."

Zora blinked, throat tightening again.

"You got people now," Mama Regina said, voice steady. "The kind that don't need you to be strong all the time. Let 'em see you."

Zora nodded slowly, even as her cheeks stayed wet.

She didn't say thank you. She didn't have to.

Mama Regina's fan swished slow beside her. The porch creaked as someone passed by in the yard. The sky was deepening behind the trees, plum and gold streaked with soft blue.

Zora sat back in the chair, and this time, she let her weight sink into it.

And this time, she didn't feel the need to catch herself.

Zora didn't know how long she sat there after Mama Regina fell quiet.

The sky had deepened to velvet. String lights flickered

above the porch, bathing the yard in soft gold. The buzz of voices had mellowed— turned low and warm, like coals settling under the grill.

She spotted him near the back steps.

Darius.

He wasn't looking at her at first. Just laughing—really laughing—with Mari, head tipped back, face unguarded. The sound of it landed somewhere deep in her chest, warm and a little sharp, like wanting and wonder tangled up together.

Then he looked up.

Saw her.

And stilled.

His gaze shifted—not startled, not panicked, but attentive. Present.

His head tilted slightly, the way he always did when he was listening without words.

He saw her.

Saw the tears drying on her cheeks. The quiet in her shoulders.

And then he came.

No hesitation. No rush.

He crossed the yard like gravity, his footsteps a steady rhythm on the porch. When he reached her, he didn't speak. Just stood beside her chair for a beat, hands in his pockets, breath even.

Then, gently, "You alright?"

Zora nodded. Then shook her head. Then nodded again.

"I didn't mean to—" she started.

"You don't have to explain," he said, voice low.

He crouched beside her—not standing over, not taking control. Just being where she was.

His hand reached for hers, slow and open.

Zora let her fingers slide into his.

No squeeze. No pull.

Just holding.

And this time, she didn't feel the need to catch herself.

She let it land.

And she stayed.

They didn't rush.

They sat there a while longer—his hand in hers, the porch settling around them like dusk folded into cotton. The music playing now was low and slow, old-school—horns, hush, and ache.

Mama Regina had gone inside with a knowing nod, a final swipe of her fan across Zora's shoulder. Like passing a torch.

Darius stood and held out his hand.

Zora looked up. "What?"

He nodded toward the patch of grass beneath the string lights. Most of the family had migrated inside. Just a few voices lingered now—faint laughter, clinking glasses, the bass of a Marvin Gaye slow jam curling around the dark.

She hesitated.

Then, she rose and slid her hand into his.

They stepped into the open together, beneath the lights.

He didn't say a word. Just pulled her close—one hand at her waist, the other laced with hers. They started to move, bodies swaying to the rhythm like they'd done it before in another life.

Zora rested her cheek against his shoulder.

The warmth of his hand at her lower back made her exhale without realizing it.

They danced slow. Unrushed. The world around them falling quiet, as if it knew not to interrupt.

And then—halfway through the song—he dipped his head low and kissed her.

Not tentative.

Not gentle.

Hungry.

Like he'd been waiting all night. Like the laughter, the porch, the space she'd taken and held—every bit of it had been winding him tighter.

His mouth moved over hers, slow and deep, pulling her into him like breath.

Zora melted against him, hand tightening in his.

He didn't let her go.

Not when the kiss deepened. Not when her breath hitched. Not when her free hand slid into the back of his shirt, like she needed more contact, more skin.

He broke the kiss first, but only just.

They were both breathing hard now, foreheads pressed together, lips brushing.

"You ready?" he asked, voice rougher now. Lower.

His thumb swept along her jaw, and then he stepped back —barely. She nodded, her voice a whisper. "Yeah."

She took his hand, grounding them both, and he stepped back—barely.

They walked to the car without speaking, bodies still vibrating with the taste of each other.

At the curb, he opened the door for her. She slid in, pulse still thrumming.

When he climbed in beside her and turned the key, the silence between them wasn't awkward.

It was charged.

He glanced at her again. "Still sure?"

Zora didn't blink. "Drive."

let me take it from here

"SAY YES" BY FLOERTY

The ride was quiet, but not tense.

Zora leaned against the passenger door, one knee drawn up, watching streetlights pass in long streaks. Darius kept one hand on the wheel, the other resting easily on his thigh, fingers tapping out a rhythm only he seemed to know.

When he pulled into the driveway, she sat up straighter.

He cut the engine and glanced over.

"You sure?" he asked, voice low.

Zora met his eyes. "Yeah."

He nodded once and stepped out, circling around to open her door before she could reach for the handle. She liked that about him—never flashy. Just... sure.

Inside, the house greeted them with quiet warmth. Clean lines. Dim light. The subtle scent of cedar and something softer beneath it—maybe the same diffuser oil he used when she was here last.

No clutter. No chaos.

Just a space that made room.

Zora toed off her shoes near the door and slipped out of her jacket, hands brushing down the front of her jeans like she needed something to hold.

Darius took her coat and hung it without a word, then turned to face her.

"You want water? Wine?"

She shook her head. "Just you."

That cracked something in his expression—something tight and waiting.

He stepped toward her slowly. No rush. No claim. Just presence.

"I don't want to move too fast," he said. "Not for you."

"You're not," she whispered. "I want this."

He studied her a second longer, then reached for her hand. Held it. "You ever talk about what you like?" he asked. "Or just hope somebody guesses right?"

Zora's smile was soft. "Guessing hasn't worked out great."

His thumb moved over her knuckles.

"I'm not gonna guess."

He let the silence stretch between them, eyes steady on hers, waiting for her to feel it fully.

They ended up on the couch without thinking—gravity pulled them there. Zora sat tucked into the corner, one leg bent beneath her, fingers still threaded with his.

Darius leaned back a little, watching her. Not intense—just tuned in.

"I wanna make sure we're on the same page," he said, voice low. "I don't do guessing games when it comes to this."

Zora nodded. "Okay."

He let a beat pass, then spoke, smooth and quiet.

"I like to lead. Set the pace. Pay attention to how your body moves, what you respond to. I'm not rough unless you ask for it. But I'm not passive, either."

Her mouth parted slightly. He kept going.

"I like control. Not to take anything from you. Just to keep you grounded while you let go."

That landed.

Zora shifted, heat rising under her skin.

"I like praise," she said, voice a little softer. "Being touched like it's not routine. Like someone's really in it."

"I don't go through the motions."

"I like being on top sometimes," she added. "But I don't want to run it."

Darius gave a quick nod. "You won't. I'll let you move how you need—but I'm still in charge of where we go."

She inhaled through her nose, eyes holding his.

"I want to make you feel really good.," she said—like she needed to say it out loud.

He leaned in a little, rubbing his hand up her thigh.

"You make it good just being here," he said, with a wink. "But yeah—you'll hear it. I don't keep quiet about what feels good."

Zora let out the smallest laugh, her breath catching in her chest. "What about if something's too much?" she asked.

"You tell me." His voice didn't change. "Say 'slow down' or 'hold up,' and I will. No ego, no attitude."

She studied him. Not just the words—him.

"You sure?"

He nodded once. "Always."

The room felt charged now—not because it was heating up, but because everything was clear. No pretending. No games.

Zora let her hand slowly fall to his thigh, fingers resting there like an answer.

"I want this," she said.

His hand came up slowly, brushing her jaw with the back of his fingers.

"Good," he murmured. "Because I'm not holding back."

He kissed her like he already had the right to—slow, deep, full- mouth pressure that said he'd been holding back too long.

Zora didn't even get a word out before he bent low, one arm behind her back, the other under her thighs. "Darius—"

"Shh." His voice was a quiet drag of heat. "I got you."

He carried her through the hall like she was weightless,

his grip unshakable. The bedroom was dim, cedar-scented, quiet. He laid her down like she was something precious— then stepped back just enough to admire how gorgeous she is.

"Don't move." His gaze swept over her, dark and hungry. "Goddamn, Zora," he murmured, voice roughening at the edges. "You don't even know what you're doing to me."

He stripped her himself. Shirt lifted. Bra unclipped. His hands never rushed, never fumbling—just steady, certain, like he'd memorized every snap and seam.

When she lay bare before him, he dropped to his knees at the foot of the bed, palms sliding up her calves, her thighs, spreading her open slow.

"Look at you," he breathed, eyes drinking her in. "Wet already, huh? Been needing this?"

Zora's breath caught, a flush crawling up her chest. "Yes… my body knows it's yours."

A deep groan rolled from him. "Damn right, it is."

He leaned in, kissed the inside of her knee, then the curve of her thigh, each press of his mouth a slow claim. "You know what I'm about to do to you, baby?" His lips brushed closer. "Gonna take my time. Gonna eat you until you forget every name but mine."

Her hips shifted, needily. "Please..."

He smiled against her skin. "Yeah... love how soft you beg." His hands framed her hips, holding her steady. "Let me taste what's mine."

Then his mouth found her.

A long, deliberate lick from base to clit made her cry out, fingers twisting in the sheets.

"Mmm." He groaned against her, tongue pressing deeper. "Sweetest thing I've ever tasted."

She tried to arch toward him, but his grip tightened, holding her open, anchored.

"Don't run from it," he demanded, looking up at her from between her thighs. "Stay right here. Let me work."

Zora's head dropped back, breath coming fast. "Yes... Darius..."

"That's it, baby. Let me hear you."

Then his mouth sealed over her clit, tongue circling, lips pulling her in like he meant to devour her. Every sound she made fed his hunger. Every tremble made him growl low in his chest.

He pulled back, lips slick, eyes blazing. "You wanna cum, beautiful?"

"Please—" Her voice broke on a gasp. "Please, I need—"

"You need?" His smile was dark silk. "Say it, Zora. Tell me."

"You—God—your mouth... you're making me lose it—"

"Good." He dipped lower, licking deep again. "I want you to fall apart for me."

"Darius—" Her thighs quivered, body straining against his grip.

"Beg me."

"Please... please, let me—"

"That's my girl." Then he sealed his mouth over her again, tongue rolling, sucking until her whole body seized, shattered.

She broke with a cry, her orgasm crashing wild and loud, and he stayed right there, working her through every aftershock until she slumped against the bed, boneless, gasping.

When her breathing slowed, he rose, towering above her, calm and dark-eyed.

"You ready now?"

Zora could barely lift her head. "Yeah," she whispered.

He stripped off his shirt, his jeans, his briefs. His dick stood hard, glistening at the tip.

"Good," he said, climbing onto the bed. "Because I'm not done with you."

He moved over her like he'd been there a hundred times before—confident, steady heat radiating off him.

"You good?" he asked, palm brushing down her thigh.

Zora nodded. "Yeah."

He slid his fingers through her folds, slow, savoring. "You're soaked for me, baby. Just waiting to be filled."

She gasped as he pressed his thumb over her clit. "Darius..."

"You ready for all of it?"

"Yes," she whispered.

He lined himself up and pushed in slow—no teasing, no rush. Just making sure she felt every inch.

"Mmm... you feel that, baby?" His voice was a low rasp, heat curling around the words. "Takin' me so damn good."

Zora choked on a moan, hands grabbing his arms. "So full—"

"Yeah, you are." He leaned down, lips brushing her ear. "Perfect fit. This pussy was made for me."

He bottomed out, hips flush, holding still so she could adjust.

Her eyes fluttered closed, breath catching.

"Keep lookin' at me," he said, nudging her chin up gently. "I want you with me the whole way."

Then he started to move—slow, deep, deliberate strokes that made her gasp beneath him.

"You feel how tight you are around this dick?"

She whimpered, legs wrapping around his waist.

"That's it, baby," he murmured, rocking deeper. "Keep squeezing my dick. I can feel your pussy pulsing."

He dropped his head to her neck, kissing the sensitive skin. "This pussy... fuck, it knows me," he muttered, thrusting deep, slowly. "Takes me like it's built for it. Like you don't want nobody else filling you up but me."

"Darius—please—"

He grabbed her leg, pulling it higher around his waist, driving in harder.

"You gonna cum again for me?"

"Yeah—oh my God—please don't stop—"

"I'm not," he growled. "Make my pussy cream for me."

Her body clenched tight around him. He felt it. Knew it. Fed off it. He dropped his hand to her clit, circling, rubbing fast, his thrusts never losing pace.

"Let go," he commanded softly. "Cum on me."

Zora cried out, back arching, body locking, as her second orgasm tore through her, wild and loud.

But he didn't stop.

He held her hips steady, moving deeper, riding out her trembling. "Still with me, baby?" he murmured, breath warm against her cheek. She could barely nod, her voice wrecked. "Yeah..."

"Good," he whispered, lips brushing her temple. "I'm not done yet." He pulled back slow, sliding out of her heat, leaving her gasping at the sudden emptiness. His hands slid down her sides, a tender drag of fingers over soft skin.

"Turn over for me," he said, voice low, steady. "On your stomach." Zora shivered, but obeyed, rolling onto her belly, lifting her hips instinctively.

"Just like that," Darius praised, smoothing his palm over the curve of her ass. "Look at you, baby... so fuckin' beautiful. So ready for me."

She felt his hands part her gently, his mouth pressing a kiss to the small of her back.

"You okay?" he checked, his voice quieter now.

"Yes," she breathed. "I want you."

He groaned softly, lining himself up behind her, one hand steadying her hip, the other guiding his length back to her slick heat.

"Deep breath for me, baby."

Zora inhaled, bracing as he pushed in slow—deeper this time, the angle sharper, the stretch fuller.

"Fuuuck," Darius hissed through his teeth, bottoming out. "Damn, you feel good like this. So tight for me."

A shaky moan spilled from her lips, hands gripping the sheets.

"Darius..."

"You takin' all of me, baby," he murmured, rocking into her with deep, rolling strokes. "Every inch."

Each thrust pressed him deeper, the sound of skin on skin filling the room, mingling with her soft cries.

"You hear that, baby?" he rasped. "That's you. That's us."

Zora's back arched instinctively, pushing into him, chasing the friction.

"Please..." she gasped.

He leaned over her, chest brushing her back, mouth at her ear. "You want more?"

"Yes—harder—please—"

His hand slid under her belly, lifting her hips slightly.

"That's it. I got you." He snapped his hips harder, deeper, the angle hitting something inside her that made her gasp louder, tremble harder. "Right there, huh?" he breathed. "That spot feel good, baby?"

"Yes—oh God—right there—"

"I know, baby. I feel you gripping me." He kissed her shoulder, slowing just enough to let the tension build. "You gonna cum again for me?"

"I—I can't—" she gasped, overwhelmed.

"You can," he murmured, rubbing tight circles against her clit, never losing his rhythm. "You're gonna. I want it. Give it to me."

Her body locked, breath caught, pleasure rising sharp and fast. "Darius!"

"That's it, baby. Let it happen."

Zora shattered beneath him, her orgasm tearing loose, raw and unguarded. Her whole body quaked as he fucked her through it, drawing it out, giving her every deep stroke until she collapsed forward, spent.

He groaned above her, hips driving harder now, chasing his own release.

"Where you want it, baby?"

"Inside," she whispered, her voice rough and soft all at once. "Please... give it to me..."

He gritted his teeth, his thrusts faltering as heat coiled tight in his gut.

"You sure?"

"I'm yours," she whispered again. "Do it."

With a deep groan, he sank in hard, spilling inside her, his body locking against hers as he rode the wave, his breath breaking against her skin.

Then he collapsed forward, chest pressing to her back, one arm sliding under her and holding her close.

Neither of them moved for a long moment. Just breathe, skin, the weight of everything between them settling in the quiet.

Finally, he pressed a kiss to her shoulder, soft and lingering.

"You good?" he asked, voice low, rough.

"Yeah," Zora murmured, utterly quiet, utterly content.

Darius pulled out slowly, carefully, and rolled onto his side, still facing her.

Zora blinked at the ceiling, chest still rising fast, her body buzzing under his touch.

"Come on," he murmured. "Shower with me."

She didn't answer right away. Just looked at him—really looked—and saw something settled in his eyes. Not softness. Not exactly. Stillness.

Trust.

Zora exhaled, then reached for his hand.

"I'm with you."

And she followed him into the shower.

The bathroom filled with heat, fog curling around them in lazy waves as Darius turned the water on.

He stepped under the spray first, letting it roll over his back, his broad shoulders slick and shining beneath the light. Then he held out his hand again, palm open, waiting.

Zora stepped in, chest to his, her cheek pressing against his damp skin. His arms wrapped around her instantly, pulling her close until there was no space left between them.

He held her like that for a long moment. Quiet. Steady.

His hand slid up her back, smoothing over her damp skin, fingers trailing slow up her spine, then down again to the curve of her waist. "You okay?" he murmured, lips brushing her hairline.

"Yeah," she whispered against his chest.

Darius kissed the top of her head. "Good."

He reached for the soap, lathering it between his palms, then rubbed gentle circles across her shoulders, her arms, her back. His touch was tender, reverent, quiet praise in every pass of his hands.

Zora's eyes fluttered closed as his fingers worked down her spine, tracing her hips, smoothing over her belly.

"Nobody's ever washed me like this," she said softly, voice wrapped in surprise.

"Somebody should've," he murmured, rinsing the suds from her skin, trailing his knuckles lightly over her ribcage. "Every time."

She tipped her head back into the water, letting it rinse through her hair, her lips parting under the heat. The words came out before she could catch them, low and raw: "I need a retwist."

His hands paused.

"My loctician's out of town," she explained. "And honestly... I'm too tired to deal with it right now."

He pressed a kiss to her temple. "Still looks good to me."

She gave a soft, worn-out laugh. "Tell that to my roots."

He didn't argue. Just ran his hands up again, slow, deliberate, smoothing over her scalp like an unspoken promise.

In the back of his mind, something rooted itself deeper.

I could learn, he thought. *For her.*

But he didn't say it. He didn't have to.

She leaned her forehead against his chest, her body soft and pliant against his.

"I haven't had anyone pay this much attention to me," she whispered. "Not during sex."

Darius turned her gently in his arms so he could see her face.

"Ever?" he asked.

She shook her head. "They might've wanted me. But not like that. Not... fully."

He studied her quietly, his gaze steady.

"You deserve that," he said. "Every time."

She looked up at him, searching his face like she didn't quite believe it—but wanted to.

He kissed her once. Then again, slower, deeper, with the same patient heat he'd carried all night.

"I haven't been with anybody in a long time," he confessed, voice low. "Didn't feel right. But this..."

"It felt right," she said, finishing it for him.

He nodded. "Yeah."

They stood there in the steam a little longer, wrapped around each other, quiet in the kind of silence that didn't ask for anything back.

grounded in care

"SWEETEST THING" BY LAURYN HILL
(ACOUSTIC VERSION)

Zora was still asleep when Darius opened his eyes.

The early light seeping through the blinds was thin. Not enough to wake her. Just enough to catch the soft, brown curve of her back, half-exposed where the hem of his T-shirt had ridden up. Her breath moved steadily against his chest, the kind of easy sleep people didn't fall into unless they trusted where they landed.

He stayed unmoving.

Let himself sink into it—the easy weight of her leg resting over his thigh, the unguarded sprawl of her arm across his stomach. She wasn't careful in sleep. Didn't brace herself like she did awake. She let herself fall. And even that was its own kind of choosing.

Darius exhaled steadily, matching the quiet pulse of the moment. His hand traced a gentle path up her spine—not to stir her, but to anchor himself.

One of her locs had slipped free during the night, trailing over her shoulder and across the pillow. Frizzed a little at the roots.

He thought of her voice last night—low, tired: "I need a retwist."

He tucked that thought away without judgment, the same

way he filed blueprints or design specs. Not because it was a problem to solve. Because it mattered.

It had been years since he woke up with someone still beside him.

Years since he let another body take up space in his bed, in his breathing room.

It felt dangerous differently—the kind of ease a man could get addicted to if he wasn't careful.

He shifted slowly, sliding out from under her, careful not to break the weight of her rest. The air outside the sheets was cooler, brushing against his skin. He pulled on a pair of soft joggers and a long-sleeved henley from the dresser.

On the way down the hall, he detoured into the bathroom. Ran the faucet low. Brushed his teeth. Washed the night off his face with cold water. Wiped it dry.

He didn't like carrying the weight of sex into other parts of the day —unless he was planning to keep it going

Freshened up, he padded into the laundry room, catching the pile of clothes she'd left without thinking—the Wild Hart t-shirt, her jean shorts, her socks, her bra, her panties. Nothing folded. No overnight bag.

She hadn't planned to stay.

But she had.

And she'd slept like she belonged.

Darius scooped the clothes up, the faint scent of her skin —lemongrass and sleep-warmed cotton—rising up as he carried them to the washer. He filled it, measured the detergent by muscle memory, set the cycle to cold.

He stood in the doorway for a second longer than necessary, the low rumble of the machine filling the air, then turned back toward the kitchen.

Today wasn't about grand gestures.

It was about showing up.

And making sure that when Zora opened her eyes, the world she woke into was already holding her right.

The kitchen stayed cool, wrapped in a quiet that filled his

chest more than any playlist ever could. That stillness moved with him, deep and grounding.

The eggs were done. The toast waited.

Darius wiped his hands on a dish towel and picked up his phone, thumb moving over the screen with slow precision.

Not to check messages.

Not to scroll.

He typed into the browser:

How to retwist locs properly?

Videos. Tutorials. Step-by-steps. He clicked through them without rush. Watched hands move steadily through thick roots. Watched how the scalp was cleaned before anything else. He saw the way clips pinned each twist into place without pulling too tight.

It wasn't just about twisting.

It was about care.

He opened a notes app and started building a list in his head. Sulfate-free shampoo first. Gentle, no heavy perfumes.

Lightweight oil—jojoba or grapeseed—nothing that would clog her scalp.

Locking gel, but not the crunchy kind. He cross-checked three brands, chose the one every loctician said left no flakes.

Rat-tail comb for parting clean lines.

Butterfly clips to hold the sections down.

Spray bottle to keep her locs damp without soaking them.

He paused, tapped his thumb against the counter, thinking.

She'd mentioned being tired.

If he was gonna do it, he wasn't half-stepping.

He added a portable inflatable washing basin—read two reviews to make sure it was soft at the edges, easy on the neck.

A bonnet-style hooded dryer attachment—low heat, even airflow.

Nothing that would overstimulate her or fry her roots.

A quiet hair dryer to connect to the bonnet. Adjustable settings. Low decibel level.

He scanned two extra product pages before settling on the one that looked the easiest to control with one hand. He filled the cart fast but deliberate, double-checked it once.

She mentioned something that she needed. He was going to do it for her.

One tap: *Expedited delivery from SwiftDrop. Set for 8 a.m. He nodded once. Right on track.*

He set the phone down, face down on the counter.

Leaned back against the cabinet.

Outside the kitchen, the washer hummed low, the kind of background noise he could live in. Inside, the house already felt different. Like it was stretching to make room for more than just him.

The house was ready. The food waiting. The order was placed.

Now it was time to wake her up right.

Darius padded back into the bedroom, no hesitation in his steps. She was still there— sprawled across the bed, the hem of his shirt barely clinging to her hips, one bare thigh thrown over the sheets like she'd claimed the complete bed for herself.

Good.

He crossed the room, dropped to his knees at the side of the mattress, and slid a hand up the inside of her thigh—slow, steady.

She stirred, murmured something soft under her breath, but didn't wake.

He bent low and kissed her knee first—barely more than breath against skin. Then higher. The inside of her thigh. Soft. Hot. Familiar in a way that made something low in his chest pull tight.

When he finally dragged his tongue through her folds— slow, deliberate—she gasped, hips jerking toward his mouth.

He smiled against her.

He did it again.

Longer this time, savoring the taste of her, the heat spilling across his tongue.

She whimpered, still half-caught in sleep, thighs spreading wider instinctively.

He sealed his mouth over her clit and sucked slow and deep, setting a rhythm before she could even think to ask for it.

"Darius—" she gasped, voice ragged and raw.

"Morning, baby," he murmured against her, voice rumbling low between her legs.

He licked her again, firmer now. Not teasing. Not soft. Just working her open, mouth moving like he had all the time in the world.

Zora's fingers clawed at the sheets, hips rocking against his mouth without rhythm, chasing the pressure he built so deliberately.

Every moan, every broken gasp, he absorbed it.

Anchored her with his hands at her hips, keeping her right where he wanted her, refusing to let her run from it.

Her thighs started trembling, muscles locking, that sharp little tremor in her belly he could feel under his hands.

"Cum for me," he ordered, voice rough.

She shattered against him—loud, helpless, back arching off the bed. He stayed with her through every twitch, every ripple, licking her slow and soft until she slumped back against the mattress, boneless and shaking.

Only then did he lift his head, wipe his mouth with the back of his hand, and push to his feet.

He crossed the room into the bathroom, brushed his teeth, washed his face quick and methodical. Didn't like carrying the weight of sex into other parts of the day unless he meant to.

When he came back, she was blinking up at him from the bed, wrecked and glowing.

He leaned down, pressed a kiss to her forehead, and whispered against her skin:

"Come eat, Zora," he said, voice low and gruff. "Before I put my mouth back on you and forget the food."

She laughed—a soft, wrecked sound—and he smiled to himself as he reached for her hand.

IN MY *Rhythm*

Zora shuffled into the kitchen a few minutes later, hair messy, skin still flushed from sleep, and everything he'd pulled out of her. His T- shirt hung loosely on her, brushing high on her thighs.

She caught his eye, smiled lazily, and dropped into the chair without a word.

Darius pulled out the chair across from her and sat down slow. Their knees bumped under the table—a soft, unthinking contact neither of them pulled away from.

He slid the plate toward her—eggs soft, toast stacked, tea steaming in the mug he thought fit her personality.

She ate in quiet, the kind of comfortable silence that didn't need filling. now and then, her foot nudged his under the table, little absentminded brushes, like she was checking he was still there.

Darius just watched her, a small curl pulling at his mouth, not rushing a thing. He waited until she set the mug down before he spoke.

"How's your scalp feeling?"

She blinked at him, surprised. "Tight. Dry. Been meaning to book an appointment, but…" She shrugged. "Haven't gotten around to it."

He nodded once. "I can wash and retwist for you."

Her lips parted, surprise flickering again—but softer this time. She didn't answer right away. And he didn't rush her.

He just stood there, steady, letting her know without saying it: *I see you. I got you. If you want it.*

She said yes with a small nod, soft but sure.

Darius didn't crowd it. Didn't celebrate it.

Just moved.

He pulled the box from where he'd tucked it by the door —already delivered hours ago because he wasn't about to offer something half- prepared. Set up the basin attachment on the kitchen sink. Adjusted the flow of water until it ran warm and easy, the way he'd seen on the tutorials. Pulled a folded towel from the laundry stack and laid it across the edge of the counter.

When he turned back, Zora was standing there barefoot, eyes a little cautious but shining.

"You sure you're ready for this?" she teased, voice low, testing him.

Darius just nodded once. Steady. Certain. "Yeah. Come here."

She climbed onto the little stool he'd pulled close to the counter, leaned forward over the sink, and let her arms dangle.

He moved slowly, threading his fingers through her locs, first to separate them gently, testing the tightness of her roots, the dryness she hadn't complained about but that he could feel with his hands.

"You good?" he asked.

"Better now," she said, voice almost a sigh.

He cupped warm water over her scalp, slow and patient, wetting her roots thoroughly before reaching for the sulfate-free shampoo. Lathered it in his palms first, then worked it through her locs from the roots down, careful not to pull, not to tangle.

He massaged her scalp in steady circles, fingers firm but controlled, the same way he'd fix a line of code or a stubborn wire—focused, gentle, unshakable.

Zora slumped forward even more, her breath coming slow and easy, shoulders loose. She didn't just let him wash her hair. She gave it to him.

He rinsed the shampoo out in sections, catching any runoff before it slid down her face. Repeated it once—no shortcuts. Toweled her hair lightly when he was done, squeezing moisture out with patience instead of force.

When she straightened back up, blinking slowly, he caught the softness in her face—the kind she didn't usually show when she thought someone was watching.

He dried his hands and motioned toward the living room.

She followed with no need of direction, the hem of his T-shirt brushing the backs of her thighs.

He sat on the couch and pulled her onto a low stool between his legs, framing her body easily, settling into the space around her like it had always been built for this.

The towel stayed draped around her shoulders. The scent of her shampoo rose between them, clean and fresh.

He started with the rat-tail comb, parting her hair into neat sections, securing each one with butterfly clips as he moved. Section. Clip. Oil the roots with a few drops of light-weight oil. Twist. Roll. Pin.

His hands stayed steady the whole time.

Zora didn't talk much. Didn't joke or fill the silence. Just sat there, spine straight but body easy, her breath syncing with the rhythm of his movements.

Every so often, she leaned back just enough to brush against his thigh or calf—small touches, unconscious, like she needed the tether.

And he let her have it.

Every twist tightened something inside him he didn't know he'd been holding.

Not because of the work.

Because of the trust.

When he finished the last loc, he slicked his hands over her crown once, smoothing the flyaways.

"You good?" he asked again, voice lower now.

She tipped her head back to look up at him, eyes half-lidded, mouth soft.

"You got magic hands," she murmured.

He huffed a small breath of a laugh, tied the satin scarf over her hair gently, making sure it lay flat and snug.

"There," he said, tapping the center of her forehead lightly. "All done."

Zora stayed still for a second, eyes closed.

Then, she turned around, still kneeling between his legs, and pressed her forehead against his thigh. Just rested there. Silent. Breathing him in. He didn't speak.

Didn't ask her to.

Just rested a hand on the back of her neck, fingers curling into the soft cotton of the scarf.

Holding her like it was the most natural thing in the world.

green doesn't lie

"I'LL BE THERE FOR YOU/YOU'RE ALL I NEED TO GET" BY METHOD MAN FT. MARY J. BLIGE (R&B REMIX)

Wild Hart hummed around her, the slow, steady rhythm she'd been easing back into over the past few days.

Plants misted. Orders packed. The diffuser whispered lemongrass and basil into the air, grounding everything in scent and movement.

Zora cradled her phone between her ear, and shoulder while taping up a box of pothos and cactus.

Her phone buzzed with a FaceTime call, Darius's voice thick with sleep on the other end.

"You really gonna multitask me like this?" he asked, voice low and raspy.

"You FaceTimed me while I was elbow-deep in dirt. You knew what this was," she said, grinning.

He was reclined against a pillow, loop earplugs around his neck, plain black t-shirt soft on his chest. He wasn't talking much — just watching her with that quiet intensity she was starting to get used to. The way he tracked her movements, like they mattered. Like she did.

"You good?" he asked, and she didn't roll her eyes this time.

"Yeah," she breathed. "I'm good."

"For real?"

She paused, glanced down at the packing slip in her hand. "Yeah. For real."

The back door clanged open hard enough to make her flinch.

Zora turned to find Keira barreling through, a tray of herb starters balanced on one arm and a paper bag between her teeth.

"I could've died," Zora muttered, hitting End Call just as Keira dropped everything on the back counter with the grace of a hurricane.

"Please," Keira said, grabbing a water bottle from the fridge like she hadn't just caused structural damage. "I come bearing gifts. Your cuttings and a bacon croissant."

Zora raised a brow. "And chaos."

"Always," Keira grinned, pulling her locs into a bun. "So... you were on FaceTime, huh?"

Zora said nothing, just turned toward the monstera shelf.

"You been smiling with your teeth lately," Keira added, suspiciously. "That's man energy. That's 'he texted back every day' energy."

Zora tried not to smirk.

She busied herself wiping down the counter, ignoring Keira's knowing grin.

"Mmhm," Keira said, pulling out her phone. "Let me go see what he's been up to."

Zora ignored her until she felt the shift in the air. Keira whistled. "Oh. Oh, he posted you."

Zora's stomach dipped. "What?"

Keira turned the screen toward her.

It wasn't a big photo. Nothing loud. Just a quiet shot of her — asleep, wrapped in one of her chunky sweaters, locs pulled back from her face, soft and still. She hadn't even realized he took it.

Just intention.

Just her.

And underneath it, a caption that made her heartbeat stutter: *She move in a rhythm I ain't had before.*

Zora didn't say anything. Didn't move.

Keira lowered the phone slowly. "Yeah. That man likes you."

Zora looked away. "It's not even like that."

"You're in a whole hard launch, sis. That's 'this woman centers me' energy."

She flipped her own phone face-down on the counter, like that would calm the heat crawling up her chest. But she felt it.

In her stomach.

In her jaw.

In the part of her that didn't know what to do with being seen this clearly, this gently.

And she wasn't sure if she was ready to name what that meant. Keira was already elbow-deep in a crate of lavender when she said it.

"This bag feel light to you?"

Zora turned, wiping her hands on her apron. "Which one?"

Keira held up one of the sealed craft soil bags, bouncing it in her palm. "This ain't your usual weight. You using a new mix?"

"No," Zora said slowly, crossing the room. "That's from last week's batch. I packed it myself."

Keira raised a brow. "Then why it feel like it's on a juice cleanse?" Zora took the bag, cracked the seal, and pressed her fingers into the soil.

At first glance, it looked right—rich and dark, flecked with perlite the way it always was. But the texture was wrong. Drier. Light. No weight to it.

She frowned. "Hold up."

She moved behind the counter, grabbed a mason jar of her control sample from beneath the shelf, and scooped a pinch from both — the sealed bag and her backup jar. Rolled the soil between her fingers. Sniffed. Felt.

Different.

Not obvious.

Not something a customer would notice.

But Zora would.

She always did.

She opened another bag from the same batch.

Same thing.

"Keira," she said, quieter now. "Something's off."

Keira's face hardened immediately.

She dropped the crate, pulled out her phone without a word.

Zora stared down at the two piles of soil, side by side, on the counter, a cold tightness creeping up through her chest.

"I haven't given this blend to anyone," she said. "Not even the recipe."

"You sure?" Keira asked, voice steady but sharp.

Zora nodded. "Deadass."

Keira scowled, scrolling fast. "Then why Loren out here talkin' about 'new custom blend' like she made dirt herself?"

Zora blinked, throat going dry. "Wait, what?"

"Cirqle," Keira said, turning her screen around. There it was.

@rooted.by.loren.

A styled product shot. Loren's signature copper-and-cream branding. A soil blend Zora recognized down to the proportions — sitting pretty on a shelf Zora knew from pop-up days. The caption screamed at her: New blend. Old magic. All mine. 🖤

Zora's stomach dropped.

Her pulse kicked up, heartbeat drumming high in her ears.

Because she knew that blend.

The mix. The weight. The care.

It was hers.

Keira exploded first.

"Nah. HELL NAH. See, now I'm mad as hell," she said, stomping across the floor like she was ready to square up with a ghost. "You build somethin' with your entire chest, and here come this recycled-ass heffa trying to sell it back to you?!"

Zora pressed her palm to the counter, grounding herself against the burn in her gut.

Memory unspooled fast and ugly: *Loren asking casual questions about her ratios. Joking about how Zora never wrote anything down. Fingering open jars a little too long when she thought Zora wasn't paying attention.*

Zora had let it slide. Had told herself not to be paranoid. Had wanted to believe.

"I should've trusted my gut," she said, voice thick with the kind of heat that didn't cool easily.

Keira spun around, furious. "You should've! But fuck that now — you're here. And we not playin' nice no more."

Zora opened her mouth, but Keira steamrolled her.

"We pulling up. Full PR crisis if we gotta. I'll tag Wild Hart in her damn post and let the streets handle the rest. I'll dox her soil samples."

Zora huffed out a tiny, broken laugh, and Keira softened — just a little.

"You ain't alone, Z," she said, low and fierce. "You ain't never alone." Zora picked up her phone again.

Her thumb hovered over Darius's name in her text thread.

She could tell him.

Could let herself be seen.

She stared at the screen, breathing shallow.

Not today. But soon.

She saved the screenshot, tucked the phone into the pocket of her apron, and closed her eyes for a long breath.

She wasn't ready to share it yet.

But maybe she didn't have to fight alone anymore, either.

The shop settled into a thick quiet.

The kind that clung to the edges of the room even after the door had slammed behind Keira.

Zora stayed behind the counter, palms flat against the wood, feeling every splinter and groove against her skin. The diffuser whispered lemongrass and basil into the air like nothing had shifted. Like the ground hadn't cracked open beneath her.

She closed her eyes. Tried to breathe around the knot tightening in her chest.

This wasn't the first time something she built had been stolen. It probably wouldn't be the last.

But it was the first time the weight of it didn't feel inevitable. Didn't feel like it had to be hers alone.

Her phone buzzed once in her apron pocket.

Then again.

She didn't move at first, just let the vibration rattle through her. When she finally reached for it, her hands were steadier than she expected.

Darius's name glowed at the top of the screen.

Not loud. Not demanding.

Just there.

Zora stared at it for a long breath.

Then tapped into their thread before she could talk herself out of it.

You up?

The response came fast — like he hadn't been waiting for permission to care.

Always.

Her breath caught.

She hesitated, thumb hovering, then typed slower this time.

> Something happened at the shop. I don't need you to fix it. I just... I need to tell someone.

There was a beat of silence on the screen — long enough for doubt to creep in, sharp and familiar.

Then his reply appeared, steady and certain.

> You ain't gotta need a reason with me. I'm here.

Zora blinked hard, the screen blurring.

She scrolled to her saved images, attached the screenshot of Loren's Cirqle post, and sent it without a caption.

Without armor.

Without pretending she wasn't wrecked.

It delivered with a soft click.

Seconds later, another message appeared

> I see it. I got you.

Her chest tightened, but it didn't feel like it was caving in anymore. It felt... held.

Before she could lose her nerve, she tapped the call button.

It rang once.

Then:

"Hey," Darius said, voice low at the edges, like he'd been bracing to answer her before it even connected.

Zora pressed the phone tighter to her ear, throat thick.

"Hey," she whispered back.

"You wanna talk it out," he asked, "or you want me to just stay?" Her eyes stung, but she blinked the feeling away.

"Just stay," she said, voice shaking more than she wanted it to.

"I'm not going anywhere."

And he didn't.

He stayed on the line with her, silent except for the low rhythm of his breathing, grounding her without asking her to explain, without trying to fill the space she didn't have the energy to patch herself.

Zora rested her head back down against her arms. The wood was cool beneath her cheek. The shop was darker now, the streetlights outside throwing soft, gold shapes against the windows.

The day still hurt. The betrayal still burned, low and steady, under her ribs.

But for the first time in a long time, the quiet didn't sound like abandonment.

soft confessions

"WANT ME" BY CHLÖE & HALLE

The studio smelled like fresh paint and worn wood, the kind of scent that clung to the floors and backs of chairs no matter how many windows they cracked open.

Zora shifted her weight, the cheap apron tied around her waist crinkling with the movement, and glanced down at the battered flower pot in front of her.

She still couldn't believe she said yes.

Last night, when Darius had asked — voice low, casual, like he wasn't sure she'd say yes — she hadn't even let herself think too hard about it.

A painting class. Flower pots. Something easy, he'd said.

Something not too loud.

Something they could just... be in.

And even though her chest had tightened the second he called it a "date," she'd said yes anyway.

Now here they were, side-by-side at a long wooden table, paintbrushes in hand, the slow hum of the studio filling the space between them.

There were only a few other people scattered around — a couple painting quietly at a table near the window, someone working slow and methodical in the back.

It felt private, even in public.

Easy.

Zora picked up her brush, dipped it into a mess of terra-cotta orange, and dragged a haphazard stripe across her pot.

It was already a disaster — bold colors crashing into each other, no plan, no symmetry.

Across from her, Darius worked slow and steady, dragging his brush in deliberate, precise lines across the clay.

Muted tones.

Structured design.

Exactly what she should've expected.

"You know you supposed to have fun, right?" Zora teased, flicking a droplet of blue paint in his direction.

He looked up, mouth twitching like he was fighting a grin.

"I am having fun," he said, voice low and dry.

"Your face says otherwise."

He shrugged one shoulder, dipping his brush into a darker shade. "My fun just look different from yours."

Zora laughed — a real, low laugh that loosened something tight in her chest.

They worked in a peaceful rhythm after that, the occasional clink of paintbrushes and quiet music from the speakers filling the room.

Still, underneath it all, a soft kind of pressure built in her chest.

Not because of Darius.

Because of how easy it was to sit next to him without performing. Because of how natural it felt to let him see her, even in this small way.

She twirled her brush between her fingers, staring down at her chaotic pot, thinking about all the times she'd kept pieces of herself tucked away because it was safer that way.

Easier to be too much before someone could decide she wasn't enough.

Her hand stilled on the rim of the pot.

Darius noticed instantly, glancing up at her from beneath the dark fringe of his lashes.

"You good?" he asked, voice softer now. Zora swallowed.

Picked up her brush.

Set it down again.

"I had this foster mom once," she said, words tumbling out rough- edged and fast before she could catch them. "Miss Essie. She wasn't permanent. None of them were. But she let me keep a plant. A spider plant. Said it'd teach me how to take care of something when nobody else knew how to take care of me."

Darius didn't speak. Didn't interrupt.

He just shifted closer, elbows resting loose on the table, his whole body bent toward her like he was listening with more than his ears. Zora kept her gaze on the pot, hands loose in her lap.

"I used to think if I loved something too much, it'd leave. Or die. Or get taken away," she said, voice lower now. "So I stopped trying to hold on to anything that could be ripped out my hands."

The silence between them stretched wide, but it didn't feel heavy.

It felt open.

Breathable.

Darius set his brush down with a soft clink, pulled off one side of his apron, and tossed it carelessly onto the table like none of that mattered compared to this moment.

"You don't gotta hold me," he said, voice steady as breath. "You just gotta let me stand next to you."

Zora blinked fast, throat burning, but she didn't look away.

Didn't run.

Instead, she huffed a shaky laugh and nudged her pot toward him. "That your way of saying your pot looks better than mine?"

The corner of Darius's mouth tugged upward.

"My pot definitely looks better than yours."

She laughed for real this time, the sound cracking open something new and frightening and good in her chest.

Something she didn't know if she could hold yet.

But maybe she didn't have to hold alone anymore.

The laughter settled between them, soft and easy, like it had always lived there.

Zora set her brush down for good, flexing her fingers, paint smudged up the side of her pinky.

Across from her, Darius leaned back in his chair, legs stretched out, one arm slung low across the table like he wasn't in any rush to leave. She liked him like this.

Open.

Unrushed.

The silence between them stretched out again — but this time, it was comfortable, breathable, filled with the kind of quiet that didn't need performing.

Zora tilted her head, studying him.

"You always this good at letting people talk first?" She asked, voice lighter now but edged with something more.

Darius's mouth tugged into something that wasn't quite a smile. "Not really," he said. He dragged a hand over his jaw, slowly and thoughtfully. "Took a minute to learn that not everybody wanna be rescued. Sometimes you just... gotta sit with 'em."

Zora nodded once, slowly, feeling the weight of that in her chest.

He stared down at the rim of his pot for a long second, thumb running over the edge like he was thinking through every word before he said it.

I ain't really used to staying nowhere long, either," he said, voice low. "Grew up where... you learned quick not to expect nobody to notice when you needed somethin'."

He paused, still tracing the edge of the pot absently.

"My mama, Jemma, she had her own mess she was dealing with. Some days, she was there. Some days it was like you was air. Saige tried to fill it the best she could. But it's hard when you a kid tryin' to raise another one."

His voice didn't break. Didn't tremble.

It was steady — but in that kind of way that told you he'd long since packed the hurt into something manageable.

Zora stayed quiet, her chest tight.

He looked up at her then, catching her gaze full-on.

"So I got used to figuring shit out by myself," he said simply. "Made it easier to breathe. Easier not to get disappointed."

Zora's throat ached with how much she wanted to reach across the table and touch him. To anchor herself to the raw, steady truth of him sitting there— not hiding, not shrinking, just being.

Instead, she swallowed hard and said the only thing that mattered. "I see you."

Darius's eyes didn't flicker. Didn't drop.

He just nodded, like maybe he needed to hear it more than he'd admit.

"And I ain't planning on going nowhere," she added, voice quieter now.

Something shifted in the air between them — small but sharp, a thread knotting tighter.

He leaned forward, elbows resting on the table again, voice almost a whisper.

"Me neither."

The studio lights buzzed low overhead, throwing soft halos across the cracked concrete floor as Zora untied the apron from around her waist.

She folded it once, careful, and placed it on the rack by the door, her movements deliberate in a way she couldn't quite explain.

Darius tugged his apron off with less ceremony, tossing it onto the hook near hers.

When he turned, his shoulder brushed hers — not hard, just enough to ground her again.

"You good?" he asked, voice low, steady.

Zora nodded, breath catching just a little in her chest. "I'm good."

The words weren't armor this time. They sat true on her tongue. Darius didn't rush her.

Just nudged the door open with his hip, holding it there for her, no grand gestures, no performance. Just care.

Outside, the night was thick with the threat of rain, the air warm against her skin.

They walked side-by-side down the cracked sidewalk, neither in a rush to get anywhere.

"You still mad your pot ugly?" he asked, a grin ghosting the corner of his mouth.

Zora bumped her shoulder into his, laughing softly.

"My pot got more soul than yours. Yours look like it came with a motivational quote pre-printed on it."

"Organization ain't a crime," he said, deadpan.

"Neither is having taste," she teased, flashing a grin.

The easy rhythm between them hummed — not tension.

Something sweeter.

Something heavier.

When they reached her car, Zora hesitated by the door, keys

clutched loosely in her hand.

Darius stood a breath away, hands tucked into the pockets of his jeans, shoulders easy but his gaze sharp and watching her. Reading her without crowding her.

"You good getting home?" he asked again, voice softer now. Zora nodded, slower this time.

"I'm good."

He studied her for a beat longer, like he was weighing something between them then took a step closer.

Slow. Intentional.

He didn't grab her.

Didn't rush.

Just leaned in, giving her time to back away if she wanted.

She didn't. Zora lifted her chin instinctively, breath tangling somewhere between her chest and her mouth.

Darius kissed her like he meant it.

His hand came up, cupping the side of her face, thumb brushing slow against her cheekbone as his mouth found hers — warm, full, grounding.

It wasn't frantic.

It wasn't soft, either.

It was certain.

Like all the things they hadn't said yet lived right there, tucked

between their mouths, between the steady beat of his thumb tracing her jaw and the low hum vibrating out of her throat.

When he pulled back, it was slow — like he didn't really want to — and he stayed close, forehead almost brushing hers.

Zora swallowed, her whole body buzzing under her skin in a way that felt nothing like panic.

He stepped back just enough to give her breathing room, his eyes still locked on hers.

"Text me when you get in," he murmured, voice thick with something that felt like a promise.

Zora nodded, her chest tight in the best way. "I will."

Darius didn't move to leave. He stayed right there, close but not crowding, hands tucked in his pockets, watching as she opened her door and slid into the driver's seat.

She looked up once more—meeting his gaze through the window— and he leaned down slightly, knocking on the glass with a crooked smile.

"Drive safe, baby," he said, voice low through the crack in the window.

Zora's smile wobbled, full and soft. "See you soon."

Only when she backed out and pulled onto the street did Darius step away from the curb, standing there steadily, watching her taillights fade down the block.

He didn't turn to go until her car disappeared around the corner.

And even then, he stayed a moment longer—hands in his pockets, eyes on the quiet road—like he was making damn sure she was really gone before he let himself move..

She didn't drive off right away. She just sat there, breathing. Not running.

Not retreating.

Just breathing.

The apartment was quiet when Zora slipped through the door, still tasting the ghost of Darius's kiss on her mouth.

She kicked off her sandals by the door and padded barefoot into the kitchen, grabbing a bottle of water without bothering to turn on the lights. The ceiling fan ticked slowly overhead, stirring the heavy summer air. She moved on instinct — keys dropped in the bowl, jacket tossed onto the chair, apron forgotten in the corner. Her body buzzed with leftover adrenaline, but her mind stayed soft, slow.

It wasn't until she curled into the couch, one knee tucked beneath her, that she let herself really breathe.

Tonight had been something different.

Something that settled into her bones, slow and certain, the kind of shift you didn't recognize until the ground beneath you wasn't the same anymore.

She cracked her phone open without thinking, scrolling Cirqle with lazy thumbs while sipping her water. She wasn't looking for anything.

Which is why Keira's DM — no words, just a link — caught her off- guard.

Zora clicked it, half-distracted, and then froze.

Rithm is Redefining Tech Spaces: Meet the Quiet Genius Behind the Boom

@wiredtothebeat — 17k shares

At the top of the article sat a photo of Darius.

Not the way she knew him — soft, loose, hoodie-slung.

This Darius wore a crisp button-down, a clean fade, a stare that didn't flinch from the camera. Professional.

Polished. Undeniable.

Zora scrolled slowly, thumb dragging down the screen, her heartbeat picking up behind her ribs.

The article wasn't messy — just loud in its admiration.

It talked about Rithm's explosive growth — the way it was reshaping online spaces for people who usually got drowned out: neurodivergent creators, disabled artists, niche communities moving at their own rhythm instead of chasing viral noise.

But it wasn't the numbers that caught her chest.

It was the story.

The article traced Rithm back to something smaller. Something more honest.

Not a venture pitch.

Not a business ploy.

It started with survival.

Eight years of therapy.

Eight years of Cognitive Behavioral Therapy teaching him how to stitch himself back together in a world built without people like him in mind.

Darius hadn't built Rithm to scale.

He built it to breathe.

First for himself — a digital space where he could move slow, set his own tempo, navigate life without setting himself on fire trying to keep up.

Then, when he realized it could work for others too — he opened it. Quietly. For free.

For parents trying to meet their kids where they lived.

For adults who didn't even know they were allowed to ask for softer spaces.

For anyone who needed a place to belong without having to shout for it.

"I wasn't trying to start a company," the article quoted him.

"Some of us just needed space to breathe. I made it 'cause nobody else did."

Now, with venture capital circling and Rithm's user base exploding, Darius Lawson's refusal to move at someone else's speed was making the world come to him.

Zora set her phone down slowly, palms pressed flat against her thighs.

The apartment felt heavier now — not with fear, but with something fuller.

Bigger.

The life he built was already spilling out into the world. And somehow, she was holding a piece of it.

The ground was shifting again.

But this time, she wasn't standing alone. It sounded like being held.

CIRQLE

**RITHM IS REDEFINING TECH SPACES: MEET
THE QUIET GENIUS BEHIND THE BOOM
BY @WIREDTOTHEBEAT**

DARIUS LAWSON DIDN'T SET OUT TO DISRUPT THE TECH WORLD —
BUT DISRUPTION FOUND HIM ANYWAY.

THE 34-YEAR-OLD DEVELOPER IS THE QUIET FORCE BEHIND RITHM, A
SOCIAL APP RESHAPING HOW SMALL CREATORS, NEURODIVERGENT
USERS, AND NICHE COMMUNITIES CONNECT ONLINE. BUILT WITH
ADAPTIVE, SENSORY-FRIENDLY DESIGN, RITHM FOCUSES ON SLOW,
AUTHENTIC ENGAGEMENT OVER VIRAL NOISE.

BUT RITHM DIDN'T START AS A STARTUP. IT STARTED AS SURVIVAL.
AFTER EIGHT YEARS OF COGNITIVE BEHAVIORAL THERAPY, LAWSON
BUILT THE FIRST VERSION OF RITHM TO HELP HIMSELF MOVE
THROUGH A WORLD THAT RARELY MADE ROOM FOR DIFFERENCE.
FIRST A TOOL, THEN A LIFELINE — AND WHEN IT WORKED, HE
OPENED IT FOR FREE.

RITHM

"FOR PARENTS. FOR ADULTS LIKE ME. FOR ANYBODY WHO NEEDED
SPACE AND DIDN'T KNOW HOW TO ASK FOR IT," LAWSON EXPLAINED.
"SOME OF US JUST NEEDED SPACE TO BREATHE. I MADE IT 'CAUSE
NOBODY ELSE DID."

NOW, WITH USER GROWTH TRIPLING AND INVESTORS CIRCLING,
LAWSON'S QUIET REBELLION AGAINST SPEED AND NOISE IS MAKING
WAVES ACROSS THE TECH INDUSTRY — ALL WITHOUT HIM RAISING
HIS VOICE ONCE.

"MY DAUGHTER DIDN'T JUST FIND AN APP. SHE FOUND A WAY TO SHARE
HERSELF — SLOW, STEADY, WITHOUT FEAR. RITHM GAVE US A BRIDGE
WE DIDN'T HAVE BEFORE."
— JORDAN M., FATHER OF A NEURODIVERGENT TEEN

you don't know me like that

"REAL GAMES" BY LUCKY DAYE

The article had changed everything. Not overnight. Not like a movie.

But steady. Relentless.

Emails stacked up. DMs flooded in. Invites came faster than he could delete.

He shrugged most of it off.

At least until Saige got her hands on one of the invites.

They were at Mama Regina's house that morning, coffee and biscuits spread across the kitchen table. Sunlight spilled lazy across the counters. Saige was scrolling her phone, Zora tucked into the corner sipping her drink, her legs curled under her like she had all the time in the world.

"You going?" Saige asked without looking up.

Darius frowned, stabbing at the butter with his knife. "Going where?" "The gala," she said, waving her phone at him like a receipt.

"Founders Night. Local tech and venture people. Big deal."

He grunted low in his chest, focused on his biscuit. "Not my scene." Saige snorted. "Tough. It's your world now."

Zora leaned forward a little, setting her mug down with a soft clink.

"You know it's not just about you, right?" she said, voice easy but sure. "You showing up at something like that... it could open doors. For the center, Rithm and the people who need it but can't get in the room themselves."

Darius's jaw flexed, his eyes still on his plate. He hated that she was right. Hated even more that he cared what that meant.

Saige jumped in before he could dodge it. "You got some money now," she said. "But having investors? Grants? Partnerships? That's generational moves, D. That's putting whole communities on your back if you want to."

He exhaled, the weight of it pressing hot against his ribs.

"It's about making sure you ain't the last one through," Zora added, voice steady and low.

Darius looked at her really looked and saw the truth sitting plain between them.

It wasn't about ego.

It was about building something that lasted longer than either of them.

Zora smiled, small, steady ,and wiped a smudge of foam from her bottom lip like nothing heavy had just been dropped in the middle of the kitchen.

"You gonna make 'em jealous," she teased, voice curling low and sweet.

Darius huffed out something that might've been a laugh. "Only care about one person looking."

She grinned wider, tapping one finger lightly against his coffee mug. "Pick me up at seven, baby."

Like it was simple.

Like she wasn't offering him something he hadn't even known he needed.

And he had.

The week slid by faster than he liked. Between meetings at the center and trying to dodge the sudden buzz after the article, Darius barely had time to breathe. Saturday came heavy and hot, the kind of day that cracked slow open into something electric by sunset.

He pulled into the narrow alley behind Wild Hart right on time — no way he was making her wait.

The truck rumbled low under him as he killed the engine. He climbed out, adjusted his jacket once, and headed for the back door.

Zora was waiting when he got there, flipping the deadbolt with one hand, the other tugging lightly at the strap of her clutch. Darius forgot everything else the second she looked up.

Emerald green, soft and heavy against her skin. Locs twisted back from her face, with a few rebellious strands brushing the cut line of her jaw. Gold hoops catching the low light.

And her eyes — bright, steady, already holding a hundred things she hadn't said out loud yet.

She smiled slow, like she could feel him staring. "You gonna keep looking or you gonna tell me I look good?"

Darius didn't smile big — he never did in public spaces — but the corner of his mouth kicked up anyway.

"You look like I should be paying you to just breathe in my direction," he said, voice low and wrecked.

Zora laughed, head tipping back just enough to show the clean, strong line of her throat. "Shut up and open the damn door, Lawson."

He grunted, tugging the truck door open with a roll of his eyes, but there was no real bite behind it.

Once she was settled inside, dress spilling over the seat like a second skin, Darius circled around and climbed in after her. The cab filled up fast, her scent, her heat, nerves humming electric between them.

She tried to smooth her dress down, fussing with the hem even though it didn't need it.

Darius watched her out of the corner of his eye — the way her hands trembled just slightly, the way she shifted her weight like she couldn't find stillness.

He didn't say anything.

Just leaned over, slow and steady, and caught her wrist in one big hand.

Zora stilled immediately, breath catching.

"You nervous?" he asked, voice pitched low, like it was just between them and the thick hush of the truck cab.

"A little," she admitted, voice softer than he usually heard from her.

Darius smiled and dragged his knuckles slow up the inside of her thigh, just under the hem of the dress where nobody would ever see.

Her breath hitched, loud in the quiet cab.

His fingers found her slick and ready . God, she was already so wet for him and he worked her slow, careful, the pads of his fingers circling just right, just enough.

His touch stayed easy, coaxing, like he had all the time in the world to bring her to the edge.

Zora's head dropped back against the seat, a soft, broken sound slipping from her lips.

Darius leaned closer, mouth at her ear. "Let me take care of you," he murmured. "Right here. Right now."

She whimpered, so soft it barely made it out into the thick air between them and her legs fell open wider in silent permission. No rush. No pressure.

Just steady, patient pleasure winding up tighter and tighter until she was trembling beside him, clutching at the seat with both hands, trying and failing to breathe through it.

"You gonna cum for me, baby?" he whispered, as he slid his fingers through her slickness. "Gonna let go like I know you need to?"

She nodded, frantic, words spilling broken from her mouth without shape.

It didn't take long.

A few more slow circles, a little more pressure, and Zora shattered, silent but sharp, her whole body locking up, heat flooding through her like a second heartbeat.

Darius stayed close, coaxing her through it, rubbing slow and gentle until she collapsed back against the seat, boneless, flushed, glowing.

He kissed her temple once tender, grounding and eased her dress back down over her thighs like nothing had ever happened.

Zora blinked up at him, dazed, her breath still shaky.

"You good now?" he asked, voice rough but steady.

She laughed that warm, wrecked sound he'd kill to keep hearing and nodded.

"Better now," she breathed.

Darius shifted the truck into drive, pulling away from Wild Hart slow and smooth.

And for the first time all week, the buzz under his skin eased just enough to let him breathe.

The drive downtown slid by under a low, humming tension neither of them tried to break. Zora sat easy beside him, her hand still brushing against his outright. When they pulled up to the valet line, Darius caught her hand before she could move.

"You good?" he murmured.

"Better now," she said, smiling.

He helped her out of the truck, slipping her hand into crook of his arm. The tips leading into the gala were lit gold and heavy under the black carpet. Suits. Gowns. Soft, expensive laughter curling against the glass walls.

Inside, the ballroom cracked open like something breathing—low music curling thick through the chandeliers dripping light down onto marble floors. The crowd buzzed thick around them—ambition, money, polished curiosity wrapped up in sequins and sharp cuts.

Eyes turned their way almost immediately.

Zora straightened beside him not loud, not posing, just

present. Darius kept his frame close to hers, their bodies moving together easy as breath.

And then—

"Well, well, well," came a voice, too loud, too bright against the polished hush.

Tamara.

She broke from the crowd like she owned the air around her, champagne glass swinging lazy between two fingers. The dress she wore clung tight and high-cut, daring in a room built for understated power. Her heels clicked sharp against the marble as she moved a little too familiar.

Darius stiffened before he could catch it, his spine straightening instinctively. Zora felt it; he knew she did. Her fingers tightened once at the bend of his arm before she let them fall away, slow and casual like nothing was wrong.

Tamara smiled wide, all teeth and broken glass. "Look at you," she said, voice syrup-sweet and sour underneath. "Got yourself all polished up for the cameras, huh?"

He didn't move.

Didn't rise to it.

"Tamara," he said, flat enough to be disrespect without crossing the line.

She stepped closer anyway, her hand brushing the lapel of his jacket like she had the right. "Never thought I'd see the day," she mused, voice lilting. "You always liked to hide in the back. Now you out here shining?"

Darius's jaw ticked, the muscle low in his cheek tightening.

Zora stood still beside him, calm, breathing slow — but Darius could feel the way her energy shifted. Watchful. Measured.

"Congratulations, Darius," Tamara said, loud enough that heads turned. "You really outdid yourself." Her eyes flicked to Zora, quick and dismissive, a flicker of something ugly cutting through the false sweetness.

Darius caught her wrist before she could lay her hand on him again.

128

The move was smooth. Polite enough to look like nothing from the outside. But Tamara felt it.

Her smile thinned.

"You need to go," he said under his breath. His voice was low, calm, and deadly. Tamara laughed, tossing her head back. "Relax, baby. I'm just saying hi."

Darius stepped back, forcing space between them. His arm found

Zora's waist instinctively, pulling her closer into his side, quiet but absolute.

"We said everything we needed to say years ago," Darius said, his voice a little colder now. "Ain't nothing left between us but silence."

For a second, Tamara's face flickered, something raw and mean flashing behind the lashes and champagne and too bright lipstick.

Then she laughed again and slipped back into the crowd, leaving behind the sharp cut of her perfume and a smear of tension thick as smoke.

Darius let the air leak out slow, forcing the burn down. He pressed a hand low against Zora's back, grounding both of them.

"You good?" he murmured against her temple.

"Better now," she whispered back.

They moved deeper into the gala — the ballroom swallowing them whole — the buzz of conversation rising and falling like waves against the shore.

Tamara's energy still clung to the edges of the night like static, but Darius kept moving forward.

He wasn't here for the ghosts.

He was here for the woman at his side.

And he wasn't about to let anybody steal that from him.

The ballroom was too warm, the lights too bright. Zora shifted on her heels, nerves buzzing low under her skin. Darius leaned down, murmuring something against her temple about getting them a drink. She smiled up at him and slipped away toward the bar before he could see the tightness in her jaw.

She needed a minute.

Just a minute.

The crowd thinned near the back corner, where the air felt cooler.

She found the end of the line at the bar, standing tall, smoothing invisible wrinkles out of her dress, grounding herself in the small, simple motions.

"You must be new," came a voice, slick and slow like honey left too long in the heat.

Zora turned slightly.

Tamara stood just a few feet away but just close enough to be a threat. Not close enough to be obvious.

The woman was tall, sharp, all polished curves and danger. Her dress was a little too tight, her smile a little too wide. She lifted her champagne glass in a lazy, mocking toast.

Zora raised a brow but said nothing, the way you do when you know something ain't right but you haven't decided yet how much energy it's worth.

Tamara didn't wait for permission. She moved closer, eyes raking over Zora's dress, her locs, the whole of her like she was a project she already had an opinion about.

"Didn't know Darius went for charity cases now," Tamara said, voice pitched too low for anyone else to hear but loud enough to land hard.

Zora's stomach clenched, heat prickling behind her ears.

She kept her face smooth. "Excuse me?"

Tamara smiled sweetly, head tilting like she was sharing a secret between girlfriends. "You're pretty," she said. "In that... unpolished way. Bet he likes that. Easy to mold. Easy to forget."

Zora's fingers curled into the fabric at her side. She could feel her pulse ticking high at her throat, the sharp burn of anger and hurt sparking together under her skin.

Tamara stepped even closer, voice dropping silkier. "Careful, baby. Men like Darius?" She shrugged, all fake sympathy. "They get bored real quick once the shine wears off."

Zora stared at her for a long, slow beat.

Something hot and thick rose up inside her, not just anger, but that old, ugly fear.

The one that whispered you're not enough, even when she fought to believe otherwise.

Tamara smiled, stepping back with a lazy sip of her champagne, like she hadn't just tried to gut her.

"Enjoy your night," she purred, then slipped away into the crowd as her hips swayed like she thought she'd won something.

Zora stood frozen for a beat longer than she should've.

Breathing too shallow.

Hands shaking just a little.

By the time she grabbed two flutes of champagne from a passing tray and turned back toward Darius, the sharp edges of the night had already changed.

She saw them. Darius and Tamara a little too close and too familiar. Tamara's hand brushing his chest as if it belonged there.

A hollow pressure bloomed in Zora's chest, sharp and wild, before she could even think what to do with it.

Darius's face was hard to read from this distance, locked down tight. Her stomach twisted, breath cinching up hard.

The champagne in her hands shook, bubbles fizzing high and angrily against the glass.

For a second, all she could hear was her own pulse thudding, thick in her ears, drowning out the music, the laughter, the whole damn room.

She blinked, slow this time, as if that might clear the burn behind her eyes—but the image stayed.

Tamara.

Darius.

Too close.

Too familiar.

Her fingers clenched tight around the glass stems, knuckles aching now.

Then before the doubt could finish hollowing her out where she stood Zora turned.

Sometimes it was just about feeling it hit you all over again. Maybe you were never built to be chosen at all.

ghosted

"LOSE MYSELF" BY AMBER MARK

The knock came sharp against the door, jolting Zora upright where she sat curled behind the counter.

She hadn't answered his texts.

Couldn't.

But she knew he wouldn't just let it sit.

Not Darius, not when he'd spent every minute showing her he didn't know how to leave things broken.

She crossed the floor, heart pounding, and pulled open the door.

He was standing there with his sleeves rolled, tie gone, his jaw clenched so tight she could see the muscle ticking under his skin.

"Zora," he said, voice low, already frayed.

Before she could swallow it down, the fear ripped frees.

"I saw you with her," she said, voice too sharp, too loud in the quiet.

Darius didn't even flinch.

He just stared at her with a flat look and waited.

"You let her touch you," she accused, chest heaving. "Like it didn't even mean anything."

He exhaled once through his nose, sharp and humorless.

"You think that's what happened?" he asked, voice clipped now. "You really think I stood there wishing for that shit?"

Zora opened her mouth, but the words crumbled before they made sense.

"You don't know half the story," Darius said, stepping closer. The porch light caught on the hard line of his shoulders, the glint in his eyes that said he was holding himself back by a thread.

"Tamara ain't just somebody I used to know," he said, each word a clean, brutal cut. "She's my mama's best friend. She was around when I was trying like hell to matter to somebody."

He shook his head once, full of something ugly and old.

"I was 25 and stupid enough to think being wanted meant I was worth something," he said. "I made that decision. And it fucked me up longer than I'm proud to admit."

Zora's chest ached.

But she couldn't pull the accusation back.

It was already there between them and it was poisoning everything.

"I didn't freeze tonight 'cause I wanted her," Darius said, voice dropping lower, more dangerous. "I froze 'cause some wounds don't close easy. I froze 'cause when you survive shit like that, it doesn't just disappear when you decide to be better."

He looked at her and this time, there was no softness left.

"You think I'd come after you, leave that whole fucking gala behind, just to be the same kind of man I spent years fighting not to be?"

The shame hit her like a slap, hard and fast.

Tears blurred her vision.

She opened her mouth, something desperate crawling up her throat but the words tangled and died before they could break free. Her fingers curled tighter around the doorframe, nails digging in, like holding on to the wood might hold everything else together.

"I just... I need time," she whispered, hating how small it sounded. Darius barked out a low laugh, sharp and bitter.

"Yeah," he said. "You need time."

He stepped back once, the night swallowing the heat off his body like a curtain dropping.

"You wanna run? Run," he said. "But don't you dare lie to yourself about who's leaving who."

Zora opened her mouth, useless.

He was already gone — boots crunching over gravel, his broad back disappearing into the dark without another word.

The truck rumbled low and angry a second later, headlights swinging wide as he pulled out fast and didn't look back.

The door clicked shut in her hands, the night pressing too hard against her chest.

She stood frozen, her pulse crashing in her ears, her breath ragged and shallow. Her knees locked, refusing to bend even though her whole body was screaming to collapse.

And this time, she didn't slide down crying.

She just stood there, shaking, staring into nothing.

Because when Darius Lawson decided he was done fighting for you? You didn't get a second chance to fix it easily.

And deep down, Zora knew it.

The door clicked shut behind him. The alley went still, and Zora stayed standing there, hand wrapped tight around the doorknob, like letting go might make everything collapse.

She didn't cry. Not yet. She stood frozen, heart hammering, breath scraping roughly against her throat.Zora tried to tell herself she was fine.

She had done the right thing. She was protecting herself. Wasn't she always supposed to protect herself first?

But the lies didn't settle like they used to.

When she finally moved, it wasn't grace or strength—it was gravity.

Her knees buckled, slow and graceless, spine sliding down the door until she hit the floor hard. The satin of her dress pooled around her like wilted petals, useless and limp.

The shop was dark except for the faint gold glow under the back office door. She stared blankly, forcing the old survival rules through her head:

Don't get soft.

Don't need too much.

Don't expect anyone to stay.

The rules she lived by.

The rules that had kept her standing.

The rules that now felt like they were squeezing her chest until she couldn't breathe.

IN MY *Rhythm*

She woke up the next morning still curled against the door. Her spine ached. Her chest felt hollow.

She checked her phon with mechanical fingers. No missed calls or new texts. Just empty space.

The fear built inside her whispered:

See? You made it easy this time. He didn't even have to walk away. You did it for him.

She stared at her empty hands, fingers curled like cows around nothing.

It wasn't anger that hollowed her out.

It was knowing she had rehearsed this ending so many times she didn't know how to write anything else.

The days blurred.

Wild Hart opened. Closed.

Plants watered. Customers served.

Zora smiled in all the right places. She said thank you and have a good one and signed her name on receipts like a woman still living her life.

But every hour felt like she was carrying dead weight stitched to her ribs.

At night, she curled on the couch, scrolling Cirqle even though she promised herself she wouldn't.

No posts. No pictures. No clues.

Just silence.

Just proof.

Good men don't stay either. Not when you show them the real pieces.

The thought made her stomach turn.

IN MY *Rhythm*

On the fourth night, the ache cracked wider.

She sat behind the Wild Hart counter, arms limp, the diffuser cold, and the playlist long since dead.

The only thing filling the shop was soft electric hum of loneliness.

She typed:

I'm sorry. I'm scared.

Her thumb hovered over Send, frozen midair, her breathe catching and scarping against her ribs. For a second, all she could hear was the loud, awful thud of her own heartbeat.

The tears came before she finished the sentence.

Not sharp or loud.

Just a slow, broken leaking of everything she'd held tight for too long.

Her phone slipped from her fingers, clattering against the counter.

Zora pressed her palms to her face, trying to breathe through the wreckage inside her, but it was no use.

The sobs raked out of her anyway — low and guttural — the kind you didn't come back from clean.

She cried until there was nothing left but silence again.

The phone screen blinked once, then faded black.

She didn't move.

Just sat there, arms wrapped around herself, letting the loneliness settle deep.

Because this time, it wasn't just fear that emptied her out.

It was knowing she'd helped build the surrounding silence with her own hands.

IN MY *Rhythm*

The bell above the door clanged, too loud for the sleepy hush of Wild Hart.

Zora didn't look up.

She just kept folding t-shirts into perfect squares, her hands moving like they belonged to someone else.

"You look like heartbreak wrapped in cotton," Keira said, her voice slicing through the silence like a blade.

Zora forced a brittle smile that barely stretched across her face.

Keira didn't wait for an invite. She dropped two coffees onto the counter and hopped up like she lived there.

Sunglasses shoved into her curls. Coffee in one hand. Concern written all over her face, even through the sass.

"You rationing sadness now?" she teased. "Or you just freelancing emotional destruction?"

Zora shrugged, tight and small. "Just tired."

Keira narrowed her eyes. She knew better.

"You," she said, slow and deliberate, "are lying. Badly."

Zora folded another shirt. And another. Pretended her hands didn't shake.

Keira didn't press right away. She just sipped her coffee and let the

silence thicken until Zora couldn't breathe through it anymore. Finally, it cracked out of her, rough and broken.

"I messed up," Zora whispered.

Keira didn't move. Just waited.

"I saw him... with his ex," Zora said, voice shaking. "At the gala."

The memory punched back hard. Tamara's hand on

Darius's arm, the frozen look in his eyes, the sharp twist of panic in Zora's chest.

"I saw her touch him," she said, voice thin and shaking.

"Soft. Familiar. Like maybe she knew him better than I ever could."

Her vision blurred, the memory hitting sharp as glass. She pressed her palm to her chest like she could smother the ache —but it only pressed deeper.

Her throat tightened until the next words scraped out raw.

"And he didn't move. He didn't push her off. He just... stood there."

Zora's fists clenched in the fabric of the t-shirt she'd been folding, wrinkling it beyond saving. And all I could think," she whispered, "was that maybe he wanted Keira's face stayed still. Anchored. Safe.

Zora wiped her palms on her jeans, heart pounding.

"He left the gala," she said, the confession spilling faster now. "He left. He found me. He came to Wild Hart and h-he explained." She gasped, voice cracking .

Tears blurred her vision.

"He told me it wasn't what I thought. That she wasn't what I wrong reasons. That he'd fought like hell to survive being wanted for the wrong reasons. That he wasn't proud of it, but he wasn't hiding either."

Her chest heaved, ribs aching like they'd been cracked open from the inside.

"And I still..." She swallowed hard. "I still pushed him away."

The weight of it crushed her in place.

"He didn't yell," she said, voice shattering. "He didn't chase me. He just walked away."

The finality of it hit harder now than it had the night she watched him disappear.

"I thought I was protecting myself," she whispered. "But all I did was rip us apart before he even had the chance to."

Keira moved then, quickly before sliding off the counter and pulling Zora into a hug, tight and unyielding.

Zora broke open against her, sobs wrecking her shoulders.

"In foster care," she rasped, shaking, "if you cried too much... if you needed too much... they moved you. Labeled you too difficult. Forgot about you."

Keira's arms locked tighter around her, grounding her.

"And Montgomery," Zora gasped. "Every time I needed him, it was like I handed him the knife to cut me loose. Like loving him made me disposable."

Her hands fisted in Keira's sweatshirt, clinging like the words could drown her if she didn't.

"I learned to survive by running first," she cried. "Always."

Keira didn't shush her. Didn't soften.

She pulled back just enough to frame Zora's face in steady, callused hands and looked her dead in the eye.

"You gotta stop punishing every good thing that tries to love you for what the old shit broke and left behind."

"Darius didn't break you. He's just trying to love you. You gotta let him."

Zora's face crumpled, tears sliding free all over again.

"And you don't gotta fix it tonight," Keira added, softer now. "You just gotta stop lying to yourself about why you're hurting."

Zora sagged back onto the stool behind the counter, heart aching, hands limp in her lap.

The shop buzzed soft and low around her, the smell of soil, the faint curl of bergamot still clinging to the air.

Her eyes landed on the coffee mug Darius had used the last time he was here, still upside down on the drying rack.

The ache cracked wider.

Not because she didn't want him back.

But because for once, she knew she had to meet him different, open, scared, real or not at all.

The fear still pulsed under her skin.

Still whispered that she was too much.

Still hissed that she was easier to love at a distance. But she didn't move.

She let it hum there.

Let it exist.

Because surviving didn't mean the fear disappeared. It just meant it didn't get to drive anymore.

It didn't fix anything. It didn't erase the wreckage. But this time, she stayed.

She sat in it.

Let it hurt.

And lived through it anyway.

the root of it all

"DON'T WASTE MY TIME" BY USHER FT. ELLA MAI

The door clicked shut behind him, and the house swallowed the sound whole.

No music. No hum from the fridge.

Just the sharp tick of the lock sliding into place, too loud in the silence he carried home.

Darius stood there for a long minute, just breathing. The kind of breath that scraped going in, like his chest wasn't built for it anymore.

Still in the half-wreck of his gala suit , tie hanging loose around his neck, collarbone visible where the shirt gaped open.

His sleeves were shoved to his elbows, the cuffs wrinkled, veins in his forearms standing out harder than usual.

The house didn't move around him.

It waited.

He kicked off his shoes, letting them clatter somewhere by the door, then dropped his keys without looking.

They hit the counter with a brittle, little sound that made his jaw clench harder.

The air smelled like clean wood and the faint ghost of laundry detergent — sterile, empty, wrong.

His shoulders pulled tight.

His body buzzing under the skin like a live wire, every nerve ending stretched thin, begging for a place to unload.

Breathe.

One in. One out.

It didn't fix the way his hands wanted to close around something.

It didn't fix the way the muscles behind his eyes ached, like they were holding back a flood.

He crossed the living room, a little unsteady, like gravity had shifted without telling him.

Fingertips brushed the edge of the couch.

The cool metal of the lamp base.

The sharp edge of the bookshelf.

Each texture real, tangible, something to catch him from floating off.

His eyes snagged on a photo halfway across the room, a frame too bright under the soft, recessed lights he never turned off.

Zora laughing in it, one hand raised like she was telling him off about something dumb he said.

He didn't touch it. Didn't dare. His hand hovered for half a second, fingers curling back tight like the frame might burn him if he got too close.

Something in his chest cracked without a sound.

Darius's hand found the little glass sculpture by instinct , a gift from a tech conference years ago, nothing special, nothing sacred.

It flew before he even thought about it, a blur of motion and breath.

The shatter cracked the silence wide open. Sharp rain of glass against the hardwood. And then—nothing. The quiet rushed back in, heavier now, like it was punishing him for breaking it.

A sound big enough to fill the hollow under his ribs.

Still breathing.

He backed up until he hit the edge of the kitchen counter, palms flattening against the cool stone, head bowed low.

Tamara's breath still clung to his skin in memory, fake and sickening.

Her hand sliding up his arm as if he owed her body something for a mistake she made years ago.

He froze back then, too.

Not out of want.

Not out of weakness.

But because the rage burned so fast, so brutal, he knew if he moved too soon he'd wreck something bigger than her.

He pulled away.

Told her plainly.

"Back up, Tamara. This ain't that."

But by the time he turned to find what mattered, Zora was gone.

Not yelling. Not slamming.

Just gone.

And the empty space where she should've been hit harder than anything Tamara could've ever done to him.

Darius slid down the cabinets, body folding, until he was sitting on the cold floor.

Suit pants wrinkling at the knees.

Hands loose in his lap.

The air around him, thin and mean.

The broken glass caught the light in a hundred tiny fractures.

He almost reached for his phone.

Almost let his hand drift toward the counter where it sat, heavy and silent.

Stopped.

His breath caught in his throat, ribs locking down. He dragged his hand back to his lap, fingers flexing like they ached from holding the line.

No.

He wasn't reaching first this time.

Wasn't pouring himself out for someone who hadn't decided if they wanted to catch him.

She knew where to find him.

If she wanted to.

He tilted his head back against the cabinets, eyes shut, letting the weight settle into his bones instead of fighting it.

The night stretched around him slow.

The ache settled deeper than muscle, deeper than memory.

Still breathing.

Still here.

For now, that was enough.

IN MY *Rhythm*

Morning didn't come calmly.

It pressed in slow and thick, the lat-spring air already dragging its weight across the house by the time Darius cracked his eyes open. The kitchen floor had lost its coolness sometime during the night, leaving his back damp where it pressed against the tiles, muscles sore from sleeping twisted under cabinets that still smelled faintly of lemon oil.

He didn't move fast.

Didn't jerk upright like a man trying to outrun something. Darius just breathed through it, letting the ache settle under his ribs didn't feel like they were cracking open with every shift. He sat up, palms flat against the floor for a long beat before he pushed himself to standing.

Upstairs, the mirror above the sink showed a man he half-recognized, face lined hard, jaw set tight, skin flushed from the heavy heat hanging inside the walls. He stripped out of the ruined suit and stood under the shower, letting the water hit him, hot enough to fog the room. The steam didn't scrub the ache out, didn't chase away the thickness in his chest, but it made him feel anchored again, enough to pull clean clothes onto his body without shaking apart.

The white tee he grabbed was thin, soft from a hundred washes, clinging to him in places the humidity seeped through the walls. His joggers slid over his hips, sticking just slightly to the damp at the back of his knees. He slid bare feet into worn black slides and leaned for a second against the counter, breath slow, measured.

From the back door, he could see Mama Regina's house sitting across the yard—the place he had built for her to ensure that she was close by.

Light spilled from her kitchen windows, golden and soft.

He pushed off the counter and walked out of the door, stepping into a wall of heat that wrapped around him, sticky and slow. The smell of biscuits and bacon cut through the thick air, sharp and grounding. The dew on the grass soaked into his joggers with every step, the blades wet and heavy under his feet.

Birdsong clattered from the trees, wild and frantic.

Cicadas buzzed high in the branches, the sound thick enough to breathe.

The front door to Mama Regina's house was propped open with a potted Colocasia. A breeze slipping across the threshold, but not enough to cut the heaviness dragging at the house. Fans whirred inside, stirring the scent of bacon and coffee into the humid air.

He paused on the porch for a second, the wood warm already under his slides, his hand braced on the doorframe. Inside, the house pulsed with life — forks clattering, chairs scraping, Saige muttering under her breath at Roman, Willow's shriek of laughter threading through it all like bright ribbon.

He didn't knock.

Didn't announce himself.

Darius stepped in, letting the heat and noise wash over him without flinching.

Mama Regina caught him immediately, her head snapping up from the skillet like she'd felt him cross the yard. She didn't smile. Didn't soften her face. She just saw him—every crack, every raw edge, the quiet choice to show up anyway. Saige's eyes lifted from her plate a second later.

Her mouth twitched — not quite a frown, not quite a sigh — but she didn't say anything, either.

Roman launched a wild story across the table, arms flailing, nearly knocking over his orange juice. Ariyah groaned and rolled her eyes. Willow giggled so hard she snorted, pressing both hands over her mouth.

Life moving.

Life refusing to pause, even though something in Darius had cracked the night before.

He dropped into a chair at the end of the table, setting his forearms against the wood like he needed the contact to stay grounded. His chest stretched tight under the thin fabric of his shirt, every breath slow, careful.

Mama Regina slid a plate in front of him without a word — scrambled eggs, bacon crisp enough to break, grits soft and steaming, a biscuit already split open and butter melting into the cracks. Her hand brushed his shoulder as she passed, a weight, brief but solid.

He picked up his fork, fingers steady even though the air felt too thick to move cleanly through it.

The first bite caught in his throat harder than he wanted, but he chewed through it.

Because that's what you did.

You kept eating.

You kept breathing.

You stayed standing even when your bones wanted to buckle.

The table rocked with laughter again when Roman made some stupid joke about dunking on his teacher during gym class. Saige cracked a grin despite herself. Willow nearly fell out of her chair, squealing.

Darius let out a breath that might have tried to be a laugh but broke into something sharper halfway out.

It scratched across his throat and fell into the noise without anybody calling it out.

Except Zion.

Except Mari.

They caught it like real ones always did: that too-tight breath, that almost-laugh that didn't quite make it to the surface.

Darius didn't meet their eyes.

Just swallowed another mouthful of grits and set his fork down slow.

Wiped his palms against his joggers once before picking the fork back up and stabbing into the eggs.

He could feel the porch calling them.

Could feel Zion and Mari shifting weight, exchanging that silent conversation across the plates and half-finished cups of coffee.

But for now, Darius sat breathing in the heavy air, surrounded by life too stubborn to stop spinning.

Eating slow, steady.

Holding himself upright without apology.

The porch door clicked shut behind them, muting the noise of breakfast. All that laughter, glass clinking, and Willow still giggling about something no one else found funny.

Out here, the heat pressed harder.

The air hung thick, unmoving, even in the shade.

Zion leaned against the railing, arms crossed, looking out over the yard like he was watching for something that hadn't come yet.

Mari sat on the steps, elbows on knees, chewing the inside of his cheek the way he did when he didn't want to be the first one to speak.

Darius stood, not quite in the middle, not quite settled.

His hands flexed once at his sides.

"You gonna tell us what happened," Mari said eventually.

Darius exhaled slow. "Tamara pulled up on me at the gala."

Mari raised a brow, just a flick.

Zion didn't move. "How close we talkin'?" Zion asked.

Not with suspicion.

Just clarity.

"Close enough to trigger something," Darius said. "She touched me. Arm. Leaned in."

"And Zora saw it?" Zion asked.

Darius nodded. "I told Tamara to back up. I handled it. But Zora wasn't there for that part. She saw what she saw."

Neither man said anything for a beat.

"That kind of moment…" Mari rubbed the back of his neck. "You can do everything right and it still don't matter if someone else already filled in the blanks."

Zion finally turned to look at Darius full-on.

"Did you freeze?"

Darius's mouth twitched, something close to shame flickering under his skin.

"Yeah," he said. "For a second. I froze."

Mari nodded slow. "You got a right to freeze. Especially when you got a history with someone who made you feel disposable."

Zion didn't blink.

"You also got the right to be disappointed when the person you love doesn't ask what happened before deciding who you are."

The silence after that didn't just sit there but it pressed in, sticky and full, wrapping around them like the humidity itself.

"She didn't ask," Darius said. "Didn't even give me a look. She just left."

"She scared," Mari said. "That ain't on you, but it's still real. Some people don't know how to stay when things feel familiar to their pain."

"Doesn't mean you stop showing up as who you are," Zion added.

"And it damn sure doesn't mean you shrink just to make yourself easier to hold."

The same ones that built things, steadied chaos, pleasure from silence.

"All I wanted was to be seen," he said.

His voice was low.

"And she made me feel like I had done something wrong by being there."

"You didn't," Zion said, firm. "But that doesn't mean it didn't hurt her. Or scare her. Both things can be true."

Mari nodded. "You gotta let her hold her fear without picking it up like it's yours to carry."

Darius closed his eyes for half a second, breathing that in. "I ain't mad," he said. "I just... I just wanted it to be different."

"It is," Zion said. "You're different. You handled that situation with patience. With control. With respect. You didn't let old versions of yourself take the wheel. That's different."

"You think she'll come back?" Darius asked, quiet.

Mari shrugged. "That's her journey. But if she does, she gotta meet the man standing still — not the boy chasing after something to prove he's enough."

Zion looked him dead in the eye. "You are enough. You been enough. Whether she comes back or not."

No hugs. No back slaps. Just three men, holding space—in the heat, in the quiet, in truth.

Men holding space for each other.

He didn't feel alright.

But he didn't feel alone.

And that was enough to end the morning.

the pull back in

"GONNA LOVE ME" BY TEYANA TAYLOR

The community center smelled like floor polish, old sweat, and something softer underneath—a place still stretching wide enough to hold every life tucked inside. Zora stood just inside the front door, letting the weight of the day settle on her. The heat clung to her skin, thick and unmoving, the late-spring sun spilling long shadows across the cracked asphalt outside.

It had been two days since she walked away.

Two days of sitting inside her own silence.

Two days of feeling that ache coil tighter, until it was too big to pretend she didn't see it.

Zora's palms were damp, throat tight. Her feet carried her forward—not fast, but without hesitation now. She moved through the center, fingertips grazing the cool concrete walls like she needed to ground herself against the decision she'd already made.

Voices echoed faintly down the halls. Kids laughing, a ball thudding against a wall somewhere out of sight but she wasn't here for the noise.

She found him in one of the back rooms, setting up folding chairs. He moved with the kind of ease that said he wasn't rushing, wasn't avoiding anything. Just steady. Just breathing. The late afternoon light slanted in through the high windows, throwing long bands of gold across the floor and across him, cutting his figure into something almost too solid to look at.

He didn't look up when she stepped into the doorway, though she knew he felt her. Darius always knew when something shifted in the room.

She swallowed against the dryness in her throat, heart hammering slow and stubborn, and crossed the threshold.

"I thought losing you would hurt less than needing you and not knowing if you'd stay."

The words broke the air between them, not loud, not soft, just there. Heavy.

At that, Darius straightened and turned to face her fully. His movements were unhurried, deliberate, the way someone moved when they had decided not to flinch for anyone, ever again. His face was steady, not blank, not hard, just open in the way that hurt more than any anger would have.

Zora stepped closer, her heartbeat rattling against her ribs but her feet sure. She could feel the sweat gathering at the back of her neck, the heat thick enough to taste, but she didn't stop moving.

"I saw you stiffen," she said, voice thick but steady. "Then saw her touch you, and instead of asking anything, instead of staying long enough to see you, I made a choice. I chose my fear."

Darius didn't speak, just watched her.

"I let my fear write a story that hurt both of us," she said. "I made you the villain because it was easier than admitting you were real and I didn't know how to survive that kind of good without bracing for the fall. That you might actually be the man you showed me you were, and I didn't know if I could survive that kind of good without preparing for the fall."

The kids' laughter faded down the hall somewhere behind

her, the whole building settling into a thick kind of quiet that wrapped around them both.

"I'm not here to excuse it," she said. "I'm here because I'm choosing you. Fully. Even scared. Especially scared."

Her voice caught at the end, but she didn't back down. She let the silence fill in the spaces between her words. She let herself be seen, raw and all the way open, the way he had stood in front of her all along.

He crossed the space between them, boots silent on the old tile, stopping close enough that she could feel the body heat rolling off him, steady as breath. His gaze was steady, seeing her, really seeing her, not rushing to rescue, not rushing to punish.

"You didn't ask," he said, voice low, even.

She nodded because there was no defense worth offering. "I know."

"You didn't trust me."

Her chest tightened. "I didn't even trust myself," she said, the words scraping out like they'd been waiting to bleed since the night she left.

He looked at her for a long beat, the kind of look that pinned her in place without needing to lift a hand. She stood in it, breathing through the shame, the ache, the raw fear that she might've already run out of time.

"You here now?" he asked.

There was no hesitation when she answered. "Yeah," she said. "I'm here."

He exhaled through his nose, slow and steady, and for the first time in two days, she felt something loosen between them, something shift.

Darius didn't reach for her. He didn't move to pull her in or push her away. He just nodded once, solid and final.

"Then stay."

She stayed there, eyes locked on his, her body buzzing from more than the heat. The quiet between them stretched, not cold now, but taut, humming with everything unsaid and everything forgiven. She knew this wasn't over, not really. But it was enough for today. Enough to keep choosing.

He moved in close, his hand skimming the curve of her waist, tilting her chin so she had to look at him.

She stood right there in the thick, humid air, sweat sticking her shirt to her back, heart hammering, fear clawing at the edges of her ribs. She stood inside all of it and stayed, anyway. Because what mattered wasn't that she was scared. What mattered was that she was choosing him, in spite of it.

They didn't speak again right away.

The surrounding room held the silence like a breath, waiting to see if it would be broken or honoured. The air was thick, clinging to Zora's skin, but she wasn't uncomfortable. Not anymore. Not in the way that meant she wanted to run. The tension between them wasn't about whether they still wanted each other. It was about what came after wanting. What came after choosing?

Darius moved first, not with urgency, but with the quiet certainty that had always been his. He walked to one of the chairs he'd set up earlier, turned it to face hers, and sat down slow. His knees spread, arms resting across his thighs, his posture relaxed but not collapsed. He wasn't performing calm. He was living inside it.

Zora followed, settling into the chair across from him. She crossed one ankle over the other and folded her hands in her lap, fingers still trembling slightly from everything she'd just said. But the fear had softened now, melted into something she could carry without it slicing open her palms.

She looked at him — not just at his face, but at the whole of him. The lines of his shoulders, the way his chest rose and fell, like the breath was coming easier now. She noticed the faint crease in his shirt, the sheen of sweat at his hairline, the steadiness in his gaze even when he wasn't trying to hold her together.

"You know what's wild?" she said, her voice softer now. "It

wasn't even what happened that night that scared me the most. It was how much I needed to believe you."

He didn't flinch. He nodded once, like he'd been waiting for her to get there.

"I spent so long being told I was too much, or not enough," she continued. "So, I started preparing for people to leave. I got good at it. At packing up first. At slipping out before the ache could settle too deep."

Darius rested his elbows on his knees, clasped his hands together, and leaned in a little. "I could feel you pulling away that night, even before you walked out."

"I know," she whispered. "And I hated that I made you feel that. After everything... I hated that I did to you what everyone else had done to me."

He looked at her then, eyes darker, not from anger, but depth. Something bruised and whole at once.

"When you left," he said, "it didn't feel like rejection. It felt like confirmation. Like, yeah... this is what happens. This is what love costs me."

Zora sucked in a breath, sharp and immediate. The weight of his words landed heavily between them, but she didn't run from it this time.

"I didn't mean to make you carry that," she said. "But I know that's not enough. You shouldn't have to be the one who always stays to prove something to the people too scared to stand still."

"You're not them," he said simply. "You showed back up. That ain't nothing."

"I want to be more than that," she said. "I want to be someone who can sit in the hard parts and not flinch. I want to be someone who sees you in all your quiet and doesn't try to make it louder just because silence scares me."

Darius leaned back slightly, letting his hands drop between his knees. He let her words settle.

"I want to stop trying to be what people can handle," he

said after a moment. "And just be what's true. Whether they hold it or not."

They stared at each other — not across a distance, not over a chasm, but in the same shared breath, the same honest place.

Then, slowly, Zora uncrossed her legs and leaned forward. She reached across the space between them, laid her hand on his knee. No trembling. No theatrics.

"I can handle you," she said. "Not because you're easy. But because I want to. I'm choosing to."

Darius didn't answer with words. He reached up and cradled the back of her hand in his palm, holding it there like it was something sacred.

They stayed like that for a long time.

Not fixing.

Not filling the air with apologies or explanations.

Just letting the truth be enough.

And this time, it was.

The back room was too exposed.

Zora felt it before Darius even spoke. The faint echo of kids' voices down the hall, the hum of the vending machines — reminders that the world hadn't gone quiet just because they had.

He moved in close, his hand skimming the curve of her waist, tilting her chin so she had to look at him.

"Not here," he said, voice low and steady. "Too many ears."

She nodded, pulse thrumming just beneath her skin. "Where?"

"My office."

A pause.

"Door locks."

She didn't ask for more. She just moved.

He let her lead but stayed close, his heat brushing the back of her neck as they slipped down the hall.

When he unlocked the heavy door to his office and pulled

it open, the difference hit immediately, the deep quiet, the soft scent of cedar still hanging in the air from the diffuser, and the faint scratch of his chair swiveling slightly on its base from where he'd left it earlier.

This wasn't a rush.

This was a decision.

He closed the door behind them, twisted the lock, and turned to her. Heat banked low under his skin, waiting to be unleashed.

Zora's body moved before her mouth could.

She braced her hands on the desk, looked back at him. Eyes dark, need heavy between them, but no fear this time. Just choice. Just want.

He came to her slow, the buttons of his sleeves brushing against the swell of her hips as he crowded into her space. His hands skimmed her sides, down to the waistband of her jeans.

"You remember when you first visited here?" he murmured against her ear. "I pictured all of the things that I could do to you."

Zora smiled, wickedly and breathlessly. "Guess you should stop fantasizing and do something about it, then."

He chuckled, rough and low, and tugged her jeans and panties down in one firm motion, leaving them bunched around her thighs.

"Mmm, that smart-ass mouth," he rasped, hand smoothing down her back, "always writing checks your body gotta cash. You ready to pay up?"

She shivered when his hand came down, sharp but not cruel on the curve of her ass. A sting that bloomed quick under her skin.

She gasped and braced harder against the desk.

"And keep it down, baby," he warned, voice thick against her ear. Smack. "That sweet mouth too loud, I'ma have to shut it for you. You feel me?"

"Yes," she whispered, barely holding it in.

Darius ran his fingers between her thighs, feeling the heat and slick waiting there for him. His groan was soft, reverent.

"Goddamn," he breathed, teasing her folds. "You feel that? All that mess already? You been needing me that bad?"

Zora whimpered, pushing back into his touch. "You're the one teasing."

"Yeah, that's because I know how crazy it makes you." he growled, guiding himself in slowly. "All that backtalk and still begging me to stretch you out." He didn't tease after that.

One steady thrust and he was buried inside her, the stretch brutal and sweet. Zora's mouth fell open around a cry, her nails digging into the desk as he held her hips still.

"Fuck, this pussy is gripping me so tight," he rasped, rocking deep, slow, like he had all night to remind her exactly who she'd come back to.

She sobbed out a yes, hips jerking, the slick sound of them meeting filling the space around their panting breaths.

He set a punishing rhythm. Deep, slow, and grinding in a way that made her toes curl.

When she got too loud, he gripped her hair, pulling just enough to arch her back more. His mouth was at her ear, hot and taunting.

"Keep that shit up, baby," he growled, fist tightening lightly in her hair. "You want me to gag you? Cuz you know you ain't coming till I say so."

She whimpered, fighting to hold the sounds back, every nerve lit up, every part of her tuned to the way he filled her again and again.

"You gonna be good for me?" he asked, his hand sneaking between her legs to rub tight, ruthless circles over her clit.

"Yes," she sobbed. "Please, Darius..please"

"Yeah, that's it, baby," he breathed, circling her clit. "You know what I need. Ask for it. Show me you can behave."

"Please," she gasped. "Please let me cum. I need it..I need you.."

"That's it," he said, grinding deeper. "That's my girl.

There you go," he groaned, driving deep. "Cum for me, baby. Wet me up."

She shattered hard, thighs clenching around him, her body trembling, her moans muffled against her forearm as she held herself together against the desk.

He chased her over the edge, hips snapping, breath breaking against her skin.

When he came inside her, it was with a broken groan of her name and the kind of shudder that said he'd been holding on just for her.

They stayed tangled over the desk, skin slick, breath shared, the office heavy with the aftermath.

Darius pressed soft kisses along the curve of her spine, slow, reverent.

After a few minutes, Darius eased back, careful not to jostle her. His hands were gentle as he helped her stand, helped her shimmy her panties and jeans back up, pulling them over trembling thighs.

"You okay?" he asked, voice low and real.

Zora nodded, still catching her breath. "Yeah. Better than okay."

He kissed her forehead, slowly and grounding, before smoothing her hair back from her face.

He didn't rush her. Didn't pull away first. His hands stayed steady, like he knew exactly how to hold something fragile without breaking it.

"Sit," he said gently, guiding her to the couch tucked in the corner of his office.

She sank down, legs wobbling. Darius knelt in front of her, hands still roaming lightly up and down her calves, her thighs, anchoring her body back into itself.

Neither of them spoke for a while.

The silence was soft now. Easy.

Finally, she looked down at him, fingers threading lightly through his hair.

"You really know what you're doing to me," she

murmured, a smile playing at her lips.

He smirked, kissed the inside of her knee. "Couldn't help myself."

The humor faded first from her face, then from his.

Zora cupped his face between her hands, thumbs tracing the line of his jaw, the curl of his beard.

"I love you," she said, voice steady. No trembling this time.

Darius's eyes didn't widen. He didn't stiffen.

He just smiled, soft and wrecked before he leaned into her touch.

"I love you too," he said, voice wrecked and sure. "Ain't never stopped."

Zora blinked down at him, heart too full to speak.

He kissed her palm once, then stood and pulled her into his arms.

They stayed there, wrapped up in each other, the world locked out behind that heavy door, two stubborn hearts finally beating in the same rhythm.

choose me out loud

"BUTTERFLIES PT. 2" BY QUEEN NAIJA

They didn't say much when they left the center that night. No big talk. No dramatic pause.

Just fingers laced, palms warm, hearts steady.

Zora walked out beside him like her body already knew what her mind had just started catching up to—that staying didn't have to feel like surrender.

"Darius opened the passenger door for her without letting go of her hand." Waited until she was inside. And when they pulled into his driveway, porch light catching the edge of his smile, she didn't hesitate.

She followed him in like she'd been doing it for years.

The first thing she noticed the next morning was how still everything felt.

Not empty. Not heavy.

Just calm.

The sheets were soft against her skin, his scent still clinging to the pillow. Cedar. Heat. Something steady. She stretched slow, the ache between her thighs a sweet, pulsing reminder of the night before. Her heart beat quiet and even. No rush. No dread.

Zora slid out of the bed without waking him, found one of

his white tees in his dresser and slipped it on before heading to the kitchen.

The space greeted her like it remembered her. Soft light through the window. Clean counters. Warmth held in the tile from the morning sun.

She didn't hesitate.

Opened the fridge, found eggs, spices and some herbs. Poured water into the kettle like she'd done it a hundred times. The pan heated beneath her hand while she cracked eggs with practiced rhythm. Her feet bare. Her body grounded.

She didn't need a reason to do it. She just wanted to.

He came in a few minutes later, quiet and barefoot, the sleep still soft on his face. Joggers hanging low. Eyes warm.

"You're up early," he said.

Zora glanced over her shoulder. "Your kitchen was calling me."

That got the corner of his mouth to lift. He stepped closer but didn't interrupt. Just leaned against the counter, arms folded, watching her because she was something worth pausing for.

"You don't have to do this," he said gently. "Zora, you don't have to prove anything. You know that I like taking care of you."

She shrugged, flipped something in the pan. "I'm not. I just..wanted to do something that felt like care. Not cleanup."

Darius stepped behind her, slid his arms around her waist, and pulled her into his chest. He kissed the side of her neck—soft, lingering—his lips pressing warmth into her skin as his thumbs traced slow circles over her hips.

"You don't have to beat yourself up," he said. "You came back and we talked. We're not in that moment anymore."

Her hands stilled over the stove, her body quieting under his voice.

"I know," she said, "I do."

He turned her slightly, just enough to meet her eyes. "We're building now. Not reliving."

She exhaled and nodded, the tension sliding out of shoulders like it had finally gotten permission to go. "Then sit down," she said, smirking slightly. "Let me take care of my man. And if you hover, I'm gonna start assigning you chores."

"Yes, ma'am." He said, grinning now. He kissed her cheek, dropped into a seat, and pulled his tablet over, scrolling through emails.

She plated the eggs, bacon and slid a mug of his favorite tea in front of him.

At one point, he reached across the table and covered her hand with his.

She didn't pull away.

When they left the house, it was still early enough for the air to feel soft against their skin. The kind of Atlanta morning that carried heat low in its throat but hadn't spoken yet.

Zora drove the van this time. Darius rode passenger, one arm resting on the door, the other scrolling through something on his phone with that familiar look—eyes half-lidded, fingers moving precisely. He didn't say what he was working on, and she didn't ask.

She already knew.

By the time they unlocked the door to Wild Hart, the day had shifted into motion.

Zora turned on the lights, flipped the hanging "CLOSED" sign to "OPEN," and moved through the space like it was an extension of her body. Darius set up in the corner of the shop, plugging his laptop into a small charger tucked beside the plant wall and pulling out headphones he didn't even use— just resting them around his neck like a boundary no one questioned.

They didn't hover around each other.

Didn't fill the room with forced chatter.

Zora pruned the Monstera near the window, wiped soil from the counter, checked invoices, display cards. Darius tapped through screens, edited lines of code, made quiet notes on the Roots & Rhythm wireframe he hadn't shown her yet.

At one point, she caught him watching her from across the room. Not staring. Just… tuned in. His mouth twitched like he was fighting a smile.

She shook her head and kept moving.

Keira rolled in mid-morning, clocked the energy within five seconds, and flung her bag down with a sigh sharp enough to cut glass.

"Oh, so we're in our domestic era now? Cute," she said, yanking off her earrings like she was ready to fight the softness. "You two been staring at each other like the Wi-Fi just hit."

Zora didn't flinch.

Just smirked.

"Don't be mad 'cause the signal's strong over here."

Keira snorted. "Mmhm. Keep it up. I'll start lighting sage in the corners again."

Darius didn't even look up. "Depends on the kind of sage."

That made Keira pause. "I know you're not about to correct my smoke game."

"I'm just saying," he murmured, eyes still on his screen, "some of y'all be burning blessings with bad technique."

Zora choked on a laugh. Keira threw a pothos tag at him.

Balance restored.

The shop buzzed with quiet movement—customers browsing, wind chimes clinking above the entrance, Zora's playlist low under it all.

And through it, they moved, Zora and Darius, never in each other's way, but never far.

Like rhythm.

Not loud.

But constant.

The shop had settled into that late afternoon hush—when the sun pooled golden across the counters and the air got heavy with stillness, not heat.

Keira had dipped already, leaving behind a half-eaten

protein bar and a text that read: Don't break anything that costs more than your feelings.

Zora laughed under her breath when she saw it, then tossed the wrapper in the trash. She was wiping down a set of hand-painted pots when Darius walked up behind the register, tablet in hand.

"You busy?" he asked.

She shook her head, brushing a curl off her cheek. "Just pretending to be productive."

He nodded. "Sit with me for a minute?"

They moved to the back table, the one near the propagation shelf. Zora tucked her leg under her, leaned into the chair like she was settling in for more than a quick chat.

Darius didn't waste time.

"What do you want?"

She blinked. "Like… right now?"

"In life."

Zora stilled.

He wasn't asking in some vague way. It wasn't a "What's your dream?" kind of question.

It was: What are you building towards? Because I need to know if I'm meant to stand in it.

She sat back slowly. "I used to think I just wanted peace. A home that didn't feel like a countdown."

Darius nodded.

"But now?" she continued. "I want roots. Not just in this shop or in plants but in people. I want to love hard and raise something that grows because of it."

"You mean kids?"

Zora paused. "Yeah. Eventually. If I'm gonna love somebody, I want to pour that into a family. Doesn't have to look like some fairytale but I want little hands in the dirt with me. I want to build something they can feel safe in."

Darius sat for a beat, then said, "Same."

She looked at him.

"I want a family," he said. "But I want it slow. Intentionally. I want to be present. I don't want to parent the way I was parented or not parented."

Zora's gaze softened.

"I've thought about what kind of father I'd be," he continued. "What kind of partner I'd have to be to not burn out trying to prove I'm not my mother."

She reached across the table and touched his arm.

"You don't have to prove anything."

"I know," he said. "But I want to show up fully. That means being real about the life I'm building."

Zora nodded. "You want that with me?"

"I wouldn't be here if I didn't."

She exhaled. "Okay. So, we talk about it. Not just in some hypothetical future. We name it. Make space for it."

Darius reached for her hand. "I want space with you. However that looks."

Her smile was soft but sure. "Then let's start here."

They didn't say much as they locked up for the night.

Zora flipped the sign to CLOSED, powered down the register, and let the quiet settle over the shop like a soft blanket. Darius checked the back door, then followed her upstairs, their footsteps soft and slow against the worn wood, as if neither of them wanted to break the quiet wrapping around them.

Her apartment was still warm from the day—windows cracked, the scent of soil and old incense lingering in the corners. Zora tossed her keys in the bowl, kicked her shoes off, and opened the fridge.

"You hungry?" she asked over her shoulder.

Darius leaned against the counter like he belonged there now. "A little. What you thinking?"

"Pasta," she said. "Maybe garlic bread, if I didn't burn it last time."

"You burn it, I'll lie," he said, grinning.

Zora rolled her eyes and grabbed a bundle of herbs. "Don't lie to me in my own kitchen."

They started moving like they'd done this before.

She chopped tomatoes. He crushed the garlic badly, the first time. She slid over and showed him how to press the flat of the knife with his palm.

"You fighting the garlic or the countertop?" She teased, bumping his hip with hers.

"Listen. That garlic had an attitude."

He cut himself just a little while slicing the bread. Nothing serious but just enough for her to grab his hand and mutter, "I told you not to rush."

She dabbed it clean, gentle but bossy and he let her fuss.

"You always like this?" he asked.

"Like what?"

"Running the whole kitchen like you're running a kitchen."

Zora shrugged, tossing chopped spinach into the sauce. "Sometimes it's just easier."

Darius stirred, without comment. But a few minutes later, while she was bent in the fridge digging for parmesan, he said, low and offhand, "You ever think about what it'd be like to do this all the time?"

She paused.

Not from panic, just surprise.

"You mean live-in garlic debates and watching you hoard the salt?"

He glanced over, smirking. "Something like that."

Zora stood up, cheese in hand. "You wouldn't last a week."

"You think I'm soft?"

"I think you like your peace too much to share it every day."

He stepped closer, brushing her hip with his. "Depends on who I'm sharing it with."

Zora didn't have anything to say that. Just handed him the cheese grater and turned back to the stove.

Her heart was steady. That was new.

When the food was done, she plated it with two forks and brought everything to the couch. No table tonight. No ceremony. Just comfort.

They sat side by side, knees touching. Shared a bite off the same fork without thinking about it. Darius wiped a little sauce from her lip with his thumb, slow and easy, and kept talking about something one of his developers broke in staging that morning like it didn't even register what he'd just done.

Zora didn't call it out. She didn't need to.

After they ate, she leaned back against the cushions, full and soft and quiet. Darius turned on a low playlist, some mellow soul, no lyrics. Just mood.

She looked at him sideways, one leg curled beneath her.

"This feels good."

Darius nodded. "Yeah. It really does."

They didn't say much after that.

The light dimmed. The room stayed warm.

And somewhere in the quiet between tracks, Zora let her head fall onto his shoulder, and Darius laid his hand over her knee.

Nothing pulled at them.

Nothing rushed.

Just peace.

The kind that settled deep. And this time, neither of them questioned if it would last.

Zora yawned, leaned into his shoulder, and murmured,

"Don't get used to me cooking. Next time you're on stove duty."

Darius chuckled, arm tightening around her. "I'll burn it on purpose.

CHAPTER NINETEEN
roots & rhythm
"OUT LOUD" BY SYD FT KEHLANI

The morning wrapped Wild Hart in the kind of quiet that wasn't fragile—it had been earned. Zora moved steady through it: misting the ferns slow, flipping the OPEN sign deliberate, pressing her palms into the warm belly of a ceramic pot still holding heat from the kiln.

The diffuser whispered lemongrass and basil into the air, curling soft around the shop's corners, weaving through the macrame and the trailing vines like a blessing she didn't have to pray for.

She wiped the counters in slow, even circles—not because they were dirty, but to smooth out the tiny hum riding her skin. A rare kind of peace sat in her chest. Not loud. Not flashy. Just solid.

Then the bell over the door chimed.

"Morning, Miss Zora!"

Mrs. Polk's voice carried across the shop before her body even rounded the corner. Bright. Cheerful. Familiar. Zora turned with a practiced smile already forming, the kind you gave to folks who'd loved you longer than they'd known your last name.

"Hey, Mrs. Polk. Whatcha got there?"

Mrs. Polk beamed like she was showing off a grandbaby.

She hoisted a sleek, cream-and-copper bag into the air, triumphant. "Look what I found at Greenhaus!"

The smile slipped right off Zora's face before she could catch it.

Mrs. Polk didn't notice. She was busy flipping the bag around, admiring it from every angle. "Isn't it beautiful? I thought it was yours at first—the colors, the packaging! But they told me it's from a new local vendor. I just knew y'all had teamed up!"

Zora's hand flexed around the edge of the counter. Her throat felt too small. "No," she said, slower. "We're not collaborating."

Mrs. Polk's eyebrows pinched, just a little. "Oh… huh. Really?" She turned the bag over again, tracing the embossed lettering. "Sure feels like you, though. I thought for sure she learned it from you." She let out a light chuckle, like it was all some cute coincidence. "Well, it's wonderful! I'm gonna try it on my fiddle leaf. And of course I had to come here for a pot to match."

She bustled off toward the planter shelves, humming like nothing was wrong.

But Zora couldn't move.

Her eyes stayed locked on the bag Mrs. Polk had set down beside the register. She stepped closer, almost against her own will, until her fingers brushed the copper foil letters.

ROOTED BY LOREN.

Her thumb traced the tagline beneath it.

"Nourish what roots you."

The words hit like a gut punch dressed up in a compliment.

A memory knocked loose: Loren years ago, grinning wide across a folding table at the back of a vendor fair, iced coffee sweating between her hands.

"C'mon, Z. You never write it down anyway. Just tell me what's in the base. We're friends."

Zora's jaw clenched. Her hand tightened around the bag.

She set it back down carefully, like she was laying something delicate to rest.

"Hey… are you guys partners?"

The question snapped her out of it.

A young woman stood a few feet away, cradling a pothos in her arms, her hopeful expression wilting under Zora's silence.

"No," Zora said, voice steady but flat.

The girl frowned, shifting her weight. "Oh. I thought she tagged you or something. Guess I misread." She drifted away without waiting for an answer.

Behind her, a soft scrape. A wobble. Then the sharp crack of a pot falling off a shelf and splitting open against the floor.

Zora's whole body jumped.

"Miss Zora? Are you okay?" another voice asked gently.

She crouched down, gathering the shards with shaking hands. "Yeah," she said, quieter. "I'm okay."

The pieces scraped together in her palm. She dropped them into the trash, then wiped her hands on her apron—just for something to do.

When she straightened, the bag was still sitting there on the counter. Silent. Gleaming. Mocking.

Zora didn't touch it again.

She moved back toward the shelves, picked up another pot, and kept working.

But the hum beneath her skin wasn't peace anymore.

It was something waiting to break.

Zora barely heard the bell chime again.

She turned, wiping her hands on her apron even though they were already clean, already worn down to nothing. The next customer smiled and nodded, setting down a small stack of pots. Zora rang them up, automatic. Her voice moved where it was supposed to move. Her lips curved in all the right places. But inside, her chest was tight, humming sharp.

When the shop finally cleared, when the last pair of

sandals clapped out the door, she leaned both palms against the counter and let her head drop forward.

The bag was still sitting there. Shiny. Warm under the track lights.

She exhaled slow. Picked it up again. Flipped it over.

A tiny QR code peeked out from the bottom.

She scanned it with her phone. Watched the page load.

And there it was: a full launch post on Cirqle.

A sleek banner across the top:

ROOTED BY LOREN

The homepage opened with a clean shot of Loren smiling beside a table lined with glass jars and earth-toned packaging. Beneath it, a scroll of praise: reposted reviews, influencer shoutouts, feature spots from blogs Zora had once dreamed of pitching to herself.

The tagline unfurled in big bold letters:

"Nourish what roots you."

Her stomach dropped.

She kept scrolling. Fingers tight.

A product page. A soil blend breakdown. Ratios close enough to make her chest ache. Tutorials shot in bright kitchens that looked suspiciously like Loren's last apartment. Press write-ups calling it "innovative," "intentional," "hand-crafted from scratch."

And then a section marked ORIGIN STORY.

Zora clicked it, pulse thudding hard in her throat.

A paragraph unfolded:

"Inspired by the community gardens of my childhood, I dreamed of creating something to reconnect people to the earth… This journey has been years in the making, blending old knowledge with fresh vision…"

The words sounded familiar. Too familiar. Like her. But not her.

A shadow of her. Wearing her story like a borrowed jacket.

Her vision blurred. She blinked hard.

The back door creaked.

"Girl?" Keira's voice floated in, casual. "You good? You been quiet all morning."

Zora held up the bag without turning around.

Keira stepped closer. Took it from her. Turned it over once. Twice. Her smile faded.

"…Is this—"

"Yeah."

Keira's jaw tightened. "That bitch."

Zora let out a breath—half laugh, half hollow.

Keira flipped the bag again, reading the tagline under her breath like it was sour. "'Nourish what roots you.' Bitch stole your whole flow."

Zora wiped her palms down her apron. "And sold it."

Keira's head whipped up. "What?"

"She didn't just copy me. She scaled me. She's on Cirqle, Keira. Got vendors lined up. I saw one of them today. They're already stocking her."

Keira slammed the bag down on the counter. "Are you fucking kidding me?"

Zora's laugh scraped raw in her throat. "Wish I was."

Keira blew out a sharp breath, pacing tight. "You want me to call her? Pull up? What's the move?"

Zora scrolled the page again. Loren's face. Loren's words. Loren's fake-ass story.

"I don't know yet," she murmured. "I don't even know where to start."

Keira stilled beside her, quieter now.

"You don't gotta start alone," she said. "Whatever you do? I'm in it."

Zora swallowed hard. Closed the page. Set her phone down face-down.

"Yeah," she whispered. "I know."

And for a long moment, they stood there together. Side by side.

Looking down at the bag between them.

Not defeated.

But bracing.

Zora's hands pressed flat to the counter, chest tight. The copper-and-cream bag sat there, shining under the track lights like it knew it didn't belong.Keira leaned in, squinting at the label. "What in the gentrified bullshit is this?"

Zora didn't answer. She just swallowed hard.

Keira picked the bag up, flipped it over, sneered. "ROOTED BY LOREN?" She said it like it tasted bad. "Oh nah. Oh nah nah nah." She slapped the bag back on the counter. "This bitch got me fucked up."

Zora let out a breath that sounded too small. "Keira…"

"No." Keira spun toward her, one hand already in the air like she was waving an invisible choir behind her. "You mean to tell me she took your blend, slapped a sexy label on it, and out here sellin' it at Greenhaus like she invented dirt?"

Zora's jaw tightened. "She's… been moving shady for a while—"

"Nah! We not doing 'shady.' She's been stealing. Call it what it is."Keira grabbed a stool, kicked it around so she could sit facing Zora head-on. "Look at me. You hear me? This ain't you losing. This is her showing she ain't got shit without you. She had to copy. She had to scheme. You? You been original."

Zora's lips parted, then pressed shut again.

Keira kept going, heat rolling now. "I swear to God, if you let this stress wrinkle that pretty ass face, I'm fighting every-body. Her, Greenhaus, the post office that delivered this shit—"

A tiny laugh cracked through Zora's chest. "Not the post office—"

"I will fight USPS, bitch." Keira grinned wide, then soft-ened just enough to reach across the counter, palm cupping Zora's cheek. "You don't gotta clap back today. You don't gotta post a damn thing. We gon' handle it. I got you."

Zora leaned into her touch, eyelids heavy. "I hate how she played me."

"I know, baby." Keira's thumb brushed under her eye, catching a tear before it could fall. "But she played herself worse. She don't even know it yet."

Zora's breath wobbled. "I'm tired."

"I know." Keira pulled her close across the counter, wrapping both arms tight around her shoulders. "But you ain't alone. You never been."

They stayed like that a long beat, Keira rocking them slightly, humming under her breath like a lullaby but with teeth.

Then Keira pulled back, a dangerous glint in her eye. "Now. You want me to go drive past her shop real slow? Or you wanna rearrange this shit in here so it look even sexier for your customers? Either way, I'm ride or die."

Zora wiped her face with her sleeve. "Shelves."

Keira cracked her neck. "Good answer. But I'm still driving by later. Just in case."

And together they moved—lifting, shifting, reclaiming the space one fierce, stubborn gesture at a time.

Keira cracked her knuckles after rearranging the last shelf. "Okay, it's officially impossible for anybody to walk in here and not see your genius. You're welcome."

Zora wiped her palms down her apron, a smile tugging at her mouth. "You didn't have to do all this."

"I did." Keira slung her bag over her shoulder. "And I'd do it again. Call me if you need anything, and I mean anything. Bail included."

"Please don't get arrested today."

"No promises." Keira winked—then paused as the bell over the door chimed again.

Darius stepped in, quiet and steady, hands tucked in his jacket pockets. His gaze flicked to Keira first, taking her in with that same calm read he gave everything.

Keira leaned against the counter, sipping from her water bottle, eyes dancing between Zora and Darius as he stepped in. "Look who finally decided to show up," she teased.

Darius's mouth quirked into a quiet smile. "Didn't wanna interrupt the hustle."

"Mm." Keira tilted her head, giving him a long look, but it wasn't sharp this time—just playful. "I been lettin' you slide, but you know I got a bat under the register, right?"

"I figured." Darius's voice stayed easy. "You ever swing it?"

Keira grinned wide. "Not yet. But there's still time." She bumped Zora's shoulder lightly. "You sure about this one?"

"Keira," Zora warned, but her mouth was already curling up.

"Nah, I'm serious. I like him." Keira jabbed a finger toward Darius. "But don't get comfortable. If you hurt her? I know your schedule."

Darius's brows lifted slightly, amusement glinting in his eyes. "Duly noted."

Keira gave Darius one last mock-narrowed glare, then pushed off the counter, grabbing her bag. "Aight. I'm out. Y'all don't do nothing I wouldn't do."

"That's a very short list," Zora called after her.

"Exactly!" Keira laughed, waving over her shoulder—then paused at the door, finger tapping the frame.

"Oh—and Z?" Her voice dipped warm, conspiratorial. "Friday. Ink & Ivy. You comin'."

Zora frowned. "Friday?"

"Yep. We celebratin'. Ain't gon' let you sit in here stewin'."

Zora hesitated, glancing at Darius.

Keira clocked the glance, smirked. "And you—" she pointed at Darius, playful but firm, "—tell your people they can pull up too. If they know how to act."

Darius's brow lifted, amused. "I'll let 'em know."

Keira's grin sharpened. "You do that." She turned back to Zora. "Don't make me show up here with a dress and no patience."

A reluctant smile bloomed. "Alright."

"Good." Keira winked. "We got you, babe. You just gotta show up."

And with that, she disappeared out the door, the bell jingling behind her.

The quiet stretched in her absence.

Darius stepped closer, setting a small paper bag on the counter. "Brought you something."

Zora blinked down at it. "What's this?"

"Dinner." He leaned against the counter, casual. "Figured you skipped again."

Zora peeled back the lid of the takeout container. The smell hit first—stewed oxtails over rice, greens folded on the side, a thick square of cornbread wrapped in foil.

Her breath caught. "You made this?"

Darius's mouth tilted, soft. "Yeah. Mama Regina's recipe. Used to fix it for me when I was little. Whenever shit felt heavy."

He watched her quietly. "Figured it might hit the same for you."

Zora stared down at the food, something thick rising in her chest. "You… cooked oxtails for me?"

Darius shrugged one shoulder. "Course." His grin flashed, boyish under all that steady. "You think I'm out here bringing you a cold sandwich?"

A laugh cracked loose from Zora's throat. "I mean… would've been on brand."

"Nah." Darius leaned in a little, eyes warm. "Not for you."

Zora unwrapped the fork, took a slow bite. The richness bloomed across her tongue, warmth curling deep in her chest.

"Damn." She let the word out quiet, full. "This tastes like… home."

Darius's smile deepened. "Good."

He watched her eat another bite. "Take your time."

They stood like that a while—Zora perched on the stool, eating slow; Darius leaning against the counter, quiet and steady beside her.

When she'd cleaned most of the container, he pulled his phone from his jacket pocket, thumb swiping it open.

"Got something else for you," he said, holding it out.

Zora wiped her hands on a napkin, took the phone slow. The screen lit up: Wild Hart. Her name beneath it.

She frowned, thumb hovering. "What is this?"

"Something to stand on." His voice stayed low.

She tapped. The app opened. Photos of her pots. Her soil blends. An easy shop interface. A bookings tab for workshops. A section labeled Ask Zora. Tutorials in her voice.

Her chest pulled tight.

"You—" Her throat closed. She swallowed hard. "You made this?"

She stared down at the screen, fingers trembling slightly. The photos glowed up at her—her work, her vision—so clear, so real. But under all that pride, something twisted low in her gut. An ache she hadn't put words to yet.

She bit her lip. "It's just... sometimes it feels like I'm building and building, and people keep finding ways to tear it down. To take from me." Her thumb traced over one of the product photos, jaw tightening. "Loren's been pushing my formula like it's hers. Slick as hell about it too."

Darius's eyes sharpened, but his voice stayed easy, steady. "Yeah? You tell me what you need."

Zora let out a breath, shaking her head. "I don't even know. I'm tryna keep my head down, keep moving, but..." She exhaled slow. "It's been sitting heavy."

Darius's hand came up, warm against the back of her neck, grounding her like always. "Let me handle it."

Zora blinked up at him, surprised. "D, no, I wasn't—"

He shook his head, gaze locked on hers, soft but unshakable. "You ain't gotta explain. I'm already watching it. Got my eyes on everything, even if you don't see it yet."

He watched her a long second, letting that settle between them, then slipped a hand into his jacket pocket—casual, deliberate. "Been working on something else too," he said, holding out his phone like an offering.

Zora wiped her hands on a napkin, took the phone slow. The screen lit up: Wild Hart. Her name beneath it.

Her brows furrowed, thumb hovering. "What is this?"

"Something to stand on." His voice stayed low, full of that quiet certainty.

She tapped it open. Photos of her pots. Her soil blends. A shop interface, clean and simple. Bookings for workshops. A section labeled Ask Zora. Tutorials in her voice.

Her chest pulled tight all over again.

"You—" Her voice broke soft. "You made this?"

Darius tucked his hands in his pockets, watching her quiet. "Been working on it a minute. Didn't wanna push it on you. Just… figured you'd need it. For when you ready."

Zora stared down at the phone. Her storefront, digital. Her work, shining. Her name, held up like something worth knowing.

A slow breath trembled out of her. "You been doing all this behind my back?"

His smile was small, warm. "Not behind your back, baby." He stepped closer, gaze steady. "Behind you."

Her lips parted, her chest too full, too tight.

"I see how much you carry," Darius said, voice softer now. "This gon' carry with you."

Something loosened deep inside her—a quiet undoing that felt less like falling apart and more like finally letting go.

She pressed the phone to her chest, stepped into him, arms winding around his waist.

"You're too good to me," she whispered.

Darius bent his head, lips brushing her temple. "Nah," he murmured. "Just loving you right."

night moves

"FIGHT NIGHT" BY MIGOS

The rest of the week folded in on itself. Quiet shifts, long hours, and small wins that didn't quite stretch far enough.

Keira's texts kept buzzing through the static:

"Don't flake."

"Already picked a dress."

"You betta show up, ho."

By Friday, Zora wasn't answering anymore. But the dress? Folded neat in her tote, anyway. Now she stood in Darius's man cave, lit low and warm, the glow of a vintage lamp skimming dark wood and worn leather.

Keira zipped her up from behind, her hands surprisingly gentle for all her usual noise. Zion perched on the arm of the couch, tossing a stress ball against the wall in a slow rhythm. Mari flipped through vinyls by the shelf, fingers tracing each spine like he was cataloging memories. Saige lounged deep in the recliner, sipping from a glass of whiskey, her gaze sharp beneath the quiet.

And Darius stood in the doorway, arms folded across his chest, watching them all with that steady patience he wore like a second skin. His cologne drifted faint in the air, threaded through the cedar and leather scent of the room. The walls held pieces of him—old photos, a framed jersey, a black-and-white portrait of Mama Regina in her garden.

A space built for him alone. But tonight, it held them all.

"You know," Keira murmured, stepping back to admire her work, "this dress gon' get Darius in a fight tonight."

Zora's mouth curved soft, a reluctant smile pulling at the corners. "He don't need to fight nobody."

Darius's voice came quiet, curling through the room like smoke. "Ain't lookin' for it," he murmured. "But I ain't lettin' nothin' slide either."

Keira turned, one brow cocked. "Mmhm. Thought so."

Zion chuckled, the stress ball thinking soft against his palm. "Man stay loaded, even on chill."

Mari glanced over, lips curving faint. "That's protection. Not pressure."

Saige's gaze flicked between Darius and Zora. "He holdin' his line. Always has."

Zora caught Saige's eyes in the mirror, felt that quiet truth settle under her ribs.

Keira gave her one last tug, smoothing the fabric flat with a little hum of satisfaction. "You look good, babe." Her voice softened, shedding the edge. "Like you."

Zora's throat tightened. "I don't know if I feel like her yet."

"You will," Keira promised, brushing her shoulder. "We gon' remind you."

Mari stepped closer, pressing a shot glass into her hand. "For courage."

Zora hesitated, fingers curling around the glass. "Mari, I—"

"Don't overthink it," he murmured. "You earned this."

Keira lifted her glass beside hers. "To showin' up."

Zion clinked his can lightly. "To makin' 'em watch."

Saige raised hers last. "To standin'."

Zora looked at each of them, warmth threading through

her chest like a scaffold. She tipped the shot back, the burn curling slow, stitching her together.

Then Darius moved. Quiet steps, heavy and sure, crossing the space between them like he wasn't asking permission.

His hands found her waist, warm and steady, pulling her back until her spine met the solid line of him. His lips brushed the slope of her shoulder, lingering, then tracing soft along her neck.

"You good?" he murmured, his breath stirring the fine hairs at her nape.

Zora's eyes fell closed, leaning into his warmth. "I'm gettin' there."

He kissed her again, slower, lips pressing beneath her ear. "You already here."

A shaky breath left her lips.

"Look at me," Darius said, his hands sliding along her waist, voice low and sure.

She turned a little, glanced up. His gaze met hers, quiet, steady.

"Ain't nobody gon' see you like I do," he said. "But they gon' try. And that's on them."

Her lips curled soft, the ache loosening in her chest.

Keira's voice cut through, playful but fond. "Alright now, lover boy. Let her breath. We got a city to take tonight."

Zora laughed, a low hum spilling from her throat. Darius smiled down at her, pressed one last kiss to her temple, then stepped back.

"Go ahead," he told her, voice easy but certain. "I'll be right here."

Her circle tight at her side. His love, steady at her back. Her chest still ached. But her feet still moved her forward.

Tonight wasn't about fixing anything. Tonight was about showing up.

The club pulsed around them, all strobe and sweat and bass, but their section stayed smooth—roped off, golden-lit, a little insulated world just for them. Plush seats. Bottles sweating in ice. Laughter rolling louder than the music.

They didn't need the whole club. They were the party.

Keira was already mid-two step, hips rolling easy to the beat, a drink lifted in one hand like punctuation. She looked back over her shoulder, eyes gleaming. "Y'all just gon' post up lookin' cute, or somebody gon' come dance?"

Zora stood, already grinning. "Thought you'd never ask."

Zion leaned against the booth's edge, head nodding to the rhythm, watching Keira with quiet amusement.

"You just gon' stare?" Keira called, walking up on him, smooth like she had all night. "Or you scared of a little rhythm?"

Zion raised his glass, that half-smile tucked deep in his beard. "I'm just being respectful. You out here dancing like you got somebody to answer to."

Keira cocked a brow. "And you out here talking like you want the job."

"Oop," Zora muttered behind her drink, catching the flicker of heat behind Zion's grin.

He stepped in—close enough to mean it. "You tryin' to make me prove something?"

Keira's smirk curled sharp. "I'm tryna see if you can keep up."

Zion tossed back the rest of his drink, set the glass down, and fell into step like he'd been waiting. Smooth. Unbothered. Intentional.

Keira laughed, low in her throat. "Okay then."

Zora watched them go toe-to-toe for a second before a warm hand curved against her back, pulling her close.

"You good?" Darius's voice dropped low at her ear.

"I'm great."

She turned to him, her body already syncing with his— slow, steady. Didn't matter what the DJ was spinning. Darius moved like he only heard her. Like the room bent around her rhythm.

Before they really got into it, he dipped his hand into his pocket and pulled out his loop earplugs, sliding them in smoothly, practiced. No drama. Just a soft boundary he didn't need to explain.

Zora clocked the movement, smiled gently, and kept right on dancing with him.

Mari raised his glass from the far end of the booth, nodding toward them. Saige tapped hers against his, posted up with that same calm energy she always carried, eyes sweeping the room like security wrapped in sisterhood.

Keira nearly collided with a bottle mid-spin. Zion caught her waist with both hands, holding her steady.

"Girl!" Zora called out, laughing. "Not the liquor!"

"I got it!" Keira shouted back, dancing through it anyway. "Let me live!"

Zion didn't let go. "You reckless," he said, smiling.

"You like it."

Zora shook her head, pressing her cheek to Darius's shoulder, the low thud of the bass threading through her bones. For once, she wasn't thinking about what came next. She wasn't bracing for the worst.

She just felt good.

The night stretched wide in front of them. Heat. Music. Her people.

Whatever came later could wait.

Right now? She was in the beat. In the love. All the way present.

IN MY *Rhythm*

The rest of the week folded in on itself—quiet shifts, long hours, small wins that didn't quite stretch far enough.

Keira's texts kept buzzing through the static:

"Don't flake."

"Already picked a dress."

"You betta show up, ho."

By Friday, Zora wasn't answering anymore. But the dress? Folded neat in her tote, anyway. Now she stood in Darius's man cave—lit low and warm, the glow of a vintage lamp skimming dark wood and worn leather.

Keira zipped her up from behind, her hands surprisingly gentle for all her usual noise. Zion perched on the arm of the couch, tossing a stress ball against the wall in a slow rhythm. Mari flipped through vinyls by the shelf, fingers tracing each spine like he was cataloging memories. Saige lounged deep in the recliner, sipping from a glass of whiskey, her gaze sharp beneath the quiet.

And Darius stood in the doorway, arms folded across his chest, watching them all with that steady patience he wore like a second skin. His cologne drifted faint in the air, threaded through the cedar and leather scent of the room. The walls held pieces of him—old photos, a framed jersey, a black-and-white portrait of Mama Regina in her garden.

A space built for him alone. But tonight, it held them all.

"You know," Keira murmured, stepping back to admire her work, "this dress gon' get Darius in a fight tonight."

Zora's mouth curved soft, a reluctant smile pulling at the corners. "He don't need to fight nobody."

Darius's voice came quiet, curling through the room like smoke. "Ain't lookin' for it," he murmured. "But I ain't lettin' nothin' slide either."

Keira turned, one brow cocked. "Mmhm. Thought so."

Zion chuckled, the stress ball thinking soft against his palm. "Man stay loaded, even on chill."

Mari glanced over, lips curving faint. "That's protection. Not pressure."

Saige's gaze flicked between Darius and Zora. "He holdin' his line. Always has."

Zora caught Saige's eyes in the mirror, felt that quiet truth settle under her ribs.

Keira gave her one last tug, smoothing the fabric flat with a little hum of satisfaction. "You look good, babe." Her voice softened, shedding the edge. "Like you."

Zora's throat tightened. "I don't know if I feel like her yet."

"You will," Keira promised, brushing her shoulder. "We gon' remind you."

Mari stepped closer, pressing a shot glass into her hand. "For courage."

Zora hesitated, fingers curling around the glass. "Mari, I—"

"Don't overthink it," he murmured. "You earned this."

Keira lifted her glass beside hers. "To showin' up."

Zion clinked his can lightly. "To makin' 'em watch."

Saige raised hers last. "To standin'."

Zora looked at each of them, warmth threading through her chest like a scaffold. She tipped the shot back, the burn curling slow, stitching her together.

Then Darius moved. Quiet steps, heavy and sure, crossing the space between them like he wasn't asking permission.

His hands found her waist, warm and steady, pulling her back until her spine met the solid line of him. His lips brushed the slope of her shoulder, lingering, then tracing soft along her neck.

"You good?" he murmured, his breath stirring the fine hairs at her nape.

Zora's eyes fell closed, leaning into his warmth. "I'm gettin' there."

He kissed her again, slower, lips pressing beneath her ear. "You already here."

A shaky breath left her lips.

"Look at me," Darius said, his hands sliding along her waist, voice low and sure.

She turned a little, glanced up. His gaze met hers, quiet, steady.

"Ain't nobody gon' see you like I do," he said. "But they gon' try. And that's on them."

Her lips curled soft, the ache loosening in her chest.

Keira's voice cut through, playful but fond. "Alright now, lover boy. Let her breath. We got a city to take tonight."

Zora laughed, a low hum spilling from her throat. Darius smiled down at her, pressed one last kiss to her temple, then stepped back.

"Go ahead," he told her, voice easy but certain. "I'll be right here."

Her circle tight at her side. His love, steady at her back. Her chest still ached. But her feet still moved her forward.

Tonight wasn't about fixing anything. Tonight was about showing up.

IN MY *Rhythm*

The next song dropped harder, bass coiling thickly through the floorboards. Keira grabbed Zora's hand, pulling her deeper into the crowd. "C'mon, babe—don't stand cute, move!"

Zora hesitated, but the sound was too rich, the air too electric. She let her body fall into the rhythm, hands tracing the beat, hips catching the sway. Keira's curls bounced beside her, Zion laughing when she spun him, Mari shaking his head but smiling.

And for a little while, Zora let the night hold her. Let herself feel weightless.

Until Keira's smile faltered. "Wait—who the fuck—"

Zora turned.

Montgomery.

Leaning against the far wall. Smile lazy. Eyes sharp. Watching her like he'd been waiting.

Her chest tightened.

Keira's face hardened. "Nope. Not tonight."

Darius's hand brushed Zora's back, his warmth steady. "Who's that?"

Zora swallowed. "Somebody who should've stayed gone."

Darius's gaze locked across the room. Still. Heavy. "Stay here."

And he moved.

Not fast. Not loud. But everything in his body said final.

Montgomery's grin flickered when Darius stepped into his space. "Oh. That's him, huh?"

Darius didn't blink. "You followin' her?"

Montgomery smirked. "It's a public spot, bruh."

Darius's jaw worked once. "You came in here looking for her. That's different."

Montgomery's smirk curled sharper. "You gon' make me leave?"

Darius's stare didn't waver. "I ain't gon' make you. I'm telling you."

Montgomery's laugh grated low. "You soft, man. Look at you."

And Zora saw it—

A slow shift in Darius's shoulders.

A quiet stillness flooding his face.

Not anger. Not heat.

A cold decision.

Darius's hands dropped from his pockets. His weight rolled onto his back foot.

"Say less," he murmured.

Then he swung.

One clean arc. Fist meeting jaw with a sound that cracked sharper than the music.

Montgomery's head snapped sideways, his glass flying, his body staggering into the wall.

The whole floor rippled.

Mari and Zion stepped up fast, blocking the fallout. Keira's shout sliced through the air. "THAT'S RIGHT."

Montgomery pushed off the wall, blinking, dazed, a smear of red at his lip.

"You done?" Darius's voice stayed low, unbothered.

Montgomery hesitated. Wiped his mouth. Looked around.

Zora watched the fight drain right out of him. Watched him see what he couldn't win.

The bouncer appeared, big and bored. "Problem?"

Darius didn't look away. "Not anymore."

The bouncer grabbed Montgomery's arm, dragging him toward the exit. His curses faded under the bass.

Darius turned back to Zora, breathing steady, hand reaching out. "You okay?"

She stepped into him without thinking, her face pressed against his chest. "Yeah."

"You sure?" His palm curved protective against her spine.

"I'm sure."

He pressed a kiss into her hair. "You ain't gotta worry, Z."

Keira slid beside them, smile fierce. "I swear to God, sis— you picked right."

Zora let out a breath that almost tasted like relief. "Yeah," she murmured. "I did."

Keira pulled her in quick, pressed a kiss to her temple. "Go on, babe. You safe."

Zion gave a nod. Saige's gaze held steady. "He got you."

Zora looked at them all, heart full, chest warm. "Love y'all."

"Love you back," Keira echoed.

Darius's hand slid into hers, quiet, sure.

Together, they stepped into the night.

The hum of his car carried them, headlights carving the dark, the city sliding past in soft, gold pools.

Inside the hush, Darius reached across the console, palm open.

Zora slid her hand into his without hesitation.

He drove silently, thumb brushing over her knuckles, his warmth anchoring her deeper with every block they left behind.

She watched him—the streetlights flickering across his face, jaw set but calm, hands steady on the wheel. And with every mile, something loosened inside her chest.

By the time they pulled into his driveway, she could finally breathe.

Darius cut the engine.

Without a word, Zora followed him inside almost like she belonged.

The door clicked shut. The night stayed outside.

Darius turned toward her.

But Zora was already moving.

She stepped into him, hands sliding up his chest, palms over the steady beat of his heart.

"I ain't here to be held tonight," she murmured, voice low and silky.

Darius's eyes sharpened, heat flashing under the quiet. "No?"

"I'm here to hold you."

She curled her fingers in his collar, tugging him down, catching his mouth with hers—slow at first, then deeper, needier, her body pressing close, claiming every inch.

Darius let her lead but his hands moved sure, gripping her hips, pulling her in tight like he couldn't help it.

She pulled back, breath hot between them. "Let me."

His lips curved, eyes locked on hers. "I'm right here. You ain't gotta ask for shit."

She shoved his jacket off, letting it hit the floor, her palms dragging down his chest, slow and sure, fingers hungry for the feel of him.

"You been my peace," she whispered. "Now, let me be yours."

Darius's hands slid down, cupping her ass, squeezing firm. "You already are, baby."

She made quick work of his belt, tugging it loose, fingers sure and steady. But his hand caught her wrist—tight enough to pause, not stop. Eyes dark and steady.

"You know what you asking for?"

Her smile was all heat and promise. "I know exactly what I want."

He let her go, settling back, hands resting at her waist like a dare. "Then take it."

She dropped to her knees, palms gliding up his thighs, feeling him hard already, thick and ready for her.

Darius hissed through his teeth, his hands clenching. "Zora…"

She undid his jeans, pulled them down, freeing his dick—heavy, hot in her hand. She wrapped her fingers around him slow, savoring the way his breath hitched, his hips flexing toward her, hungry already.

"You always so quiet," she teased, lips brushing the head, tongue flicking over the slit, tasting him. "But I hear you just fine."

His hands slid into her locs, gripping close, grounding himself. "Z… fuck…"

She took him into her mouth, slow and deep, eyes fluttering closed as she sank down, the weight of his dick stretching her lips. Drew back, then took more, hollowing her cheeks, tongue slick along the shaft, working him like she meant it.

"God damn, Zora," he groaned, head tipping back, his fingers tightening in her hair. "You ain't gotta—"

She hummed around his cock, pulling deeper, stroking what her mouth couldn't swallow, eyes lifting to catch the wrecked look on his face.

"I want to," she murmured against his dick, then swallowed him down again, slow and deep. "Let me love you like this."

Darius's breath shuddered, hips jerking once before he steadied himself, voice ragged. "Shit… baby… you got me."

She sucked him deep in her throat, savoring the way his thighs tensed, the way he cursed low and broken, his hands tight in her locs but never forcing.

When his breath started catching sharp, body tight and coiled, she eased back, kissed the tip soft, and rose up slow, her eyes still locked to his.

"You ain't finna cum without me," she teased, pushing him down to the couch, straddling him easy.

Darius's grip was tight on her waist, his eyes burning. "Nah, baby. We finishing together."

She guided him to her pussy, hot and dripping, and sank down slow, taking every inch of his thick dick, her breath shuddering as he filled her deep.

Darius's groan rumbled low, his hands sliding up her back, gripping tight. "Fuck… you feel so good, baby. This pussy…" He cursed again, jaw tight, voice wrecked. "Goddamn."

She rocked slow, grinding deep, palms braced on his chest, eyes locked to his—watching him feel her, watching the flicker of heat ripple through every tense muscle.

"You feel this?" she whispered, rolling her hips, making damn sure he felt every inch. "All yours."

Darius's arms locked around her, his lips brushing her neck. "Always been mine," he growled, deep in his chest. "Ain't never been no question."

She moved faster, chasing that sharp edge building, the tight coil low in her belly. Every grind of her hips met with his strength, his grip steady, his mouth finding every gasp, every moan.

When her thighs trembled, her breath breaking ragged, Darius pressed his lips to her ear, voice deep and coaxing.

"cum on, baby," he murmured, hips grinding up into her. "Let it go. I'm right here."

She shattered, her cry rough and raw against his throat, her body clenching hard around his dick as the orgasm tore through her, deep and wild.

Darius held her through it, one hand braced at her back,

the other gripping her thigh tight as he rocked up into her once, twice more before he stilled, groaning into her skin as he let go, thick and full inside her.

They stayed close, chest to chest, sweat cooling between them, breath syncing easily.

He stroked a hand up her spine, lazily and warmly. "You good?" he rumbled, lips brushing her temple.

Zora let out a breathless laugh, eyes half-closed. "Boy... I feel like you cracked my whole soul open and stitched it back together."

Darius smiled against her skin. "So... that's a yes?"

She chuckled, tucking her face in closer. "Yeah. That's a yes."

His arms squeezed tighter, his breath warm at her ear. "You always do too much."

She lifted her head, gaze heavy-lidded but sharp. "And you love it."

Darius smirked, eyes soft but dark. "Damn right I do." He kissed her cheek, voice dropping low. "Ain't nobody ever seen me like you do, Z."

She brushed her forehead to his, eyes warm and sure. "That's 'cause I see you. Always have."

He didn't say thank you. Didn't need to.

He kissed her instead—slow, deep, no hurry at all.

And she melted into him—right there in the hush where words didn't even matter.

lines drawn

"THE LIGHT" BY COMMON

The sun was folding low over the block, casting that warm gold across the street that made everything look softer than it really was. Music bumped lazy through the air—old-school tracks sliding under the buzz of conversation, dominoes slapping sharp on tables, grill smoke curling up like prayers.

Darius stacked empty crates behind Zora's truck, wiping his hands on a rag as he turned. His shirt clung damp across his back, but he moved easy—already reaching for the next load before Zora could ask.

She was bagging soil at the counter, lips pressed tight in focus, answering three customers at once without missing a beat. Her locs swept over her shoulders every time she bent forward, and the sight of her standing tall in her hustle made something deep in his chest settle.

She didn't even know how damn good she looked like this.

Darius slid a fresh stack of empty pots to her elbow before she could call for them. She caught his eye, gave him a quick, tired smile, and kept moving.

Mama Regina sat a few feet away, fanning herself slow from a folding chair, sipping something cold out a Styrofoam cup. Every few minutes she flagged somebody down, posting proudly toward the truck. "That's my boy's girl right there. Got magic in them hands, doesn't she? Just watch."

Darius felt a smile twitch at the corner of his mouth. He ducked his head so nobody saw it.

Mari leaned against a crate nearby, arms folded, watching as Willow stood beside Zora at the booth, carefully placing tiny pots in a neat line like it was the most important job in the world. Zora gave her a quiet nod of approval, and Willow beamed, proud and focused.

Roman was off down the block with some boys, shooting hoops under a crooked rim bolted to a light pole. Ariyah passed by once with her friends, grabbed a water bottle from Saige's cooler, tossed a grin at her mama, then vanished back into the crowd.

Saige posted up by the truck window, one arm braced against the frame, sipping sweet tea, eyes scanning the block like she was taking inventory.

Darius wiped the back of his neck with the rag, grabbed another flat of seedlings from the truck bed to the front table without breaking stride.

"You good?" Zora called over the bustle, tossing a smile his way even as her hands stayed busy.

"Yeah," he said, setting the tray down. "You?"

Her hand brushed his chest as she passed him an order slip, already ringing up the next sale.

For a moment, everything held. Familiar. Steady. The block moving in rhythm around them.

He felt it before he saw them.

The air tightened, the warmth draining clean out of the gold afternoon.

Jemma.

Tamara.

Walking up, loud already, like they'd been circling the lot waiting to make an entrance. Jemma led, bracelets jangling with every swing of her arms, her grin stretched wide but hollow. Tamara trailed behind, gaze sliding over the setup, that old, slow curl pulling at her mouth.

Darius's jaw locked.

Saige's voice cut low beside him. "Oh, hell no."

Zora's hands stilled on the register, her shoulders pulling square.

Mari shifted Willow's weight on his chest, his eyes narrowing.

And the crowd?

They started turning. Heads tilting. Conversations dipping low, small pockets of silence blooming as Jemma's voice carried high over the music.

"Well ain't this somethin'!" Jemma called, loud enough to make folks glance twice. "Look at you, D. Whole setup. Big man now."

Tamara's smirk sharpened, her eyes sliding up to Darius. "Mmm. Saw that article. Full write-up. Got your name buzzin' now."

Darius didn't blink.

Jemma's smile turned sharper, leaning forward a step. "Told Tamara—you was gon' come up, eventually. And now look. City watchin'. Papers talkin'. Sponsors sniffin' around." Her voice dropped lower, syrupy and smug. "You gon' take care of your people now, right?"

Tamara chuckled under her breath, rocking her weight onto one hip. "We been waitin' on you to remember where you come from." Her gaze flicked to Zora's booth, lingering. "And who been there."

Darius shifted forward, quiet but solid, his body blocking their line of sight to the booth.

"Not here," he said, voice low but firm.

"Oh?" Jemma lifted her brows, lips curling up. "Big man don't want nobody hearin'?"

"I'm not givin' nobody a show." His words stayed even, cutting clean. "Walk with me."

He didn't wait.

Didn't ask.

Just turned, already moving, already pulling them off the lot, away from Zora's space, from the watching eyes.

And he felt those eyes.

The boutique rep near the tent, pausing mid-bite.

The garden sponsor was whispering behind her clipboard.

The district councilman standing by the drinks table, half-turned their way.

He wasn't about to let their mess stick to Zora's name.

Behind him, Jemma and Tamara followed, footsteps sharp against the pavement. Saige close on their heels, quiet shadow.

He led them behind the vendor tents, into that half-shadow where the music faded softer, the lights stretched thinner.

He stopped.

Turned.

"Alright," Darius said, steady and cold. "Say what you came to say."

Jemma crossed her arms tight, eyes narrowed, her lips twisting like she was gearing up to spit poison. Tamara leaned back against the fence, arms folded, gaze slow and smug, watching Darius like she already knew his moves.

"You gon' act like you don't know why we here?" Jemma started, voice low but biting.

"I know," Darius said, his tone flat as stone. "I always knew."

Jemma huffed, sharp and bitter. "We saw that article, D. You out here lookin' like Mr. Success. Don't act brand new."

Tamara's smile deepened, her eyes gleaming. "Mmm. Lookin' good in print, baby. Got folks sayin' your name. Got people askin' all kinds of questions."

Darius stayed still, didn't blink.

"You out here big time now," Jemma kept pushing, stepping closer, her voice dripping fake warmth. "Money's comin'. Sponsorships, partnerships. And when it's your time?" Her eyes hardened. "You take care of your people."

Tamara straightened, stepping in close, her voice softer, slinking. "You ain't forgot who had your back, huh?" Her fingers brushed his sleeve, lingering like she had a right. "Ain't forgotten who had you first."

Darius stepped back, slow and sure, shaking her off like she was nothing. "I ain't forgot nothin'," he said, eyes locked. "I remember exactly who was there. And who wasn't."

Jemma's smile soured. "Oh, so now you act like we ain't never done shit for you?"

"You didn't," Darius shot back, his voice cutting sharper now. "You watched. Watched me struggle. Watched me scrape. You ain't lift a damn finger when it mattered. Saige carried me. Mama Regina carried me. Zora?" He cut his gaze to Tamara. "She been showin' up. You? You ain't show up till it smelled like money."

Tamara's eyes narrowed, her mouth curling. "Don't get cute, D. You ain't always been so high and mighty. You forgot who you ran to when shit got rough?"

Saige stepped forward then, her voice like a whip. "Girl, shut up. You talk a big game for somebody who only shows up when the bag's close."

Tamara's smirk twisted. "And you still ridin' his coattails, huh? Always playin' mama when your own life a mess."

Saige's jaw clenched, her hands balling tight. "Say one more thing."

"Oh, don't act brand new," Tamara sneered. "We all know who kept him warm when nobody else would. That little saint act Zora's got?" She snorted. "Won't last forever."

Jemma jumped back in, louder now, her voice rising just enough to turn heads near the edge of the lot. "That's right. You think she's different? She here for the glow too. Just like we were. Let's see how long she stick around when that money runs out."

A hush slid over the nearest circle of vendors. People paused mid-sentence, eyes darting their way, the music still pulsing but the air thick now.

Darius's jaw flexed, his stare drilling into Jemma. "You done?"

Jemma's mouth opened like she had more, but Saige stepped in hard, right up in her face. "No—you done. You don't get to come here, act like you raised him, then tear him down the second he's winning."

Jemma's face twisted, but Saige didn't flinch.

"Say what you really mad about," Saige hissed. "You ain't mad he up. You mad you ain't sittin' next to him while he rises."

"Watch your damn mouth," Jemma snapped.

"No," Saige spat back. "You watch yours."

Darius stepped between them, his hand firm on Saige's arm, his voice low but loaded. "Enough."

They froze.

He looked Jemma dead in the eye. "You ain't family just because we share blood. Family shows up. They stay. Family lifts but you? You leech."

Jemma's lips pressed tight, fury flashing.

He turned to Tamara, voice ice cold. "And you? Whatever fantasy you got in your head? Let it go. That door's been closed. Locked. Sealed."

Tamara's smile cracked. "You really think she's better than me?"

"She's in a whole different lane," Darius said, his voice quiet, final. "Don't ever confuse it."

Tamara flinched like the words hit raw.

"You pull up on Zora again at her booth, her work, anywhere, you won't like how it ends," Darius said, his voice like steel now. "We're done here."

They didn't move at first.

Then Tamara let out a sharp breath, spun on her heel, muttering under her breath as she stomped off. Jemma lingered, jaw tight, eyes burning like she had something else nasty to throw but nothing came.

Finally, she followed.

Darius watched until the crowd swallowed them, the surrounding hush slowly unspooling as people turned back to their drinks and laughter.

Saige exhaled hard, wiping a hand down her face. "Lord."

Darius didn't say a word. He just stared at the spot where they'd stood, his shoulders tight.

Saige put a hand on his back, voice softer now. "You good?"

"Yeah," Darius muttered. "It's done."

He turned, and there was Zora. Still behind the booth, eyes locked on his, steady and sure.

No smile.

No questions.

Just that quiet, unshakable gaze and seeing all of him.

Darius gave her a small nod.

Handled.

And stepped back into the light.

Darius let his breath out, rolling his shoulders once to shake it off.

Saige stood beside him a beat longer, eyes still locked on the path where Jemma and Tamara had disappeared.

"Bout damn time," she muttered, her voice clipped but proud.

He didn't answer right away. Just tipped his chin once, grounding himself before turning back toward the lot.

The noise of the block party swallowed him again, the music thumping, laughter spilling but it felt thinner now. Like the sound was stretched over something tight, like folks were waiting to see if the tension would crack open again.

He felt their eyes. Quick glances. Whispers. But none of it mattered.

His gaze locked straight on Zora.

She was still at the booth, standing steady, her hands moving even though her eyes were pinned right on him. No smile. No questions.

Just... seeing him.

Darius made his way back, keeping his shoulders loose, his face blank, Saige falling in step beside him like a shadow.

When he stepped behind the booth again, Zora passed him a water bottle without a word, her fingers brushing his hand, her gaze searching his face.

"You good?" she asked quietly.

Darius cracked it open, took a long pull, then nodded. "Yeah." His voice came, rough at the edges. "It's done."

Zora didn't look away. She studied him like she could feel the leftover weight under his skin.

Her hand brushed his forearm lightly. "You wanna sit for a second?"

He hesitated, then nodded, following her around the side of the truck where the shade stretched long and the noise dipped low. She sat on the crate, patting the spot beside her.

Darius lowered himself down, elbows on his knees, water bottle hanging loose between his fingers.

For a while, they didn't say anything. Just sat in the hush between the beats, the music bleeding around the edges of their quiet.

Then he spoke, his voice low. "I should've seen it earlier. The way Tamara moved. The way she.." He shook his head, jaw working. "It wasn't about love. Never was."

Zora stayed still, her eyes on him, waiting.

Darius's thumb ran along the ridge of the bottle cap. "She knew how to say the right things. Act like she was down. But it was always… conditional. Always what she could get."

He paused, shoulders tensing. "And the crazy thing is..I was so used to that. I thought… that's just how people were. I ain't even realize how much it looked like Jemma until I was deep in it."

Zora's brow creased, but she didn't interrupt.

"She'd show up when shit looked good. Disappear when it didn't. Made me think I was the one messin' up. Tamara had that same pattern. Same empty promises. Same little digs."

He huffed a bitter breath. "I kept lettin' her back in. Over and over."

His eyes flicked up, locking on Zora's face. "Till you."

Zora's gaze softened, her hand slipping onto his knee, grounding him with quiet pressure.

"You ain't never asked for nothin' but honesty," Darius said, his voice thickening just a little. "Never once made me feel like I had to earn your respect. Or buy your loyalty."

She squeezed his knee, her thumb brushing slow. "That's how it's supposed to be, D."

He let out a long breath, shoulders loosening under her touch.

"It's wild," he murmured, eyes locked on hers. "I ain't even know what solid looked like until you."

Zora's lips curved, eyes shining, her voice steady. "Well… you know now."

He leaned in then, his forehead pressing gently to hers, the water bottle dropping from his fingers as his hands found her waist.

They sat like that for a while. Still, quiet, breathing the same air until the noise of the block faded back into focus around them.

Darius pressed a kiss to her temple, then pulled back just enough to meet her eyes. "Thank you."

Zora's smile deepened, her thumb brushing along his jaw. "Always."

And when they stood, when Darius slotted himself back beside her at the booth, his shoulders felt a little lighter. The weight of old ghosts still there—but no longer steering the moment.

He was back where he needed to be.

By her side.

Solid.

CHAPTER TWENTY-TWO
the reveal

"BOSSY" BY KELIS FT. TOO $HORT

Four days since the block party, and Zora still felt that shift in her bones.

Not just calm—clear.

Business was moving. The Wild Hart app buzzing. Orders flowing faster than they had all month. And under it all? That steady hum of knowing Darius had her back—no questions, no hesitation, no mess bleeding into her space.

She was adjusting a row of planters near the window, half her mind on her next workshop, when the door flew open hard.

"Zora Simone Hart, get your ass over here!"

Zora didn't flinch. "Good afternoon to you too, Keria."

Keria barreled in, eyes blazing, waving her phone like it was about to explode. "Nah, we don't have time for cute. You seen this? You. Seen. This?"

Zora wiped her hands slow on a rag. "Seen what?"

Keria damn near slammed her phone on the counter Loren's smug-ass face stared up at them, headline screaming:

ROOTED BY LOREN: NATIONAL POP-UP EVENT.

"Jasper Street. TODAY," Keira barked. Then she started pacing, hands flying, eyes wide with fire. "She really got the nerve to stand out here actin' like she cracked some secret code —girl, that's YOUR recipe with a new label slapped one on it!"

Zora's jaw locked, eyes scanning fast—Loren's face everywhere. Ads. Cirqle posts. Influencers hyping her up in the comments. The kind of viral moment people paid big for.

Keria shook her head, pacing hard now. "I swear to God, Z, she is asking for it. Bold as hell. And people really falling for it like she's Mother Nature herself."

Zora's chest went tight but it wasn't panic. It was purpose. She unlocked her phone, pulled up the Wild Hart app. The traffic spike hit her like a wave, the searches, orders, and all of it jumping since Loren's press release. And underneath that? The quiet hum of Darius's blackened work solid and smooth.

"She making noise," Zora said, voice low.

Keira spun on her heel, eyes wild. "Noise? Naw, this is full-on disrespect. You need to throw a punch or a plant pot? Say the word."

Zora's mouth twitched. "You free this afternoon?"

Keira's eyes gleamed, wicked. "Girl, what you think? I was born free for this. You want Mari and Zion on deck too? Shit, we can roll deep if we gotta."

Zora laughed, but her eyes sharpened, sliding her phone back into her pocket. "No drama. No chaos. Just facts. She wanted attention? We're gonna give it to her..with receipts."

Keira hooted, practically bouncing. "Say less. I've been waiting to eat this girl alive."

But Zora paused, her fingers tightening around her phone. She stepped outside for air, thumbing through to Darius's name and hitting Call.

Two rings.

"Hey beautiful." Darius answered, that steady warmth already anchoring her. "What's up?"

Zora breathed in deep. "It's Loren. She's out here, bae. Full-blown pop-up on Jasper Street. Cirqle's there, influencers, the whole thing. We're about to head over."

A beat of quiet. Then his voice, calm but loaded. "Figured she'd pull this sooner or later."

"Yeah," Zora said, eyes locked ahead. "I just…wanted you to know. It's time."

She could hear him inhale slow, steady. "Good. I've been watching. Been stacking everything we need. Proof, logs, filing…shit she thought was buried. It's all ready."

Zora's eyes closed, her chest loosening. "I knew you'd be ready."

"I told you," Darius said, voice deep and smooth. "I'm not just a handsome face. I'm ready to finish this. You stand tall. I'll handle the rest."

Her lips curbed, soft but fierce. "See you soon."

"Always."

She hung up slow, slipping her phone away with a deep breath.

Keira leaned in the doorway, eyes sharp. "We good?"

"Zora locked the shop door with a sharp click. "We're perfect."

She gave the Wild Hart sign one last look, heart thumping steady.

"Time to remind her," she said, voice like a blade, "exactly who she's playing with."

And together, they stepped into the sun, shoulders squared, steps in sync. Just ready.

IN MY *Rhythm*

Jasper Street was buzzing when they arrived. Vendors posted up tight along the sidewalks, music humming through portable speakers, the scent of BBQ and fryer oil threading through the air. People milled around casual, shopping, laughing, snapping photos for the 'Gram.

And right in the center of it all? Loren's booth.

It was slick. Zora had to give her that much. Big-ass

banners in that same copper-and-cream palette, shiny new displays stacked with jars and bags, polished to look high-end. She even had a damn photo backdrop set up, with her brand hashtag scrawled across it in looping script.

Keira squinted, letting out a slow, exaggerated sigh. "Oh, we in delulu territory now. Not the full influencer lounge and fake-ass rustic setup."

Zora's lips curled just slightly, eyes scanning the scene. "Look at all this polish. Girl out here screaming money but the soil? Still trash."

Keira cackled, looping her arm through Zora's as they walked closer, weaving through the crowd unnoticed for now. "And is that a DIY macrame wall behind her? Please. Not her tryna sell 'earthy and authentic' when she couldn't keep a succulent alive last summer."

Zora's eyes stayed locked in. "It's cute how she dressed it up, though. Like a bad recipe with fancy plating."

Keira let out a little snort. "Garnish don't fix garbage, babe."

They slid in closer, holding position near a table of planters, pretending to browse but keeping Loren in their sights. Loren was mid-pitch, voice syrupy sweet, leaning in toward a couple of eager shoppers.

Keira side-eyed hard. "She really got her whole backstory rehearsed, huh? Talkin' about 'crafted with care' like she ain't copy-paste your formula and slap her name on it."

Zora's jaw flexed, voice low. "She's bold, I'll give her that."

Just then, a familiar heat pressed up close behind them. It was steady and warm.

"Y'all already started without me?" Darius's voice came low at Zora's ear, and her chest loosened immediately, her lips twitching into something soft.

"You know we had to get our jokes in first," Keira said, grinning wide as she glanced back. "And whew, you're just in time. We about to serve a plate."

Darius's gaze locked onto Loren's booth, sharp and assessing. "She's got a whole circus out here."

Zora hummed, eyes still focused. "All show, no roots."

Darius slid his hand to the small of her back, grounding her. "You good?"

Zora looked up at him, her jaw set but her eyes bright with fire. "Better now."

He leaned in, kissed her temple quick, voice low. "Whenever you're ready."

Keira clapped her hands together once, eyes sparkling. "Ooooh, we really in it now. Y'all ready to shut this all the way down or what?"

Zora smiled, her breath even, chest full. "Yeah. Let's end this."

They stepped forward as one, weaving through the bodies until they were right at the edge of Loren's booth. No noise yet, no scene…just standing there, waiting.

And then Loren clocked them.

Her eyes caught on Zora first, and even from a few feet away, the shift was obvious. That too-bright smile faltered for half a second before she pasted it back on, voice tightening just a hair.

"Well, well, well. Look who decided to stop by!" Loren chirped, too loud, her tone dripping fake sweetness. "Zora! So nice to see you out and about."

Zora stepped forward, cool and unbothered. "Wouldn't miss it."

Keira crossed her arms, leaning in with a grin. "Had to see the circus for ourselves."

Loren's smile twitched, eyes darting quick between Zora, Keira, and then Darius. Her whole body tensing just a little. "I'm not sure what you're implying, but today's about celebration. Growth. Community."

Zora's smile sharpened. "Mm. Is that what we're calling it now?"

And just like that, the temperature of the whole scene

changed. Heads started to turn. Phones lifted, subtle at first, but creeping higher, as the crowd sensed something brewing.

Darius slid his phone from his jacket pocket, screen already lit, his gaze locked solid on Loren. Calm. Ready.

Loren's eyes caught the movement, and her breath hitched. So quick most wouldn't notice. But Zora did.

And she stepped in closer, her voice smooth but sharp as glass. "You ready to tell them where you really got this formula? Or should we?"

For a breath, everything held.

Loren's smile stayed stretched, tight, shiny and fake as hell but her eyes? Her eyes flicked sharp between Zora, Keira, and Darius, calculating, scrambling for balance she was clearly starting to lose.

"I'm not sure what you mean," Loren said, tone dipping just a little too fast, too high. "This is my blend. Fully developed, fully original. And today's not really the space for… negativity."

Keira barked out a laugh, folding her arms tighter. "Negativity? Babe, we are the space. You built this whole little setup on Zora's back. Let's not get shy now."

A ripple moved through the crowd. More phones lifted now and more whispers weaving through the tension.

Loren's smile twitched, her hand brushing down her banner like she could smooth the energy out. "I think there's been some misunderstanding," she said, eyes locking on Zora, voice sickly sweet. "I've always been transparent about my inspiration."

Zora's head tilted, slow and sharp. "Inspiration is one thing. Stealing's another."

Loren's lips pressed tight, but before she could spin something slick, Darius stepped up beside Zora, his phone already glowing bright.

He lifted it just high enough for the crowd to see. "Let's clear up any confusion, then."

A hush dropped, thick and electric.

Darius's voice stayed calm, each word sharp enough to cut. "We've got timestamps. Soil blend formulas. Product photos dating years back. Every piece of proof showing this formula was created, developed, and perfected by Zora Hart. Not Loren. Not this brand. Zora."

He swiped once, documents filling the screen behind Loren . Another swipe—emails, Loren's name right there in the headers, asking Zora for "help with the blend." Another swipe—side-by-side photos of Zora's originals and Loren's knockoffs, damn near identical.

The crowd sucked in a breath. Whispers snapped sharp now, heads whipping between Loren's booth and Zora.

Keira grinned wide, eyes locked on Loren. "Whew. Ain't no influencer fake apology video is fixing this mess."

Loren's hand shot out, voice cracking under the weight of her fake calm. "These are private documents..you can't just… This is harassment!"

Zora stepped forward then, eyes hard and clear, her voice slicing through the noise like a blade. "No, Loren. This is exposure. And you did it to yourself."

A beat of silence. Then someone in the crowd muttered, loud enough to catch: "Yo, that's wild…"

Another voice. "She really out here stealing?"

Loren's team scrambled, whispering fast, pulling at her arm, but Loren stayed frozen, eyes darting and lips pressed so tight they nearly disappeared.

Darius's voice dropped low, final. "We can end this here or we can take it legal action. Your call."

Loren's mouth opened, but nothing came out.

Zora's gaze stayed locked on her for one last beat, chest lifting slow and even. Then she turned, sliding her hand into Darius's, Keira falling in step beside them.

The crowd's noise surged behind them. Phones buzzing, people shouting, and cameras flashing.

Zora didn't look back.

They turned the corner, slipping down a quieter side street

where the noise from the crowd started to fade, replaced by the steady thud of their footsteps and the pulse of adrenaline still crackling under Zora's skin.

Keira was the first to break the silence, letting out a long, shaky breath before she burst into laughter. Loud, wild, and sharp. "Baaaaby! Did you see her face?! Oh my God, I've been waiting for that moment my whole damn life."

Zora laughed too, the tightness in her chest finally starting to ease. "You were wild in there."

Keira wiped her eyes, breath catching. "Please. That was me being respectable. I coulda set the whole damn tent on fire with my words, but you? Girl, you cleared her so smooth. Straight boss shit."

Darius let out a low hum, his hand brushing Zora's back, warm and steady. "You handled it perfect. Didn't have to say much, just let the truth hit."

Zora looked up at him, her smile softening, heart swelling full. "Only reason I could was 'cause I knew you had the rest."

His eyes locked onto hers, thumb tracing slow at her waist. "Always. You know that."

Keira rolled her eyes, laughing. "Ugh, y'all make me sick with this love story shit. Meanwhile, I'm over here hyped on justice."

They all laughed, the tension finally cracking apart completely.

Zora leaned into Darius's side, exhaling deep. "It feels… good. Not just winning, but being done. Like, really done."

Darius pressed a kiss to her temple, voice low and full of warmth. "You are. That chapter's closed."

Keira nodded, stepping in to wrap her arms around Zora's shoulders. "Closed, locked, and burned to the ground. Nobody's touchin' you now."

Before Zora could answer, a voice called out from behind them—hesitant but clear.

"Excuse me… Zora?"

They all turned, eyes landing on a woman weaving

through the lingering crowd, clipboard tucked under one arm, sleek lanyard bouncing at her chest. The logo gleamed: Garden & Greenhouse Collective.

Zora straightened a little, brushing a loc from her face. "Yes?"

The woman smiled, stepping closer. "Sorry to interrupt, but I caught what happened back there. Honestly? That was… impressive. I'm with GGC—we're launching a new regional spotlight campaign soon, and Wild Hart would be perfect for it."

Zora blinked, heart thudding. "Wait… really?"

"Really," the woman said, her smile brightening. "We'll follow up soon, but please expect a call. Your brand—your voice—we've been looking for someone just like you."

Zora's lips parted, her breath catching. "Thank you. I— wow, thank you."

The woman gave a small nod, then disappeared back into the crowd, her clipboard bouncing as she moved.

Keira was quiet for a beat—then let out a long, low whistle. "You see that? You see how the universe stays showing up when you do?"

Darius grinned, pressing closer to Zora's side. "Told you. This was bigger than her mess. Always has been."

Zora let out a breath, shaking her head in awe, her fingers curling around Darius's hand. "Damn. Okay."

She looked back toward Jasper Street one last time—at the noise, the lights, the little kingdom Loren tried to build.

And then she smiled, eyes bright, voice sure. "Let's go home."

what's owed

"DEAD TO ME" BY KALI UCHIS

It had been weeks since Darius shut them down at that block party, but Tamara still replayed it: every clipped word, every sideways glance, every time he stood between them and his little booth like they were strangers off the street.

He didn't even raise his voice. That's what made it worse. Just looked at them like they weren't worth the surrounding air.

Now, she sat across from Jemma in a booth with a chipped salt shaker and a flickering bulb overhead. Cheap-ass diner. Real familiar. Tamara stirred her coffee slow, even though it'd gone cold. She wasn't here for breakfast.

Jemma looked tired. Wig slightly crooked. Eyes mean with something she wasn't naming. Her fork tapped at her plate, untouched eggs going rubbery.

"You hear from him?" Tamara asked, knowing damn well the answer.

Jemma shook her head, jaw flexing. "Ain't even been a text. Nothing."

"He really think he better now," Tamara muttered, more to herself than anything.

Jemma scoffed. "That's Regina's fault. Got in his head early. Told him he was special."

"She treated him like a damn prince," Tamara said. "Even when he ain't have shit."

Jemma's voice dropped low, bitter. "She made him forget who birthed him."

Tamara didn't argue. Couldn't. She just sipped the coffee and let that bitterness mix with her own. She'd seen the way Darius looked at Regina—like she hung the moon. Like the woman who changed his diapers didn't exist.

"She the reason he don't answer calls. She the reason he talkin' 'bout boundaries like we strangers," Jemma snapped. "She taught him to cut people off and call it growth."

Tamara leaned in. "And that's why we stuck sittin' here like some damn outsiders while he out there actin' brand new."

Jemma finally picked up her glass of water. "You still want him?"

Tamara didn't flinch. "Want? No. But I remember when he didn't flinch for me. When I said jump, he moved."

Jemma smirked, just barely. "That was before you left."

"That was before he started thinking he had options."

They both went quiet.

The hum of the old fridge buzzed in the background. Somebody in a booth behind them cracked a joke too loud.

Tamara leaned back, arms folded. "You say you want your money. Your piece."

"I do," Jemma said flat. "That man got a spotlight now. I helped bring him into this world—he owe me something."

Tamara nodded. "And the girl?"

Jemma shrugged. "Don't care about her. Don't know her. But she the one sittin' next to the bag."

Tamara's lips curled slow. "Then maybe we shift the weight."

Tamara leaned in, voice low and sharp. "You wanna get his attention? We don't need to make noise. We just need leverage."

Jemma frowned. "Leverage?"

"She's the soft spot," Tamara said. "You touch that? He'll pay to get her back."

Jemma stilled. "You talkin' ransom now?"

"I'm talkin' what's owed," Tamara said. "He cut us off like we ain't part of the story—fine. But money don't forget. You make him sweat, make him scared, he'll pay whatever it takes to feel safe again."

Jemma looked away. "That's a real line to cross, Tam."

Tamara nodded slow. "And once we cross it? Ain't no goin' back. But you said you wanted what you were due. This is how we get it."

Jemma's jaw worked. "How long you thinking?"

"Just long enough," Tamara said. "She disappears for a night. He gets the call. He pays. She comes back fine."

Jemma's voice dropped. "And if she don't?"

"She will." Tamara's smile was cold. "We ain't killers. Just cashing in."

Jemma didn't say yes.

But she didn't say no either.

And Tamara? She already had a name in her back pocket. Someone who owed her. Someone who knew how to move without leaving tracks.

IN MY *Rhythm*

The corner store looked the same. Faded posters in the window. Neon light half-flickering above the Lotto sign. But the energy? That was different. Like even the walls knew she wasn't just here for snacks.

Tamara stepped inside slow, letting the door creak behind her. A bell jangled overhead, tired and offbeat.

Dre was posted up behind the plexiglass, same way he always was—leaned back, arms crossed, eyes that didn't miss much. He didn't flinch when he saw her. Just blinked once and said, "Ain't seen you in a minute."

"Been busy," Tamara said, stepping closer. "You still got folks who move quiet?"

He didn't answer. Just watched her. Waited.

She sighed. "Not lookin' to start a war. Just need somebody snatched. One night. No blood, no bruises. Clean in, clean out."

Dre scratched the side of his jaw. "You don't call me for years, and now you want ghosts?"

"You owe me," she said, voice flat. "Unless you forgot who took that heat in '09 while you ran off clean."

He didn't blink. "Ain't forget."

"Then don't act new." Tamara rested her elbows on the scratched-up counter. "She don't get touched. Just moved. We get the money, she goes home."

"And if the money don't come?" he asked.

"It will." Tamara's jaw tightened. "He'll fold before she even finish screamin'."

Dre didn't look impressed. "Sounds personal."

Tamara smiled, but it didn't reach her eyes. "Ain't nothin' personal about collecting what you owed."

A pause. Then Dre popped the drawer, slid out a burner phone wrapped in a rubber band, and dropped it between them.

"Number's saved. You get one ask. No names. No callbacks."

Tamara took the phone, heavy in her palm. "Good. I don't want conversation."

He gave her one last look. "You sure this gon' end how you want it to?"

"No," she said. "But it'll end how I need it to."

And with that, she turned and walked out; the burner tucked in her jacket and the weight of the next move already settling in her bones.

The kind of peace that crept in after the noise—not because the world got quiet, but because she stopped waiting for the next hit. That's what this felt like.

It had only been a few days, but something in the air felt still. Like a pause before a note you ain't heard yet.

Zora walked barefoot across the warm pavement, the last of the spa steam still clinging to her skin. Her shoulders were loose, her smile unforced. For once, she wasn't holding anything up but herself.

Keira pushed the glass door open with her hip, bare feet hitting the sidewalk with a satisfied slap. "Okay but that man in the linen shirt with the sleeve tattoos? The dark chocolate one with the locs and arms built like Sunday sin? Whew. Those hands alone looked like they've held a whole lotta tension—and released it just right."

Zora didn't even blink. "He was lighting aromatherapy candles."

"Exactly," Keira shot back. "That man got forearms and follow-through."

Saige followed behind, already shaking her head. "Y'all let one hot stone and a playlist get y'all talkin' reckless."

Zora laughed, warm and full. "Reckless is Keira's default setting."

Keira grinned. "I'm just sayin'. I came here for self-care. Didn't expect to find salvation on two legs and a massage license."

They strolled toward the car, sun dipping low and gold across their skin, the scent of oils still clinging soft to their clothes. Zora's body felt loose in a way she hadn't known she needed. Like someone had finally cut the strings she'd been holding tight just to keep upright.

Keira reached into her tote, pulled out a half-smashed pack of peach rings. "Y'all want some? They organic."

Zora took one, amused. "You say that like it cancels out the sugar."

Keira popped two into her mouth. "I say it like God ain't judging me today."

Saige snorted, tossing her bag in the trunk. "He probably side-eying both of y'all."

Keira winked. "He made me, so what that say?"

Zora leaned against the car, smile soft. "This was good. Real good."

Saige folded her arms, resting her weight into one hip. "It's been a long time since I did something like this. Last time was with my best friend—Raven. She moved overseas with her husband three years ago. After that… it just felt easier to keep my head down."

Keira tilted her head. "You miss her?"

Saige nodded once. "Every damn day."

Something thick settled between them—not sad, just real.

Zora stepped in gently. "Well, you got us now."

Keira smirked. "And we come with snacks and chaos. You're welcome."

Saige smiled for real then, a small thing but solid. "I see that."

Keira looked around, mock dramatic. "Wow. Look at us. Vulnerability. Shared trauma. Softness. I swear if someone cue a SZA track right now, I'm gonna ugly cry."

Zora threw a gummy at her. "You been ugly crying."

"Lies," Keira said. "I'm radiant."

They cracked up together—loud, unbothered, the kind of laughter that wrapped around your ribs and made the world feel a little safer.

Zora unlocked the car. "We doing this again."

"No question," Saige said.

"Next time mud baths," Keira added, sliding into the passenger seat. "I wanna get dirty and healed."

They piled in, still buzzing with that soft high only peace can give you.

And for a few more minutes, everything was whole.

The ride buzzed with soft laughter and leftovers of eucalyptus oil, hips still loose from steam rooms and skilled hands. Keira had the aux, of course, narrating over the playlist like the host of her own late-night radio show.

"I'm sayin' quesabirria and a frozen margarita with a Tajín rim? That's self-care," she declared, turning half around in her seat.

Zora hummed, tapping the wheel. "You had me at birria."

"Girl, you stay full off two bites," Saige said from the back, arms folded but smiling. "Let's not act brand new."

"That's 'cause y'all be strong-arming me into sharing dessert."

Keira cackled. "Like we not all gonna split the damn flan anyway."

Their laughter filled the car like heat from a good meal—slow, satisfying, something to carry home with them. It didn't rush. Didn't need to.

Zora pulled into the lot behind her shop, right where Keira had left her car earlier. Streetlight glow bathed the concrete in soft orange. The quiet wasn't eerie, just regular nighttime quiet. Familiar. A cat darted across the alley. Something buzzed nearby—maybe a streetlamp humming, or a bug zapper doing its job.

She cut the engine.

Keira stretched like she'd just come off a massage table, her curls catching a glint from the rearview. "I'ma go home, lie to myself about laundry, and fall asleep in my robe."

"You mean my robe," Zora muttered.

"Details."

Saige chuckled, reaching for her bag. "Y'all ridiculous."

They got out one by one, Zora locking the car behind

them. She headed toward the shop's back entrance, keys in hand, Keira beside her, still half-talking, half-yawning. Saige lingered at the back, checking something on her phone.

It didn't hit all at once.

It was more like the air decided not to move.

Like a room that suddenly remembered it had a secret.

Zora's key scraped the lock.

Keira fell quiet mid-sentence.

Saige's steps paused.

Zora didn't know what made her turn..maybe nothing. Maybe instinct. Maybe that tight pull low in her gut that didn't have words yet.

She looked over her shoulder.

Two figures.

Close.

Not walking like they were passing through.

Walking like they knew who they were coming for.

Hoodies up. Hands down, at their sides. Calm. Too calm.

Zora blinked. Her mouth opened.

"Kei—"

Then everything moved too fast.

"What the f—" Keira started, stepping forward.

Zora barely got her hand up before someone snatched her from behind—an arm around her ribs, sharp and tight. Her body jolted back like a rag doll.

"What the fuck?!" Keira's voice cracked the night wide open.

A second man came in from the side—hood drawn low, footsteps heavy. He shoved Keira hard enough to send her sprawling, her hands catching pavement as she hit. She groaned, dazed, but rolled to her knees, already trying to get back up.

"ZORA!"

Saige didn't hesitate. "Get the fuck off of her!"

She cracked her elbow into the man's temple—clean. He

stumbled. Zora thrashed. Screamed. Kicked her heel into somebody's shin and felt the hit—but not the release.

Hands gripped tighter.

Then metal flashed.

"Back the fuck up!" one of them shouted, voice tight, no hesitation. He flashed his gun,

Not raised. But visible. Real.

Everyone froze.

Keira froze mid-step, lip bleeding.

Saige's fists clenched at her sides. "Put that shit away before you make it worse."

"You really wanna find out?" he hissed.

The gun turned toward Zora.

Her body locked up. Her breath caught in her throat.

The hand around her waist dragged her back. Another hand slapped over her mouth.

"ZORA!" Keira screamed again, lunging forward.

Another shove knocked her sideways. She hit the car, shoulder-first, and slid down hard.

Zora's vision blurred as her back hit metal. She clawed, caught a hoodie, ripped it, but they were stronger. Faster.

The side door of a van flew open.

"NO—!" Saige shouted.

Zora's legs kicked, one heel catching the edge of the door before they yanked her inside. Her knees scraped metal. Her shoulder slammed a wheel well.

A hood dropped over her head.

Dark. Hot. Breath bouncing back in her face.

She couldn't scream now. Could barely breathe.

The door slammed.

Tires peeled.

They were gone.

Back in the lot, Keira sat stunned against the tire well, her lip split, breathing fast and too shallow. She looked down at her hands—scraped, bloodied, shaking.

Then she snapped out of it.

"Phone," she rasped. "Where's..fuck.."

Saige was already dialing. Her voice was ice, tight and focused even as she limped toward the street.

"Black van. No windows. T9R—part of the plate. Headed west on Candler. Fast."

Keira stared at her. "You got all that?"

"Of course, I got all that."

The phone rang.

Once.

Twice.

Three times.

Click.

"Darius—"

the hunt

"NO LOVE" BY AUGUST ALSINA FT. NICKI
MINAJ

His phone lit up.
Saige.

He answered fast. "Yo—"

Her voice cracked through the line as if it didn't want to be heard. "Darius… they took her."

The world slowed.

Not stopped. Just… shifted. Like sound moves underwater now.

"What?"

Not angry. Not confused. Just hollow.

"Zora. They took Zora."

Saige's voice was shaky, but steady enough to finish.

"We were behind Wild Hart. Keira was grabbing her keys. Zora had just hit the lock—barely touched the door—and this van pulled up. Black. No windows. Two men. Hooded. They moved like they knew exactly what they were doing."

His keys hit the floor. He didn't even realize he'd dropped them until he bent down to pick them up and noticed his hand was trembling.

"She screamed, D. Fought hard. We tried to help. I got a hit in. Keira's arm is bleeding. One of them had a gun."

His tablet was already under his arm. No hoodie. No shoes. Just motion.

"Plate?"

"T9R. Georgia tag. They turned down Candler. Headed west."

"You and Keira?"

"Bruised. Shaken. But we're breathing."

"Go home," he said. "You hear me? Go straight to Mari. Lock the door. I'll meet you there."

"Darius—"

"I'm on my way."

The truck felt too small.

He gripped the wheel tighter than necessary, fingers curling until the leather bit back.

Everything in his chest was tightening. Not like panic — more like pressure. Too much information at once. Too many directions he needed to go.

His mouth was dry. Eyes too sharp. The streetlights were too bright, and the radio too loud, even though it wasn't on.

He didn't remember the turns.

But her touch lived under his skin now.

Last night, they lay tangled in his sheets, with the city humming outside his window. She'd kissed the corner of his mouth just to see if he'd smile, then did it again when he didn't.

"You ever gonna relax with me?" she'd whispered, brushing her nose against his cheek.

"I am relaxed," he'd murmured, even though his hand was curled around her hip like she might disappear.

Zora laughed — low and soft — then kissed his neck. "You don't gotta guard me while I sleep, D. You're safe here, too."

That memory lived behind his ribs now.

Burning.

Now she was gone.

The porch light at Mari and Saige's house burned too brightly against the night.

The door opened before he even reached the steps. Saige stood there, barefoot, hoodie halfway zipped, like she couldn't decide if she was hot or cold. Her eyes were puffy. Split lip. Shoulder bruising. She looked like she was still in the fight.

Mari was behind her, steady. One hand on her back. The other, near the doorframe like he was holding the house together by sheer will.

Darius stepped inside. The air hit differently. Like grief had cracked the windows open and let the cold in.

Keira sat on the couch, arm elevated, blood soaked through a Quick-Wrap towel. One eye was swelling. She looked up when he walked in.

Didn't speak.

Didn't need to.

He didn't say anything. Just crouched beside her for a beat.

"You good?"

She nodded. "Still got my teeth. Still pissed."

That was enough.

He stood and turned to Saige.

"You?"

She hesitated. Her shoulders quivered, as if fighting back tears.

"I'm alright."

He touched her wrist, real soft. Not to comfort. Just to connect. To say, I see you.

"You called me fast. That counts."

She swallowed hard then nodded once.

Mari cleared his throat. "System's up. Feeds waiting."

Darius didn't answer right away. He moved toward the table but stopped halfway there. His hands were twitching— two fingers tapping a rhythm against his thigh, just to keep him level.

The fridge kicked on, and the sound made his skin crawl. He blinked hard. Couldn't focus.

The pressure was rising again. Breath getting too short. His brain spinning too fast—plate number, camera grid, app backend, GPS signal, threat level, gun, Zora screaming—

Mari stepped in close, but didn't crowd.

"D," he said quietly. "Look at me."

Darius didn't.

"Just breathe, man. You don't have to solve it all in the next minute. One step."

Darius clenched his jaw, shoulders rising as if the air were trying to crush him.

Then—one breath.

Then another.

He moved to the table, sat down, cracked his knuckles once, and dropped into the feed.

Not because he was calm.

Because he had to be.

"I'm pulling everything west of Wild Hart," he said, voice flat now. Steady, even if his hands still twitched between taps. "If the van's still moving, I'll find it."

Zion's name popped up on his phone. Missed call.

He didn't answer yet.

He stared at the screen, watching code blur into movement.

"I'm bringing her home," he said.

Not to them.

Not to himself.

Just into the air.

Like a vow.

IN MY *Rhythm*

The room was still thick with shock. The kind that doesn't scream — it hums under your skin.

Keira was silent on the couch, arm braced, towel soaking through. Saige sat next to her, wringing her hands in slow, anxious circles like she didn't know they were moving. Zion had just stepped out to make calls. Mari stood by the table, drawing invisible routes with his finger on the wood, already tracking roads in his head.

Darius tapped through city feeds, half-lit footage dragging pixel by pixel on the screen. Every clip was a window too late. Every blink of the cursor, another second too far.

Then his phone buzzed.

Unknown number.

He stared at it for a beat.

Everything in him tightened.

He answered.

No hello. No voice he recognized. Just static and breathing.

Then a voice, filtered. Flattened.

"Two million."

No intro. No pretense.

"Wire transfer. No cops. You'll get instructions. Twelve hours."

Darius didn't say a word.

"You try anything," the voice added, "she bleeds."

Click.

That was it.

He kept holding the phone long after the line went dead.

The silence came in hard. It felt as if something sucked the air out of the room.

Mari looked up from the map. "That it?"

Darius nodded.

Zion re-entered, phone still in his hand. "What happened?"

"Ransom call." Mari didn't miss a beat. "Two million. No cops. Twelve-hour clock."

Zion's brows lifted. "So, it's about the money?"

Darius didn't respond.

Because he couldn't.

His hands were still on the phone, too tight now. Shoulders locked. Jaw clenched so hard that it hurt.

Light and sound, not physical pressure from the walls, created a sense of confinement. The buzz of the fridge. The subtle tick of the fan. Keira's shallow breathing. The flicker of a poor connection in the tablet screen. Too much input. Too fast.

His chest felt like it was filling with wet sand.

Mari saw it. Moved in slowly.

"Darius," he said, calm but direct. "Hey."

No response.

"You're here. Right now. Eyes on me."

Darius blinked once. Then again. But the air still felt wrong. The data on his screen was wrong. Time was wrong.

Mari didn't push. Just dropped a hand on his shoulder. Firm. Still.

"Breathe in. Count four."

Darius did.

"Hold it."

Another second.

"Now out. Four again."

The pressure didn't vanish but it leveled. Enough.

Zion had gone quiet. Saige watched from the couch, hands still in her lap, guilt etched across her face as if it had teeth.

Darius finally spoke. Quiet. Even.

"They're serious."

Mari nodded. "Yeah. They are."

"They're not bluffing," he said. "They knew I'd pay it."

"Will you?"

Darius looked at him then. Something sharp behind the eyes. Not rage. Not panic. Just truth.

"I'll pay it," he said. "But I'm not giving it to them."

He turned back to the screen. More traffic cams. Warehouse feeds. Side street footage. All too grainy. All too late.

Then something caught in his chest — a thought, a spark.

"She had her phone."

Saige looked up. "What?"

"Zora. She never put it down. She was checking her messages when y'all left the spa."

"Yeah," Keira said hoarsely. "She had it out in the car. Still laughing. Talking about some comment she saw."

Darius was already moving. "The Wild Hart app. It's on her phone. I built the backend."

Mari raised a brow. "You can trace it?"

"I can try."

He launched the admin dashboard. Entered the dev portal. Bypassed his own multi-factor lockout — fingers flying faster now. Like his system knew who he was working for.

GPS ping: Weak.

But there.

His whole body tensed again. But this time, it didn't freeze. It locked in.

"She's still broadcasting."

"Where?" Mari asked.

He zoomed in. The signal was flickering—but present.

"Chastain Industrial Corridor," Darius said. "Could be inside a warehouse. Cement walls — that's probably why the signal's shit."

"But she's still got the phone?" Zion asked.

Darius nodded. "Yeah. Or they don't realize it's active."

"Then we move," Zion said, already pacing. "We move now."

Darius leaned in, watching the signal blink like a pulse.

They had a location. A clock. And no more patience.

"She's close," he whispered. "We're not letting her disappear."

Her mouth was dry.

That was the first thing she noticed when the hood came off — not the flickering light or the sting in her knees, but the desert feeling in her mouth. Like she'd swallowed fear, and it had soaked up all her spit.

The room wasn't a room. It was a shell.

Concrete floor. Cinder block walls. No windows. One flickering fluorescent light overhead and the faint smell of gasoline and piss.

She was zip-tied at the wrists and ankles. Kneeling. Like she was supposed to pray.

The man who dragged her inside was still by the wall, hoodie up, arms crossed. She hadn't heard him speak yet. Didn't need to. The way he'd yanked her from the van said enough — efficient. Emotionless. Like grabbing groceries.

Her heart hadn't slowed down since they took her.

But she hadn't screamed again. She wouldn't. Not yet. Maybe not at all.

She needed to listen.

She needed to watch.

The rope bit into her wrists—tight, coarse, cut from the kind of cord used to tie down freight. Her arms ached, her ankles felt worse, and her neck stung from where the tape had been ripped off her mouth hours ago. But she was still here. Still breathing. Still thinking.

The warehouse was cold now. Not winter-cold. Just empty. Abandoned. Like it'd been holding its breath for something to go wrong. Metal groaned overhead with every wind shift, and the single bulb swinging above her made every shadow feel like it had teeth.

Zora blinked hard, keeping her eyes sharp even though the light kept swaying. Fear sat hot in her throat, but she refused to let it climb higher.

Stay focused. Breathe. Think.

This wasn't the first time life had cornered her.

But this was the first time she didn't know if she'd make it out whole.

The door creaked open. She didn't jump.

Tamara stepped through first, all hips and poison. She still had her lashes on, still strutted like the concrete beneath her was a runway. Jemma followed, less polished—wig tilted, lip gloss smudged, rage tucked under every line of her face like static.

Tamara stopped a few feet away, tilting her head. "You lookin' a little less goddess-like now," she said with a smirk. "Still holdin' that spine up, huh?"

Zora didn't answer. Her mouth was dry, her pulse loud— but her silence was deliberate.

Tamara circled slowly. "You ever think about how you got here? How a little side hustle turned you into a target?" She leaned in, mock-confidential. "All that soil, all those pots, and now look—you sittin' in a warehouse like cargo."

Jemma said nothing, arms crossed tight, jaw working like she was chewing glass.

Tamara walked over to the table on the far side. Zora's phone sat there, face-down. Tamara flipped it over and clicked the screen.

"Still blowin' up," she said. "Let's see—twelve missed calls from 'Baby.' Damn. That man is desperate." She held it out so Zora could see. "Text says he's on his way. So sweet. Think he'll bring the two million?"

Zora's stomach flipped. Two million?

Tamara laughed. "Oh yeah. You worth that much now,

babe. Ain't that somethin'? Two mil by midnight, or he starts gettin' pieces of you in the mail."

Jemma flinched. "Tam…"

But Tamara ignored her. She turned back toward Zora, crouched low so they were eye to eye.

"You think you're special?" She said, voice low and mean. "He was mine before you ever came sniffin' around. You out here claimin' something I built. That soft look he gives you? That thing he does with his tongue?"

Her grin sharpened like a blade.

"Yeah. I taught him that."

Zora blinked slowly, keeping her face neutral.

But Tamara wasn't done.

"You just got him after I broke him in. Took him long enough to learn how to act right. And now you walk around like you're the prize?"

Jemma finally snapped, stepping closer. "That's enough."

Tamara stood, brushing imaginary lint from her coat. "No, it's not."

Zora's voice finally cracked through the quiet, hoarse and clear. "You think this is love?"

Tamara turned fast.

"This ain't love," Zora said, her mouth dry but her gaze unshaken. "This is desperation wrapped in old bitterness. He chose me. That's the part you can't stand."

Tamara's nostrils flared, but she didn't strike her again. Not yet.

Jemma stared, her mouth twisting. "He should've looked out for the people who raised him."

"You didn't raise him," Zora said. "You watched him grow from a distance and waited to collect when he bloomed."

Tamara's smile was gone now. "You got all the answers, huh?"

"No," Zora said. "But I know this—when Darius finds me? He's not comin' to negotiate."

They both stood quiet for a beat too long.

Tamara cracked her neck, then looked at Jemma. "We'll move her to the back if he doesn't pay by eleven. That gives us time."

Zora watched them go. Their footsteps echoed sharply. The door slammed behind them.

And the silence returned.

She let her head fall forward. The ropes digging deeper, her pulse thudding in her ears.

She didn't know how close Darius was. But she knew he'd come.

And when he did?

This warehouse was going to turn into a graveyard.

The signal locked.

It didn't glitch. Didn't stutter. Just blinked once, settled, and stayed still.

Darius stared at the screen as if it might disappear if he looked away.

Warehouse. Chastain industrial strip. Just east of the old train yard. The warehouse sits tucked behind fencing untouched since before the recession. No public access. No reason to be there unless you didn't want to be found.

She was there.

Zora.

Still. Unmoving.

He didn't speak right away. Just set the tablet down with care, then stood.

Mari glanced up from the route he'd been sketching across a street map. "That it?"

Darius nodded once. "She hasn't moved in almost ten minutes."

Zion leaned against the wall, cracking his knuckles. "Then it's time."

Mari folded the map, already sliding it into his bag. "One entrance. No exterior cams except the one I hijacked. Back lot's got a fence that looks half-collapsed. No real cover. You'll need to move fast."

"We won't need long," Darius said.

Zion popped open the trunk of Mari's SUV. It wasn't a gear stash — it was a small armory. Padded hard cases. Tactical vests. A set of ear comms. Two sidearms. A knife that looked like it had been used more than sharpened.

"Go bag's ready," Zion said. "Pick your poison."

Darius stepped up and grabbed the SIG from the center slot. Checked the weight. Racked it clean. No hesitation, but no flair either — just a man who'd practiced until the unfamiliar got quiet.

Zion raised an eyebrow. "You sure you good?"

He didn't mean it as a challenge. He meant it like the range. The way he used to look at Darius after every third shot, waiting to see if the rhythm had clicked in yet.

Darius locked the clip, holstered the gun.

"Mari and you ain't take me to the range just to keep me company," he said. "I'm straight."

Zion grinned. "Cool. I'll be loud. You be precise."

Mari handed Darius a comms mic. "Stay in contact. I'll be in the car, monitoring all exits. If you lose signal, you've got ten minutes to get out. After that, we have to assume fallback."

"Copy," Darius said.

He took the comm, slid the earpiece in, double-checked the frequency.

Zion strapped on a vest, popped a clip into his Glock, and gave it a spin before holstering.

Darius turned toward the door—and stopped.

Saige was standing there. Arms crossed, eyes glassy. Shoulders tight like she'd been holding herself still too long.

"You sure this is the only way?" she asked, voice tight.

"No," Darius said. "But it's the one I've got."

She stepped forward, fingers twitching at her sides. "Just… don't lose yourself in this. Don't come back with blood on your hands and nothin' left in your chest."

He didn't answer. He didn't know how to.

So instead, he said, "I'm bringing her home."

Saige's chin trembled. "You better."

Mari touched her back as she stepped away.

Darius turned and walked out the front door like it owed him nothing.

The car ride was silent except for the road.

Mari drove like he'd done this too many times to count. Focused. No nerves. No wasted motion. Zion tapped against his thigh, tension humming through him like static.

Darius sat in the backseat, shoulders loose, mind locked. Not spiraling now. Not frozen.

Just waiting for the green light.

Mari turned down a side street near the warehouse and cut the headlights. They coasted slowly past the fence line, scouting shadows.

"East wall," Mari said, eyes scanning. "Weakest point is behind the service stack. Zion takes left. Darius, you're on point. I'll sweep wide and cover the rear approach."

Darius nodded. "Copy."

Mari killed the engine. Reached back and handed Darius a second clip.

"Let's bring her home."

Darius took it without a word.

Zion popped his door. "Time to clean house."

They stepped into the dark together.

The warehouse loomed ahead, ribs of steel cutting the sky, every edge sharp with silence.

The wind blew, and the whole place creaked like it knew what was coming.

Darius adjusted his grip on the gun. Took one long, quiet breath.

And then he moved.

IN MY *Rhythm*

The metal groaned as the front door caved in, years of rust giving way to fury and force.

Darius moved like muscle memory. Gun drawn, eyes scanning, every footstep placed with purpose. Zion cut left, slicing through shadows with clean, quiet speed. Mari took the right flank, precise and methodical — not flashy, but unshakable.

Inside smelled like oil, mildew, and bad intentions.

The first guard came into view—rifle loose in his hands, too relaxed.

Darius fired before the man even saw him.

One to the chest. One to the head.

Done.

Zion didn't speak. Just moved deeper into the maze of crates.

Mari called out low through the comm. "Two more in the back. One pacing. One posted."

Darius turned a corner. Saw the second—mid-step, gun swinging up.

He didn't make it.

Zion's shot cracked through the warehouse like thunder.

"Dropped him," he said.

Third guard tried to run.

Mari caught him from the side. Disarmed. Disabled. One quick shot to the leg. Another to the head.

They were methodical. Not merciful.

Darius turned down the hallway that ran along the edge

of the floor plan—half memory from Mari's layout, half instinct.

And then—

A sound.

Soft. Hoarse.

Not a scream. A breath.

"Zora."

He broke into a run.

The storage room door was half-open. A sliver of light. A heartbeat behind it.

He kicked it in.

There she was.

Tied. Bruised. Rope biting her wrists. Knees raw. Tape residue on her cheek.

Eyes locked on him as if they never left.

He crossed the room fast. Dropped to his knees. The knife Mari gave him was already in his hand.

The cords snapped with two pulls. One at her wrists. One at her ankles.

She collapsed forward, and he caught her like it was the only thing he knew how to do.

"You came," she breathed.

"Always."

Her fingers dug into his shirt like she didn't trust the floor anymore.

He didn't rush. Just held her. Just breathed. His hand slid up the back of her head, cradling her, steadying them both.

"I've got you," he murmured. "You're okay now. I got you."

Footsteps.

He shifted Zora behind him, still holding her, still shielding her.

Tamara stepped into the room, arms up, voice trembling under practiced calm.

"We didn't mean for it to get this far. You found her. She's alive. That's what matters."

Darius didn't blink.

"She's alive," he said, raising the gun, "because you're bad at this."

"Darius, wait—"

He pulled the trigger.

Tamara dropped like a string had been cut. Dead before she hit the ground.

Zora didn't flinch. Just leaned into him, like she was rooting herself there.

Then came the sound of running.

Darius tightened his grip on Zora.

Mari stepped into the hallway, gun raised, but paused as Zion jogged past him, calm, efficient.

"Runner," he muttered.

They saw her at the far end—Jemma. No grace now. Wig askew. Face twisted.

She turned when she saw them. Hands up. Voice high.

"Wait—wait, please—Darius—"

Zion didn't stop.

Two shots.

One to drop her.

One to end it.

Darius didn't say a word.

He just looked at Zion and nodded.

Zion nodded back. No smile. No victory. Just understanding.

Zora shifted against his chest. "They're gone?"

He looked down at her. Brushed a smear of dirt from her temple with the edge of his thumb.

"They're done," he said.

Mari returned after he cleared the rest of the space.

No more movement.

Just silence. Cold and final.

Darius stood slowly, keeping Zora with him. Her weight leaned into his side like her body knew where she belonged.

He didn't rush. Didn't speak.

They stepped out of the warehouse into the wind.
No sirens. No noise.
Just the three of them.
Zion behind. Mari beside.
And Zora in his arms.
Alive.

CHAPTER TWENTY-FIVE

bloom

"GARDEN (SAY IT LIKE DAT)" BY SZA

The ride back was quiet.

Not peace-quiet. Just the kind that hangs in the air when four people share the weight of something none of them can put down yet.

Mari drove like he still had to — threading them through a war zone, not a neighborhood. Calm. Sharp. Every stop calculated.

Zion rode up front, elbow on the window, one knee bouncing. Every so often he looked back toward Zora. Like he had something to say but couldn't find the shape of it.

Darius was in the back with her.

Close, but not too close.

His thigh brushed hers. His hand lay open between them, palm up. Not pushing. Just there.

Zora took it without thinking.

Her fingers found his like they always had. Familiar. Final.

He hadn't let go since he cut her loose.

And he wasn't going to now.

The house came into view and her stomach twisted.

It looked the same. Porch light on. Shadows shifting behind the front windows. But something in her still braced —

like the van door might slam again, like the tape might come back.

She stopped breathing.

Darius leaned in, voice low. "You ready?"

"No," Zora said. "But I want to go in anyway."

Mari pulled up. Parked smooth.

The front door opened before the car even stopped.

Keira.

Then Saige.

And behind them — Mama Regina. Waiting in the doorway, hands folded, head held high.

Zion stepped out first. Mari behind him. Neither said anything.

Darius came around to Zora's side and opened her door.

She moved slow. Every step a memory.

Her feet hit the porch and her knees wobbled. Not from pain — from weight. From trying to carry what just happened into a place where it didn't belong.

They stepped inside.

She made it five steps before her legs gave out.

Zora collapsed in the middle of the living room. No warning. No pause. Just gone.

Keira caught her halfway down, and they dropped together.

Zora sobbed. Loud, ugly, chest-wracking cries that sounded like they'd been waiting to be let out since the warehouse.

Keira held her. Cried with her. "I thought—I thought I lost you—"

Saige hit her knees next, silent at first, but her face crumpled before the sound could follow. "I should've fought harder."

Zora reached for her. Pulled her in.

"You stayed," she gasped. "You stayed."

Then Mama Regina knelt — slower than the rest, but just as sure. She gathered Zora into her lap like she had Darius

240

once, like love didn't care how old you were when you needed holding.

"You're home now," she said. "That's all that matters."

Darius stood a few feet away, hands at his sides, eyes never leaving her. He wanted to touch her. Needed to. But this wasn't his moment yet.

The crying slowed, eventually.

Not because it was over.

Just because they were out of breath.

Later, Mama Regina passed Zora a cup of tea. Zion offered a throw blanket and muttered something about "soft-ass comfort rituals," but he stayed close. Mari sat near Saige on the floor. No words. Just presence.

Zora stayed curled on the couch, her head resting against Darius's chest, her body still trembling in places.

The room began to breathe again.

Keira looked up, her voice soft. "Do we know how they found her?"

Saige asked, "Tamara and Jemma—are they…?"

The air tightened.

Mari didn't even look up from his mug. "Not now."

Zion's voice followed. "Not while she's still in the room."

Mama Regina nodded. "Let her rest."

Keira nodded, eyes wide. "Yeah. Yeah, of course."

Zora didn't say a word. But her hand tightened around Darius's, and she didn't let go.

A little while later, Zora stirred.

"I need to go outside."

Darius kissed the top of her head. "Then let's go."

He helped her stand. She winced but didn't fall. He stayed close as they stepped out the back door—quiet, careful.

No one followed.

The backyard was wild. Unkempt. Everything in bloom and overgrown all at once.

Zora walked slow, her fingers brushing stems and leaves

like old friends. She crouched beside the mint, touched it gently.

Still alive.

Still growing.

Darius stood nearby, not saying anything. Just holding the space with her.

Zora looked up.

"I'm not waiting for the next storm anymore," she said.

His eyes never left her.

"I'm planting anyway."

IN MY *Rhythm*

It had been three weeks since Zora came home—to his home. Their home, now, though neither of them had said it out loud. The shift had been quiet: first her clothes, then her teacups, then her silence finding peace in his spaces. They hadn't drawn a line in the sand or signed a lease. She just never left after the night he brought her back—and he never asked her to.

Her body still remembered the pain. Her mind still flicked through shadows when the room got too quiet. But her heart? Her heart was waking up. And today, it was blooming.

The botanical garden wasn't crowded. Late afternoon sun stretched lazy across winding paths, and the air smelled like lemon balm and late spring. Zora walked ahead, curls catching the light, her linen dress dancing around her calves with every step. She stopped often—sometimes to smell, sometimes just to breathe.

Darius watched her like she was the centerpiece of the whole damn garden.

She looked over her shoulder. "You gonna keep staring or you gonna come hold my hand?"

He moved quick—closed the space between them with a small, quiet grin—and took her hand like he'd never let it go again. Their fingers interlocked. She gave him that look, the one that said everything and nothing all at once, and kept walking.

They wandered slow through arches of roses, into the deeper shade of the herb garden. Zora pulled him down beside her on a bench nestled under a tree with soft-hanging limbs. The air was thick with lavender and mint.

Darius ran his knuckles along the back of her hand, slow and steady. "You feel like yourself again," he murmured.

Zora leaned into him, resting her head on his shoulder. "Not quite. But I'm starting to feel like ourselves again."

That made him pull her closer. One arm around her shoulder. The other hand resting low on her thigh. He didn't need her to keep talking. He just needed to feel her weight against him—warm, safe, here.

Her fingers played at the edge of his collar, light and aimless. Then they slipped beneath it, tracing the skin there like she was grounding herself.

"Can I kiss you?" she asked, voice low.

"You don't ever have to ask," he said.

She shifted, turning toward him on the bench, and cupped his face in both hands. The kiss wasn't hurried. Wasn't fragile. It was home. The kind of kiss that quieted every room in her head. The kind that pressed the past down beneath the roots and left her wanting more.

Darius deepened it, one hand sliding behind her neck, thumb brushing the line of her jaw. He tasted like peppermint and the steadiness she hadn't known she craved this deeply.

When they pulled back, breath mingling, Zora's eyes were still closed.

"You still with me?" he asked, voice warm against her lips.

She smiled. "Too much. Might need you to slow down or take me home."

"Say the word."

She curled into his lap then, unapologetic. One leg slung across his, arms around his neck, like the garden wasn't there.

Like the whole world had narrowed to this bench and his heartbeat against her chest.

They didn't talk much after that. Just let the quiet stretch, their hands moving without thought—her thumb tracing circles on his shoulder, his fingers drawing lazy lines across her thigh.

At some point she whispered, "You're my soft place."

Darius kissed her shoulder. "You're my whole damn garden."

Eventually, they circled back to the little shaded side patio tucked behind the greenhouse, half-secluded and perfect for the kind of date Darius had quietly set up weeks ago.

There was a folding easel already waiting. Two chairs. A low table with a bottle of wine, paint palettes, water jars, and canvas boards. Sunlight filtered through the trellis overhead, casting soft gold across everything.

Zora paused and looked at him.

"You serious right now?"

He popped the cork without flinching. "I said I owed you a real date. Not just sunlight and vibes."

She laughed—loud, bright, unguarded. "So this is what we're doing now? Sip and paint in the garden like we bougie and bored?"

"You said you wanted soft," he said. "I'm giving you soft."

She slipped her sandals off and sank into the chair like she belonged there. "You better pour that glass then."

He did—generous pour, no hesitation. She raised an eyebrow. "You trying to get me loose out here?"

Darius grinned. "Nah. You're already loose. I'm just helping the art flow."

They painted for a while. Not seriously—just play. Zora dipped her brush into the green like it was a dare and started sketching the shape of Darius's beard with broad, chaotic strokes.

"Why you look like you fighting the canvas?" he teased.

"Why you look like you posing for a church mural?" she fired back.

"Because I know my angles."

They cracked up. Zora leaned in to flick paint at him—soft, just a little speck on his cheek. He didn't move.

He dipped his fingers in the blue and swiped a line across her collarbone.

"Oh, it's war now," she whispered.

But she didn't move either. She just let the silence catch up again, watching him like he was something rare and alive.

Their paintings were a mess—his was all wild color and abstract flowers. Hers was mostly Darius's hands. Just his hands. Holding a bloom. Reaching. Protecting.

He stared at it for a long time when she flipped it toward him.

"You drew the part of me I didn't know you saw," he said.

She sipped her wine. "It's the part that never lets me go."

They didn't clean up right away. Just sat there, a little wine-drunk, smudged with paint, feet tangled under the table. Zora moved her chair closer until their knees bumped, then climbed into his lap like it was the most obvious next step.

"I love you, D," she murmured, forehead against his.

He kissed her slow.

"I love you louder than that."

IN MY *Rhythm*

The sun was starting to dip by the time they packed up their things. The paint was still wet on their canvases, their wine glasses half-full, their hands stained in color and closeness.

Zora leaned back in her chair, stretched her arms overhead, and sighed like her body had just remembered it belonged to her again.

"You ready?" Darius asked, watching her with a gaze that

had shifted from gentle to hungry somewhere between the second laugh and the third glass.

Zora didn't answer right away. She just stood, slow and easy, and stepped between his legs where he sat. Her fingers slipped under his chin, lifting his face.

"You taking me home," she said, "or are we pretending we ain't been eye-fucking since the third flower bed?"

Darius grinned, slow and sure. "Let's go."

He gathered the sketchpad and their bottles, tucked everything back into the bag like it didn't matter if the paint smudged or the brushes dried wrong. Zora didn't even bother putting her shoes back on — just slid her hand into his and followed.

They didn't talk much on the ride.

She played with the hem of her dress, watched the city pass by like it was somewhere far away. Darius drove with one hand on the wheel and the other resting on her thigh, thumb tracing slow circles that said everything his mouth didn't need to.

By the time they pulled into the driveway, the air between them was thick with silence that wasn't awkward—it was charged.

Darius cut the engine, but neither of them moved right away. Zora stared straight ahead, lips parted, chest rising slow. Darius looked over at her like he was already undressing her in his head—but still letting her lead.

She turned toward him, slow. Steady. Smiling like she knew exactly how the rest of the night would end.

He didn't say a word.

They got out of the car in sync. No rush. No hesitation. This wasn't the start of something new. This was the continuation of something theirs.

Zora unlocked the door with the ease of someone who lived there. Because she did. She stepped inside like her body already knew the way back to him, and he followed like gravity.

They were still laughing when they got inside. Not loud, not clumsy—just that quiet, lingering kind of laughter that lives between lovers when the air is full of what's coming.

Zora tossed her bag near the door, then walked barefoot through the kitchen, trailing her fingers across the counter like she was touching a memory. Darius leaned against the doorway and watched her with a hunger that had nothing to do with food.

She turned, wine-warm and soft-eyed, and caught him staring.

"What?"

"You know what," he said, already pushing off the frame.

She met him halfway. Mouth found mouth. Soft at first, then greedy. Her hands slid under his shirt, palms hot on his skin.

He pulled back just enough to whisper, "You ready to let me wear you out tonight?"

Zora grinned. "Been ready. Thought you was takin' your sweet ass time."

That lit something in him. Dark. Intentional.

He didn't take her to the bed—not yet. He spun her toward the counter, bent her just enough to have her breath catch. One hand slid up her back, the other hooked her panties to the side.

"Put your hands flat. Don't move till I tell you."

Before she could speak, his palm came down on her ass— sharp, just enough to make her yelp and clench.

"Darius—"

"That was for actin' like you wasn't already drippin' for me."

She moaned, tried to turn.

"Uh-uh. Stay."

He dropped to his knees and ate her like it was the only thing that could save his soul. She gasped, back arching.

"D—oh fuck. Baby."

His tongue worked slow circles, then fast flicks, his fingers joining in, teasing her entrance.

"That's it. Make that mess on my face. You earned it."

"Shit, I'm..baby, I'm—"

"Cum for me. Right now."

She shattered with a scream.

Then he stood, kissed her shoulder, and said, "Bed. Now. Don't make me say it twice."

She made it down the hall before he caught her wrist and spun her into him, lips on hers, his other hand already pulling open the bedside drawer. A vibe. Lube. A soft silicone plug she'd told him once she liked but hadn't been ready for.

"Tonight you take all of me," he said against her throat.

She didn't hesitate. "I want it."

He helped her onto the bed, onto all fours. One hand gripped her ass as he spread her, the other slicking the plug and easing it in with care.

Zora groaned, back arching. "Shit—okay—damn."

"Good girl. Look at how full you already are."

He slid two fingers into her pussy, slow, just to watch her squirm.

Then came the vibe—low setting, pressed right against her clit.

She whimpered. Twitched. "D..baby, I can't hold all that."

"Yes, you can. And you will."

He teased her with the head of his dick, then pushed in slow.

Her whole body seized. The plug. The vibe. The stretch.

"Oh my God."

"Nah. That's all me. Now breathe and take it. Don't run."

He moved with slow, deep thrusts. One hand at her waist, the other holding the vibe in place.

Zora moaned nonstop, her voice caught between pleasure and disbelief.

"I'm gonna...fuck...baby, I'm gonna cum."

"Cum on this dick. You need it. Let it take you out."

She came hard, clenching tight around him, thighs shaking.

He kept going. Pulled the plug out, slow and careful. Flipped her over, slid back inside.

"You not done. I want that next one, too."

"Babe..fuck. I don't even know if I can—"

"You can. You mine. I got you."

She cried out, coming again within seconds, nails digging into his arms.

Only then did he let go. Buried himself deep, held her there, and let the orgasm take him.

They collapsed together. Gasping. Spent.

He wrapped himself around her from behind, kissed the back of her shoulder.

"Still wit' me?"

Zora didn't even open her eyes. Just smiled.

"Still yours. And you ain't shit for that plug. But I love you anyway."

"LOVED BY YOU" BY KIRBY

6 months later

Spring came back different this year.

It wasn't just the weather—though the breeze moved softer, and the sunlight stuck longer. It was in the way Zora walked. The way she stood still. The way the world made more space around her now, instead of asking her to shrink.

She tugged gently at the edges of the blindfold wrapped around her eyes. "I swear, Darius, if you're walkin' me into a juice bar, I'm goin' back home."

He laughed behind her. "You got trust issues."

"You blindfolded me. In heels."

"You look fine as hell in 'em."

She smirked. "Flattery don't mean my ankles won't sue."

His hand held hers as they crossed the sidewalk. The sounds got louder. Music. People. Laughter. The smell of something fresh—flowers, citrus, and cinnamon. Her steps slowed.

They reached a set of steps. He paused, then guided her gently up. One, two, three.

She could feel it before she saw it. Joy. Energy. That buzz of celebration in the air. Darius exhaled softly beside her.

"Alright. Take it off."

Zora slipped the blindfold free—and froze.

The storefront stood wide and new in front of her. Copper signage, tall glass windows, balloons bobbing in the soft breeze. The name gleamed above the door: Rooted.

The sidewalk was full. People laughing, talking, and snapping pictures. Kids from the center in their Sunday best. Zion by the curb, nodding like he knew he was part of something big. Keira near a flower cart, handing out little bouquets wrapped in paper stamped with Zora's name. Saige stood next to her, chatting with guests while Willow clung to her hand, Roman handed out flyers with his usual charm, and Ariyah stood confidently by the welcome table, running check-ins like it was her own event.

Mari held a clipboard near the side entrance, coordinating deliveries like he'd been born doing logistics. And tucked beside a cluster of sunflowers near the glass doors stood Mama Regina, her hair wrapped in deep plum, eyes already full.

Inside, the shop glowed from within. Shelves of soil blends: Wild Bloom, Quiet Thunder, Raised by Rain, sat beneath a sign that read: Now Stocked Nationwide. Branded tote bags. Gift boxes. A soft jazz playlist drifting from speakers near the ceiling. Every detail intentional. Every inch hers.

Zora stared, speechless. Her chest rose, tight. For a moment, she felt that same blur she'd felt her first day at Wild Hart—but this time, it was steady. This time, she wasn't wondering if she belonged. She was the reason the door opened.

Darius leaned in close. "Before you start crying and I know you're about to..there's one more thing."

He nodded toward the far window.

And that's when Zora saw her.

Miss Essie stood tall in a soft blue dress, bouquet in her arms, a little shaky in the knees but steady in the eyes.

Zora gasped. "Darius—"

He smiled, quiet and sure. "You said she's the one who taught you how to listen to the earth. Figured she oughta see what you've done with it."

Zora's feet moved before her thoughts caught up. She crossed the shop in a blur and threw her arms around Miss Essie, burying her face in the woman's shoulder. Her tears hit like relief, not grief.

Miss Essie held her tight. "Look at you. Look what you built. I always knew you'd find your way back to the dirt. But this? This is somethin' else."

Zora laughed through it. "You showed me the way."

They rocked there, quiet in their reunion. The rest of the celebration pulsed around them—music, laughter, kids weaving through legs, arms full of tiny potted succulents.

Willow wandered up with a plate of snacks, her dress a little wrinkled, curls bouncing. "Miss Zora, Mama said you need to eat or you gon' pass out like Miss Keira did that one time."

Zora burst out laughing, crouched down, and took the plate. "I appreciate the medical advice."

Willow beamed, then skipped off with a cookie in hand.

Zora finally turned to Darius, her face wet but shining.

"You did all this?"

He slid his hands into his pockets, gave that small, satisfied smile. "Nah. You did it. I just made sure the right people were here to see it."

Inside, the celebration bloomed. Zion made a toast. Half-serious and half-roast. Keira passed around cupcakes. Saige snapped pictures of everything. Ariyah filmed content for socials. Roman tried to sneak another cupcake until Mama Regina caught him mid-bite.

Zora moved through it like light. Hugged everyone. Touched every shelf. She overheard a teen at the back say, "My aunt drove all the way from Macon for this soil," and it made her pause. Made her inhale.

She read the plaque above the counter three times: To Zora—who taught us how to bloom and believe.

She stood still for a moment, her fingers brushing the wood. The music rolled on around her, sweet and slow.

Darius came up behind her, arms sliding around her waist. "You good?"

She leaned back into him. "I'm better than good."

He kissed her temple, didn't say anything more.

They stayed like that for a while—surrounded by joy, rooted in something real.

And she was ready.

IN MY *Rhythm*

Later that week, Zora stepped through the double doors of the newly expanded community center. It looked different now. Brighter. Bigger. The walls had been painted in deep greens and rich golds, with a mural stretching across the east side that showed hands planting seeds into soil and children's silhouettes growing out like sunflowers.

The new garden courtyard sat right at the center of it all —her design, her touch, her dirt. Raised beds lined the path, full of herbs, edible flowers, and vegetables. Even the youngest kids had their own row to tend.

She walked through slow, waving to parents, volunteers, and new staff. Inside, classrooms buzzed with energy. One room had teens gathered around computers, learning how to build digital portfolios. Another had kids hunched over compost bins, learning how banana peels could bring life back to dirt.

Zora crouched beside a wide ceramic pot, her hands already brushing at the soil. A girl named Laila sat nearby, no more than ten, clutching a sketchbook.

"I tried to draw you," Laila said, holding up a page where

Zora's curls were rendered like a crown of vines. "But then I drew your garden instead."

Zora took the sketch like it was holy. "This yours?"

Laila nodded.

"Can I hang it in my office?"

"Really?"

"Yeah. Every queen needs a gallery."

She smiled, standing again, dusting off her palms.

The center wasn't just bigger—it was blooming. With life, with hope, with future.

In one of the new workshop rooms, a sign read: Soil Sisters: Youth Entrepreneur Program sponsored by Rooted.

Zora stepped in, watched a group of girls repotting lavender plants, their hands in gloves, their laughter full and unbothered.

This was what it was all for. Not just selling soil. Not just success. But creating something that lived longer than she would. Something that gave other girls a chance to choose joy, to choose growth, to choose themselves.

She took one more look around the room and exhaled. Long. Full.

The sun was starting to dip outside. And somewhere, Darius was waiting.

And she was ready.

The community center looked different now, but it still felt like home.

The new wing stretched wide from the original building— glass walls, solar panels, a rooftop garden that Zora had helped design herself. Where there'd once been cramped offices and overworked classrooms, now there were clean lines, open spaces, and a warmth that didn't come from sunlight alone.

Zora walked the halls slow, one hand trailing along the freshly painted wall. Kids streamed past her, laughing, their sneakers squeaking on the floors. She caught glimpses into rooms—one filled with teens at a coding station Darius had helped fund, another with toddlers planting marigolds in painted pots.

In the center courtyard, the garden buzzed. Raised beds overflowing with herbs and leafy greens. A rain barrel system. Compost bins. A row of fruit trees just beginning to bud. The plaque near the entrance read: In Honor of Mama Regina: For the Seeds You Gave Us.

Zora crouched next to a little girl who was patting soil around the base of a sunflower. "You know the trick to keep it growing tall?" she asked.

The girl looked up at her, wide-eyed. "Water and talk nice to it?"

Zora smiled. "Exactly. Plants know when you mean it."

She stood again, brushing off her hands, and scanned the courtyard. Staff were moving with ease, kids planting, laughing, learning. It felt alive. Sustained. Like it could go on even if she walked away.

Keira approached, clipboard in hand. "You see the greenhouse yet?"

Zora raised a brow. "Y'all added that already?"

Keira grinned. "You say it, Darius funds it. That man's got a whole trust labeled 'Zora's ideas.'"

They both laughed. Zora glanced toward the glass greenhouse in the back corner. She could already see rows of starter plants, stacked shelves, irrigation tubes. Ariyah waved from inside, holding up a tray of sprouts.

Saige and Mari stood near the edge of the courtyard, watching Willow try to teach Roman a planting chant she'd made up. Mama Regina sat in a wide wooden chair beneath a canopy, sipping from a tea mug like she'd claimed her throne.

Zora made her way to Mama Regina, crouched beside her chair, and looked out over the courtyard. "It's beautiful," she said, voice soft. "Like everything we prayed it could be."

Mama Regina opened her eyes just enough to meet hers. "It's real now, baby. You made it real."

Zora breathed in deep. Sun, soil, sound.

Legacy.

She wasn't just watching things grow anymore.

She was planting for real.

And the roots were holding.

The house was quiet by the time they got home.

After dessert—some kind of buttery, cinnamon-dusted pastry Darius pulled from the oven like it was a secret weapon—they stayed out on the patio, legs tangled beneath the table, wine glasses catching the porch light.

Zora rested her head on his shoulder. Her body was warm, heavy with peace. "You really planned all this," she murmured. "The shop, the party, Miss Essie... You thought of everything."

"I just paid attention," he said.

She laughed lightly. "I ain't even know I wanted half of it till I saw it."

"That's 'cause you been too busy takin' care of everybody else."

There was no accusation in it. Just fact. Just love.

A cricket chirped somewhere in the yard. Zora closed her eyes.

"You ever scared we'll lose this?" she asked quietly.

Darius didn't answer right away. His hand found hers under the table, thumb tracing the bones of her knuckles.

"I'm not scared," he said. "I'm present. I know what it took to get here. I know what we had to survive. And I know if anything comes for us again..." He turned to press a kiss into her hair. "We'll handle it. Same way we always do. Side by side."

Zora exhaled. Her other hand came up to rest on his chest. "I believe you."

They sat like that for a while. No pressure to fill the silence. Just them, surrounded by what they built—inside and out.

Eventually, Darius stood and pulled her up gently.

"Come on. Get some rest. We movin' early tomorrow."

"Early?" She groaned but followed. "You makin' me get up at dawn again?"

He grinned. "You'll see."

Zora narrowed her eyes, suspicious. But when he tugged her close and kissed her slow—like promise, like steady rhythm—she let it go.

Whatever tomorrow was, she trusted him with it.

IN MY *Rhythm*

They left the house before the sky even thought about turning blue.

Zora was bundled in a cream-colored sweater tucked into high-waisted jeans, with thigh-high black boots that clicked softly against the sidewalk. Cute but warm, cozy without losing her edge. Her locs were under a soft knit cap, and her hands curled around a thermos of too-sweet coffee. She didn't ask where they were going. She just let herself be led—out of the driveway, into the quiet city, past sleeping streets and blinking stoplights.

Darius drove with one hand on the wheel and the other resting lightly on her thigh, the way he always did. No words. Just a steady presence that said, you're safe here.

They pulled off the road onto a gravel path. Zora blinked hard against the dark, watching shadows turn to shape.

Then she saw it.

A hot air balloon. Tethered. Towering. The basket low and waiting. A small crew moving like ghosts in the dawn.

She turned to him slowly. "Darius."

He raised his eyebrows like it was nothing. "You said you'd never been up before."

"I thought you meant like… a rooftop. Or a hill."

He stepped out of the truck, came around to open her door. "I meant up."

She stared a second longer, then laughed, wide and breathless. "You're insane."

He offered her his hand. "Only for you."

She took it.

The balloon lifted just as the horizon started to split open. Gold streaked across the clouds, and the city below softened to shadow and shimmer. The wind was quiet. The basket creaked under their weight, and Zora held the edge like it might disappear beneath her.

Darius stood beside her, both hands tucked into his coat pockets, eyes on the skyline.

Neither of them spoke for a while.

Zora leaned out, watching buildings shrink beneath them. Her breath caught when they passed over a patch of land—small, overgrown, fenced off in chain link.

She narrowed her eyes. "Wait... I know that garden."

Darius glanced over. "Yeah?"

"I forgot that was still there. We used to ride our bikes past it. Thought it was magic."

"It was magic," he said. "Still holding on."

She turned to look at him.

He was already watching her.

"I didn't bring you up here just to see the view," he said, pulling in a breath. "I brought you up here because this... this is the highest I could get without leaving the earth. And you— Z, you keep me grounded, but you lift me at the same time. You make things grow even when it's hard. You give the kind of love that stays in the soil and still manages to bloom again when the seasons shift."

He reached into his coat. Pulled out a ring box. "You changed me. Not just the way I move—but the way I feel. I didn't even know I was waitin' for you until you showed up and made the silence make sense."

He opened the box.

Inside sat a radiant-cut diamond, large and luminous,

haloed in rose gold. It caught the sunrise like it had been made for this moment.

"I want this life with you. All of it. Not just the garden. Not just the good days. I want every season. Every root. Every storm and bloom and rebuild."

He looked at her, steady. Soft. Unshaken.

"Be my rhythm. Marry me."

Zora didn't cry. She didn't gasp. She just stepped forward and pressed her forehead to his.

"You been mine," she whispered.

He slipped the ring onto her finger. Her hands didn't shake.

Below them, the world rolled out quiet and endless.

They stood at the edge of the sky, palms pressed together.

And for once, neither of them needed words to know they'd been chosen.

The end

This story started with soil.
With hands in the dirt. With breath held tight. With grief and softness and a woman who dared to bloom where nothing was promised to grow.
Zora is a piece of my heart. Darius, a rhythm I've heard in the silence between pages for a long time. Writing them meant holding space for healing, for Black love that's messy and rooted, tender and loud when it needs to be. It meant letting them rise, not because life made it easy—but because they kept choosing to try again.
If you've ever loved hard. If you've ever lost. If you've ever built something out of the pieces you were told to bury—this book is for you.
Thank you for walking this journey with them.
Thank you for believing in a love that doesn't just survive—but grows.
With full heart and muddy hands,
C.M. Campbell

C.M. Campbell is a stay-at-home mom, lifelong reader, and storyteller who finally decided to take the leap in 2025. Though she's been writing for years, it wasn't until recently that she gave herself permission to treat it like more than just a dream.

For her, stories have always been a place of healing—a way to find light in the shadows and softness after survival. Through every character and chapter, she writes with purpose: to honor Black love, growth, and legacy. Her books are rooted in real emotion, rich intimacy, and the quiet power of choosing yourself.

When she's not writing, you can find her in the thick of motherhood, curled up with a book, or building the kind of life she used to only imagine.

Let's connect

Social Media
and Signed Paperbacks

also by cm campbell

Colliding Into His Arms

www.ingramcontent.com/pod-product-compliance
Lightning Source LLC
Chambersburg PA
CBHW071415300726
48976CB00006B/2105